# Annelise was wed to a demon.

She had pledged to remain by his side until death parted them. He returned her gaze impassively and Annelise struggled to quell her fear.

What would be her fate? Did her spouse intend to devour her? Or would she have to kill him first?

Annelise wanted the truth. Regardless of how unattractive it might be. Her voice dropped as she squared her shoulders, holding her husband's gaze unswervingly.

"And *what* you are," she said deliberately. "I want to know *what* you are."

Rolfe held her gaze for a long moment, as though assessing the strength of her will.

"And if I refuse?"

"I will leave." Simply saying the words lodged a lump in Annelise's throat. How could she be so attracted to this man of mystery?

Dear Reader,

Longtime Harlequin Historical author Claire Delacroix continues to delight audiences with her stories of romance, passion and magic. And this month's title, *Enchanted*, has more than its fair share of all three. *Enchanted* tells the story of a valiant knight who can be rescued from a wicked curse only by the love of a beautiful noblewoman. Don't miss this captivating tale of lovers bound by destiny.

A duke with a tainted reputation must learn to forgive himself before he can accept the love of the woman of his dreams in *The Dark Duke,* the second title in award-winning author Margaret Moore's terrific new MOST UNSUITABLE... series set in Victorian England.

Our other two titles this month are both from very popular authors. *The Secrets of Catie Hazard,* by Miranda Jarrett, is another Sparhawk story, this time with a secret baby and lovers who must overcome not only a troubled past but a turbulent present in order to reunite. And *Sweet Sarah Ross,* by Julie Tetel, follows the next generation in the author's ongoing NORTHPOINT series, a Western adventure with enough perils to keep Pauline happy.

We hope you keep a lookout for all four of these wonderful books wherever Harlequin Historicals are sold.

Sincerely,

Tracy Farrell
Senior Editor

Please address questions and book requests to:
Harlequin Reader Service
U.S.: 3010 Walden Ave., P.O. Box 1325, Buffalo, NY 14269
Canadian: P.O. Box 609, Fort Erie, Ont. L2A 5X3

# Claire Delacroix

# ENCHANTED

## Harlequin Books

TORONTO • NEW YORK • LONDON
AMSTERDAM • PARIS • SYDNEY • HAMBURG
STOCKHOLM • ATHENS • TOKYO • MILAN
MADRID • WARSAW • BUDAPEST • AUCKLAND

ISBN 0-373-28966-9

ENCHANTED

**Books by Claire Delacroix**

Harlequin Historicals

*Romance of the Rose #166
Honeyed Lies #209
†Unicorn Bride #223
*The Sorceress #235
*Roarke's Folly #250
†Pearl Beyond Price #264
The Magician's Quest #281
†Unicorn Vengeance #293
My Lady's Champion #326
Enchanted #366

*The Rose Trilogy
†Unicorn Series

## CLAIRE DELACROIX

An avid traveler and student of history,
Claire Delacroix can be found at home when she has
a deadline, amid the usual jumble of books, knitting
needles and potted herbs.

For Michele,
who laughed (mercilessly!)
while Annelise changed
this story to suit herself.

# Chapter One

*November 1101*

Rolfe felt the cold as he never had before.

The wind wound its way beneath his heavy cloak, its fingers creeping under his tabard to chill his flesh. He shivered as he rode, knowing that winter had only just bared its teeth.

Clearly his six years in the Holy Land's sun had thinned his blood overmuch.

Wolves howled, their voices at greater proximity than Rolfe might have liked. He had forgotten that a winter forest like the one surrounding him could be so bleak and brooding. The trees' barren branches scratched the dark bellies of the clouds scurrying across the sky. A few dry leaves scuttled over the ground, seemingly muttering to each other of unwelcome intruders.

Not a creature stirred; not a bird sang.

Rolfe huddled lower in his cloak. He was not given to whimsy, but he had the odd sense that the forest was loath to let him pass. Maybe this shortcut through the woods to the main road had been less than an inspired idea, for there was unlikely to be a welcoming inn close by.

He deliberately thought of home, Château Viandin, still a week's ride ahead. His elder brother, Adalbert, should feel secure in his seat as Lord de Viandin by now. Rolfe permitted himself to hope that Adalbert would be inclined to grant him a favor.

Certainly, as a younger brother, Rolfe had no right to any of the family holdings, but fulfilling his family's obligation to the Crusade had to have earned him *something*. Six years was a heavy price to pay.

Rolfe wanted something for himself. Not much, just a small property to manage—one that Adalbert wanted securely beholden to his hand; perhaps one on the perimeter in need of vigorous defense. Rolfe was tired of traveling, tired of having nothing but his blade and his steed. He wanted only to have a hearth and home of his own, however humble it might be.

A man who had done his family proud deserved no less, to his mind.

Adalbert, of course, might not share his view.

Rolfe's gaze fell to the black decanter fastidiously lashed to his saddle. He had known from his first glimpse that this would please Adalbert's taste for the unusual. Rolfe hoped yet again that this exotic gift might be enough to dismiss any reservations from his elder brother's mind.

It was a marvelously unusual bottle and one that could only have come from afar. The very sight of it conjured fanciful tales from vague childhood recollections. Unfortunately for Rolfe's curiosity, the magical decanter was sealed. He had itched to open it for months, but was determined not to insult his brother with a used gift.

That would rather have defeated Rolfe's purpose.

But still, the months and the miles had fed an imagination he had not known he possessed. He had grown more and more certain that there was a treasure inside, simply waiting to be discovered. He imagined a liqueur captured from pomegranates, or an exotic healing potion, or even a perfume the like of which had never been smelled west of Byzantium. Rolfe ran a finger down the neck of the decanter.

Suddenly, he noticed that the wax seal had lifted cleanly away from the bottle.

His heart skipped a beat with the awareness of what he could do.

Rolfe pulled his black destrier to an unceremonious halt before he could question his impulse. Mephistopheles' ears flicked, as though the beast made a comment about stopping where there was no sign of shelter, but Rolfe ignored him.

He freed Adalbert's gift with impatient fingers, halting with wonderment once the weight of it filled his hand. The dark bottle fit perfectly into his gloved palm, and he sat, transfixed by its beauty, for a long moment.

The bottle was blacker than obsidian, blacker than anything Rolfe had seen before, and its surface danced with strange opalescent lights. Its slender neck curved gracefully to a bulbous base, which was etched with unfamiliar designs. The stopper was made of the same dark material, its heavy cork jammed solidly into the neck.

A fine silken cord of silver and gold was knotted around the stopper, then secured to the decanter's neck with a healthy dollop of red wax.

But now the wax had lifted from the cold bottle without cracking. The glittering cord swung free; the seal was still whole.

He could satisfy his curiosity without Adalbert ever knowing the difference.

Rolfe did not need to consider the matter twice.

The cork was more resolutely anchored than he might have expected. Rolfe grimaced as he pulled, but to no avail. Mephistopheles nickered, impatient with their delay, and when the beast danced sideways, Rolfe's grip on the bottle slipped.

God's wounds, but the stopper was tight!

It was obvious he needed a sure footing for this task. He dismounted and braced his feet against the ground. Rolfe winced, grunted and twisted the dark top savagely.

The cork popped with sudden vigor, its release sending Rolfe sprawling backward. When he hit the ground in a clatter of chain mail, the bottle danced from his grip as though it had a will of its own.

"Addlepated fool!" he muttered to himself.

Rolfe lunged after the bottle, but it hit the ground just beyond his reach. Adalbert's gift would be broken! The decanter rolled across the hard ground and stopped an arm's length away, apparently undamaged.

Rolfe exhaled shakily in relief and brushed himself off. But as he reached for the bottle something was spewing forth from its mouth. It was neither elixir, nor liqueur, nor exotic scent.

As he watched, an ominous dark cloud billowed from the bottle with alarming speed. It was unnatural, to say the least. Rolfe stumbled to his feet as he inched backward.

The shadow erupting before Rolfe swirled into the shape of an overly tall woman with long dark hair. She was before him, yet she was not. Her features were clearly etched in the insubstantial cloud, but Rolfe could see the silhouette of the trees through her form. His heart skittered to a halt as she loomed high and her blazing gaze fixed upon him.

Rolfe swallowed carefully. This sight could not be real.

The vision leaned closer as Rolfe fought to make sense of what he saw. Obviously, this was some trickery, like that caused by certain mushrooms. Obviously, his previously unfanciful mind had outdone itself in this eerie forest.

"You!" the shadow roared.

Rolfe jumped in shock at the volume of her voice.

As far as he knew, visions from mushrooms were silent.

But he was not the only one to have heard the vision's cry. His palfrey, usually content to follow Mephistopheles, whinnied in fright and tugged vehemently at its reins. It snapped the leather from Rolfe's astonished grip and bolted into the woods.

Curse the skittish creature! His supplies were in the palfrey's saddlebags! That salient fact wiped any fanciful nonsense from Rolfe's mind. He turned angrily on the vision responsible for his woes.

"You have frightened one of my steeds and now my supplies are lost! What do you mean to do about this outrage?"

"I?" she purred, and Rolfe shivered unwillingly. The specter leaned closer suddenly, and Rolfe was granted a view of wickedly sharp teeth.

Perhaps he should have worded his question more politely.

The scents of saffron, cinnamon, cloves and ambergris flooded Rolfe's nostrils as her dark cloud embraced him. He struggled to logically explain the presence of smells that had no place in this northern forest and failed.

Rolfe had a sudden certainty that losing his palfrey was the least of his problems.

"Confess to me your name, mortal," she growled.

"Rolfe de Viandin." He answered before he could question the wisdom of doing so. He was dismayed to find his voice no more than a shadow of its usual bold tone.

"So, Rolfe de Viandin condemns me to leave my beloved palace in this desolate place. Trust a mortal man to complicate matters!"

The specter spat. The ground melted with a hiss where the missile landed, just to Rolfe's left. He jumped in alarm as a cloud of steam rose from the spot.

He should have set that old cheese aside at midday, he reasoned wildly. Clearly, the cheese had been past its prime. He had suspected as much at the time.

Rolfe eased a little farther away from this manifestation of a sour stomach.

Caution was the better part of valor, after all.

Before he got far, the vision flung her arms wide with a bellow of astonishing volume. The cloud, still erupting from the bottle, boiled angrily beneath her.

"A curse upon you, Rolfe de Viandin!" she screeched, pointing a finger directly at him. The fury of her gaze made him quiver in his boots, despite all he had faced in the past. "A mortal man is at the root of my woes and you shall pay the price of the faithlessness of your kind!"

That did not sound promising, but Rolfe had little time to reflect upon her words.

The dark cloud began to swirl like a tempest, picking up dirt and leaves and casting them in all directions. Rolfe's indigo cloak whipped around him, its hem snapping across Mephistopheles' side, and his dark hair blew across his brow, obscuring his vision.

Rolfe snatched at the cloak, closed his eyes and lifted his arm to protect himself from the unexpected assault. He huddled against his destrier, who snorted indignantly and lowered his head. Rolfe was halfway certain that every scrap of clothing he wore would be ripped apart. He did not dare to consider how cheese could manage such a feat.

Then, as suddenly as it had begun, the raging wind fell silent.

Inexplicably, Rolfe heard a bird sing.

His garments seemed suddenly too warm, and he felt the heat of the sun upon his helmet. Rolfe lowered his arm and blinked in shock at the sight that greeted his eyes.

He stood in a garden, surrounded by lushly fragrant and exotic blooms, although that seemed decidedly against the odds. Golden sunlight poured on the blossoms around him and the air was alive with the hum of insects. The bleak autumn forest where he had ridden just moments past was nowhere to be seen.

Truly, the cheese had outdone itself.

Surrounding the garden was a high wall made of an unfamiliar white stone, artfully fitted and gleaming silver in the sunlight. A low palace stretched out behind him. A long pool lined with blue tiles guided the eye directly to its doorway, and the scent of Eastern cooking teased his nostrils.

Rolfe blinked, but the illusion stubbornly remained.

As did the specter before him. She tapped her toe and folded her arms across her chest, dissatisfaction clear in the harsh line of her lips.

It was true that the best offense was a solid defense. Rolfe braced his booted feet on the ground and faced the vision squarely.

"What manner of trickery is this?" he demanded. "I insist that you return me to the forest and restore my palfrey."

She arched a brow. "Make no mistake, mortal, my palace is as real as you are."

Rolfe eyed his surroundings skeptically. The garden did appear to be real enough. He doffed his helmet and gloves, sniffed a bloom, fingered the leaves of a shrub and found nothing amiss. A type of insect he did not recognize ambled along the shrub's leaves and he touched it.

It stung him. Rolfe cursed and leapt backward, shaking the creature from his hand.

He eyed the specter warily. "Where are we? What have you done?"

"You are precisely where you were before," she sniffed. "It is my palace that has moved here, to satisfy the curse laid upon me. I hope that you are satisfied with what you have done."

Wolves bayed in the distance, their howls carrying over the walls in support of her claim. She shivered and glanced about with distaste.

Rolfe thought quickly. There were no wolves in the East, from whence this palace seemed to have sprung. And he had heard wolves in the forest just before opening the bottle.

Could there be some truth in her claim?

But no! It was beyond preposterous! This must be a deception, and he had only to figure out how it had been accomplished.

"What I have done?" Rolfe frowned in disbelief. "To be sure, I had nothing to do with this."

The spirit granted him a chilling glance. "Of course it is your doing!" she snapped. "Do you imagine that I would *choose* such a dismal locale?" She shuddered and fixed him with an accusing glare. "It was you who opened the bottle and you to whom I am indebted for my release."

"You seem less than pleased," he retorted. "Surely to be released from confinement is no small thing?"

"Perhaps it would be a relief if I did not have to pay such a heavy price! Who would be pleased to give their greatest treasure to a mere mortal?"

At that, Rolfe was insulted. *Mere* mortal? "I asked you for nothing!"

The specter rounded on him furiously. "And what you *want* is of no consequence! Trust me, mortal, if I could betray my obligation, I most surely would, for no one ever deserved such a gift less than a mortal man!" She straightened and folded her arms across her chest once more as she glared at him. "But a curse required me to grant possession of my palace to whoever freed me from my prison. Even jinns must adhere to some code of honor."

A jinni?

She tossed her hair as she glanced about. "Though nothing was said of doing so with grace."

This palace was to be given to him? Rolfe snorted in disbelief. A tale too fair was seldom true. This was a trick, of a manner that he could not explain, but a trick nonetheless.

It was a trick designed to rid him of his possessions; he could see that. Yes. The palfrey was already gone, and with it a goodly quantity of his supplies. Rolfe's eyes narrowed and he glared at the inexplicable being before him.

He had heard strange tales of certain plants in the East. Maybe that cheese had not turned foul, but had been brushed with some concoction designed to confuse him and grant him visions. Yes, that could be it. Rolfe's grip tightened stubbornly on Mephistopheles' reins.

No one would take from him what was his.

"You grant nothing to me," Rolfe argued. "This is merely a trick."

The jinni's eyes blazed. "A *trick?* You spurn my glorious gift?" Her voice trembled with anger, but Rolfe did not waver.

"I have no need of your spells and sorcery," he retorted. "Return my palfrey and let me continue on my way."

"No need?" the jinni sneered. Another wolf howled beyond the walls and a glint suddenly lit her eye. Dread trickled down Rolfe's spine, and he took a step back before he could stop himself.

The jinni pursued him with lightning speed. Her face filled Rolfe's vision, and when she smiled, he saw that her teeth were sharpened points of brass.

"Perhaps you will soon see the need of spells and sorcery," she hissed with an intent that made Rolfe shiver. "You were warned that I would take my vengeance." She drew herself up taller and flung her hands skyward, her growing size making both Rolfe and his black destrier slide cautiously backward.

Rolfe wondered if they could make it to the gate while her attention was averted.

"Rolfe de Viandin," she roared, and the ground trembled at her words. "Ingratitude for my gift has earned you this strife: as a wolf you will live out your life!"

The jinni smiled with malicious satisfaction.

A wolf!

Despite his conviction that this was nonsense, Rolfe

waited with baited breath for a moment. His gaze danced over himself in anticipation.

When nothing changed, he dared to feel relieved. And his relief was quickly followed by scorn. He had been a fool to lend any credence to her words!

"A wolf?" he asked skeptically.

The jinni's eyes narrowed. "You do not believe me?"

Rolfe shrugged with a bravado born of fear averted. "I am a man who believes in what he sees, and I see that nothing has changed. I suspect that you and this—" he gestured to the palace "—are a reminder that the cheese I ate at midday was past its prime."

"Cheese?" the jinni roared. Rolfe jumped in surprise, and even Mephistopheles' eyes widened. "Cheese? You dare to attribute my presence to *cheese?*"

Her eyes flashed and the clear sky was abruptly obscured by dark clouds. Thunder rumbled overhead. Lightning crackled in the distance and the ground stirred restlessly beneath Rolfe's feet. The black destrier stepped sideways with a nervousness more typical of the lost palfrey.

"More than mere cheese am I, and soon enough will you see the truth!"

"Perhaps I should have been more tactful," Rolfe murmured under his breath. Mephistopheles pointedly ignored him. The jinni grew to the height of a mountain before them and Rolfe could not help but dread her pronouncement.

Surely it was the cheese at work.

*Cheese.* Rolfe repeated the word like a litany, but as he watched the ominous cloud grow, his conviction faded.

When the jinni spoke again, her voice made the ground shake. The trees quivered from the tumult of her breath. The flowers abruptly closed against the storm.

"Powers vested beneath the earth, hear my words and attend my curse. Teach this one to respect my powers and leave him trapped outside these towers. Condemn him to howl and prowl near, this place a reminder of all he held dear. Mortal ways he shall pursue no more, but doomed is he to remember forevermore. Let the one who crosses this threshold first, be condemned to wed him despite his curse. And let the one in whom he confides, lead a killer to his side.''

The wind ripped at Rolfe's cloak as her voice fell silent. When he opened his eyes, he was outside the smooth white walls. The silent forest surrounded him again, and snow fell thickly around his head. There was no sign of the jinni, although winter had fallen with a sudden vengeance.

''May you be as miserable as I have been, mortal!'' The jinni's voice came from every side, though she was gone from view. Rolfe spun around, but he was alone.

''Look for your change by nightfall.'' Her ominous laughter filled the forest, coming from everywhere and nowhere at all.

Rolfe shivered, telling himself it was only the unexpected change of temperature he felt. The sky was darkening, though he refused to let himself dread the night.

''Cheese,'' he stated flatly to Mephistopheles. Although he spoke to the destrier, he knew his words were meant to reassure himself as much as any.

''The vision is clearly over,'' he continued with a resoluteness he was far from feeling. ''We are in the forest, just as we were before and, undoubtedly, just as we have been all along. It is not surprising in the least that I did not see this palace wall, for it is as white as the falling snow.''

Rolfe waved his hand dismissively, deliberately ignoring the fact that it had not been snowing earlier. ''Perfectly logical,'' he concluded stubbornly.

Mephistopheles gave his knight a glance that might have been skeptical, had it come from a man instead of a beast. Then the horse's gaze fell pointedly on the space behind Rolfe. Mephistopheles snorted and tossed his head.

A curious tickling sensation made Rolfe dread what he

might see. He turned and caught a glimpse of a silver-gray tail.

Rolfe twisted, and the tail danced merrily out of sight as he turned in ever tighter circles, trying to get a better look at it.

"No! It cannot be!"

He grabbed at it, his eyes widening in shock at the answering tug he felt. The tail trapped within his grip was long and quite firmly affixed to him. It was graced with thick silver hair that shaded to white at the tip.

Precisely like that of a wolf.

Before he could utter another sound, Mephistopheles nickered a warning.

Rolfe swiveled to see the bottle rolling across the ground, seemingly of its own volition. He leapt backward and collided with the palace wall.

Rolfe knew he should flee, but he could not tear his gaze away from the bottle. It rolled first this way and then the other, leaving a trail in the thickly falling snow.

Suddenly a voice rose to Rolfe's ears.

"Drat this bottle! In all truth, one would think that to be freed of her company would be blessing indeed, but *no!* This cursed bottle has to hamper my departure in a most uncomfortable way. Too many centuries waiting for rescue has a way of going to one's hips, I suppose, but *truly...*"

Rolfe's eyes widened. Mephistopheles flicked his ears when the feminine voice squeaked. "*Oh!* I never thought I had indulged that much. Certainly *she* consumed twice what I did, if not more, but perhaps malice is better for the figure in the long run. Would *that* not be a sad statement on the world, if such were the case! I cannot imagine it, but certainly it would appear to be so."

It was another jinni. And Rolfe had had enough of jinns and their interference for this day.

"Away with you!" he bellowed. "Trouble another if

you must, but leave me be! I have had my share of jinns and their curses to last a lifetime!"

The voice fell silent, but still Rolfe intended to put as much distance between himself and the cursed bottle as possible. He landed a solid kick to the dark vessel and it sailed through the air.

It did not travel as far as Rolfe might have hoped before bouncing on the rapidly accumulating snow. Another muffled squeak had Rolfe reaching for his saddle, tail or no.

He had no intention of waiting like a fool to see what this jinni's response might be.

A rosy cloud unfurled from the bottle's mouth, making the air around Rolfe and his destrier glow with a soft luminescence reminiscent of the first light of dawn.

It was not unpleasant.

Rolfe hesitated despite his intention to leave, and found himself glancing back over his shoulder in curiosity.

"Much better, oh yes, much better indeed," that feminine voice declared. "What a relief it is to have room to stretch."

The glow grew high and wide, stretching out to encompass all of the surrounding woods, before rolling back into a tight ball. The cloud radiated a curious opalescent light, but beyond its periphery, the sky grew steadily darker.

Knight and destrier exchanged dubious glances until a resonant *pop* drew their attention back to the cloud.

A plump, perfectly ordinary looking woman of indeterminate age sat on the upturned bottle. She smiled sunnily at Rolfe and propped her chin on her hand.

Well, perhaps she was not quite ordinary, for her garments were of a curious combination. She wore the sheer trousers and upturned leather shoes prevalent among Eastern women, topped by a high-necked, heavily embroidered tunic the like of which Rolfe had never seen. Her hair was dark and hung on either side of her face in thick braids. She wore a round fur hat ornamented with red woolen balls dangling from its rim, which danced as she moved. A broadsword much like Rolfe's own hung by her side.

She returned his curious regard intently for a moment before she stared suddenly down at herself. It was as though she was unaware of what she wore.

"Oh, my," she whispered and one hand rose to her lips.

A shimmer of light blinded Rolfe for a moment. He blinked, and incredibly, in that short interval, the woman's garb changed.

She now wore a fitted blue kirtle over an undyed chemise and a fur-lined cloak that fell all the way to her boots. She looked like any noblewoman Rolfe might have seen before, with the exception of her strange fur hat, which remained.

She touched it and smiled confidentially at Rolfe's glance. "It is warm," she informed him. She had a certain girlish charm, but he would not be swayed from his suspicions.

"Another jinni, are you?" he demanded.

She blinked in surprise at his hostile tone. "Yes, that I am. I must say your manner is decidedly forward."

"My manner is nothing compared to that of the last jinni I met," Rolfe declared. His eyes narrowed in suspicion as he glared at her. "Just how many of you are in there?"

She looked taken aback at his question. "No more than two, mercifully, for she was company enough for me." She rolled her eyes. "I can tell you quite confidently that several centuries take considerably longer to pass than one might think."

Rolfe wondered if he had heard her aright, but then she was chatting merrily.

"I must say that I am so relieved to be released. I should even grant you a wish." She frowned and tapped one finger on her lip. "Was that how it worked?" she mused to herself. "One wish? Three wishes?" She flicked a glance at Rolfe. "One must follow the rules, you know."

The last jinni had spoken similarly just before she had

taken her vengeance upon Rolfe. Clearly, it was time to leave.

"It does not matter," he said hastily. "I thank you, but have no need of any favors from jinns." He took several quick steps backward and reached for his saddle once more. Could he mount and ride away without her stopping him? It was certainly worth a try.

"Oh, but I must insist—"

"No, it is best saved for another. If you will excuse me?" Rolfe turned smartly and had one foot in a stirrup before she tut-tutted under her breath.

"Oh, she is good, is she not?" she commented appreciatively.

Rolfe knew this jinni had spotted his tail, and he felt his neck heat in embarrassment. Something tingled at his fingertips before he could speak, and he glanced down to find his nails had turned dark.

Like claws. Panic sent him spinning back to face the jinni, for lack of other alternatives.

He was changing to a wolf! And right before his very eyes!

"You said you could grant me a wish?" he demanded. The jinni nodded amiably. "Can you undo her spell?"

"Undo?" The jinni recoiled in shock and shook her head adamantly. "No one can *undo* anything. That is not the way."

"Then you cannot help me?"

The jinni sat up straight. "I did not say that," she asserted proudly. "I will help you, despite your manner, because I think she was ungracious in cursing her liberator. We had hopes, you know, that time would cure her of her malicious tendencies, but it seems she has only become more vengeful."

The jinni sighed, then fired a pointed glance at Rolfe. "And *I* was always taught that there was no excuse for rudeness, under any circumstance."

Rolfe averted his gaze guiltily, for he knew his own manners had been decidedly lacking in this meeting.

Even if there were extenuating circumstances. The wind riffled through his new tail as though to remind him of the precise nature of those circumstances.

"Of course," the jinni continued brightly, "I have always been burdened with an *inexplicable* affection for mortals."

Rolfe did not miss her slight emphasis. He felt himself color and decided his charm had picked a poor time to desert him. The jinni, however, seemed to have forgotten his presence.

"Let me see…" she mused. She kicked her feet playfully and tapped one fingertip against her lips.

Suddenly, Rolfe's ears felt odd. He lifted one hand, hoping against hope that he would not find what he feared, but fur greeted his touch.

The jinni did not appear to notice, and frustration rolled through Rolfe. Was he to be no more than a pawn in these jinns' foolish games? What had he done to merit such a fate?

"God's wounds, woman!" Rolfe roared, impatient with her inactivity. She jumped in a most satisfactory way. "Think if you must, but do it quickly!"

The jinni's gaze landed on him and her mouth rounded to a little O of surprise. Without further ado, she squeezed her eyes shut and pursed her lips, looking all of six summers old as she concentrated.

"Powers above and powers below, attend my words as never befo'e. Cursed by day is enough to pay…." She hesitated and nibbled on her bottom lip as she clearly fought to make a rhyme.

Trust the malicious one to have had a greater gift with words.

"Befo'e?" Rolfe repeated dubiously.

The jinni shot him a hostile glance. "Spells are not my

foremost ability," she informed him archly. She straightened and closed her eyes again before Rolfe could respond. "Now, I have forgotten where I was." She frowned, and he did not dare interrupt again.

"*Ala-kazam*," she concluded finally. "By night be a man."

Rolfe caught his breath.

He waited.

He watched.

Nothing changed.

If anything, his tail seemed a little more luxuriantly thick. Rolfe exhaled impatiently and glared at his newest companion.

This jinni's powers were apparently less than compelling. And little wonder, given the quality of her rhymes.

"*Ala-kazam*," Rolfe echoed skeptically. "Now there is a spell." He rolled his eyes, jumping backward when some invisible assailant swatted him across the shoulder. Rolfe yelped in pain and glanced wildly about.

The jinni smiled at him innocently.

"A completely inexplicable affection," she reminded him. Any urge Rolfe might have felt to apologize was swept away by her next words. "But quite a nice spell, I think, all the same."

"That is all? You mean to do no more?" Rolfe was astonished. "What manner of solution is that? Being a wolf by day is little better than being one all of the time! With all respect, I must say that I had hoped for more!"

The jinni straightened her shoulders and tossed her hair. "I told you that I could not undo the charm," she maintained proudly. "In truth, for spontaneous work, I thought it was not at all bad." She slanted a hostile glance in his direction. "My best work is not performed under duress."

Rolfe cleared his throat as he fought to maintain his temper. He reminded himself that half his time as a wolf was better than all the time.

Maybe she could do better, if his manner was sweeter than it had been so far. His charm had brought him good fortune in the past, if not the grace of more than one maiden's favors. He might do well to spare some of his charisma for this jinni.

Mindful that he could easily make his situation worse, Rolfe took a deep breath and eyed the jinni.

"You have indeed outdone yourself in aiding me on such short notice," he began. The jinni granted him a wary glance, clearly skeptical of his change of tone, and Rolfe spared her his most winning smile.

She thawed slightly, though her gaze flicked nervously away. The feminine gesture was heartrendingly familiar and fed Rolfe's confidence as nothing else could.

It was reassuring that jinns and mortal women were not that dissimilar.

"Make no mistake, *madame*," he continued smoothly, "I do appreciate your endeavors. Undoubtedly the shock of this change made me speak hastily." Rolfe locked his gaze with hers when she turned to him, and deliberately let his voice deepen. "I would thank you with all my heart for your assistance."

The jinni granted him a smile. "I could try again," she offered.

"You cannot imagine how greatly I would appreciate your efforts," Rolfe said wholeheartedly. Encouraged by her manner, he dared to suggest once more, "Perhaps we could remove the entire curse?"

"Oh, no." The jinni dismissed his suggestion yet again without giving it the consideration Rolfe thought it deserved. "It is not the way. You must earn your salvation with the conditions you have been granted. I cannot change that, but I can grant another point in your favor."

"Earn? I did nothing to *earn* this curse!"

A tingling sensation halted his protest. Rolfe looked down to find silver fur sprouting all over his flesh. He gasped aloud, but his voice sounded more like a muffled yelp.

He looked to the jinni in shock, but she only smiled.

She shook a finger beneath Rolfe's nose, which he was alarmed to see had turned black. "*You* opened the bottle," she explained. "Do you not see? That deed earned you this."

"But can you not do something? I beg of you, *madame*, help me however you can!"

"Well, perhaps a little more," the jinni mused, her expression considering.

"Then hurry! Please!"

"I told you that I do not work well under pressure."

Rolfe was going to interrupt her, but his voice was a bark this time. Panic raged through him, but the jinni merely squeezed her eyes shut again.

"Though when cursed by day, in the garden he cannot play, let him in at night to avoid the forest's plight. And whether he feel good or ill, the palace shall reflect his will. Finally, by grace of the powers above, let this curse be broken by the blessing of love."

She opened her eyes and smiled with satisfaction. "That was rather a good one, was it not?"

Rolfe could not confess to be in the least pleased by the jinni's intervention. He thought he had won her assistance! Forest's plight? Blessing of love?

What manner of solution was this?

He barked in frustration, but it was too late. He ran upon all fours in the snow around the jinni. Too late, too late!

And what of her spell? It was night and he was a wolf! Rolfe howled deliberately at the moon beginning to rise in the sky, then fixed the jinni with an accusing glance.

Had she not said that he would be a wolf only by day? Her power was a sham!

The jinni's lips twisted with uncertainty as she eyed the moon. "It is just a question of timing," she assured Rolfe with a confidence that was not convincing. "That is far and away the most complicated part of casting spells."

Rolfe had thought it was the rhymes she found troubling, but he could hardly argue with her. Instead, he snarled for the first time and rather liked the feel of it.

He especially enjoyed the way the jinni jumped away from him when he did it. She retreated behind her bottle and eyed him speculatively.

"You know, it is not very fitting to have her flying freely," she said hastily. "There was a reason why she was confined to this bottle in the first place, as you can well imagine. It might be wise to see her thus confined again."

That was enough. Rolfe had been patient beyond belief. He was finished with jinns and their curses.

And there was one good way to tell her his opinion.

He lunged toward the jinni and bared his teeth. He snapped, and though his jaws closed on empty air, he savored the knowledge that he had made his feelings clear.

"Well, well." The jinni sniffed indignantly from several feet away. "I see I shall have to find someone else to aid me."

She snatched up both the bottle she had vacated and its cork. With a vicious spin, she turned and stalked off into the forest, those red balls bouncing indignantly as she walked. Her footsteps left no mark upon the surface of the snow, and in the twinkling of an eye, she had disappeared into the trees.

And Rolfe was left alone. Mephistopheles regarded him with wariness. The silence of the forest surrounded them, and the moon made the snow glitter ethereally.

Were it not for his changed form and the palace wall behind him, the entire incident might not have happened.

Wolves howled in the distance again and Rolfe felt a primal urge to lift his voice along with theirs. The forest was more alien to him than it had ever been, but he settled resolutely back on his haunches.

If nothing else, Rolfe could protect his destrier from his hungry brethren while he pondered the first jinni's spell.

He hated that he had few other options.

Cheese, indeed.

## Chapter Two

*December*

"I tell you, Yves, the most sensible course would be to wed Annelise to Hildegarde's son."

Bertrand de Beauvoir clapped Annelise's younger brother on the shoulder companionably. Though his manner was friendly—indeed markedly more friendly than he had ever been to Yves in the past—Annelise wondered what the old mercenary sought to gain for himself from this match.

Come to think of it, she was not certain that Bertrand had ever before addressed Yves directly. Yves was a bastard, true enough, but their wretched sire had let Yves be raised within the walls of Château Sayerne.

Of course, he had not been without his own motives, either.

With their sire deceased, Bertrand could hardly have discussed this offer for her hand with anyone else, Annelise mused. A bastard brother was all the family she had left.

That is, besides her rumored legitimate brother, Quinn, who had left Sayerne to earn his own way before Annelise had even been conceived. She shivered in recollection of the tales their father had told of the cruelty of his firstborn. She and Yves had been right to leave Sayerne to the wind and the wolves when they had heard that Quinn had been summoned back there.

It suited Annelise's sense of justice to leave the man who had inherited her sire's character a legacy not worth having.

For Château Sayerne, the traditional holding of Annelise's family, was no prize. Jerome de Sayerne had let the estate fall into neglect, and with his death, the last of Sayerne's tenants had fled before an uncertain future. This past year, not a single seed had been sown in Sayerne's fields. The holding had declined so greatly from its original state that Annelise and Yves had not even needed to discuss the merit of leaving once they learned of Quinn's pending return.

And neither of them had looked back.

Beauvoir was, in marked contrast to Sayerne, a comfortable keep, despite its remote location. Bertrand, the new Lord de Beauvoir, had been entrusted with the strategic task of guarding the Beauvoir Pass. Here the old Roman road passed out of the Lord de Tulley's holdings on its straight route south. Château Beauvoir itself was perched on the apex of the pass like a commanding finger pointed heavenward.

Beauvoir's tower was as narrow as a needle, construction restricted by the rocky terrain on all sides. There were windows only at the very top of the tower, in Bertrand's solar and the guard's watch above. To say that the keep was heavily garrisoned would have been a gross understatement.

It was the most military keep in all of Tulley's holdings, which said much about this critical point on the road. Annelise and the lord's wife were the only women to be found within these walls, and Annelise had been painfully aware of the soldiers' eyes following her every move.

But Beauvoir, despite its unwelcoming nature, was a

sight more friendly, she was certain, than Sayerne would be on Quinn's return.

Bertrand's office, adjacent to the solar, was a sparsely furnished room, although the pieces there were fine ones. The shutters were fastened tightly against the chill fingers of the wind, and a merry fire blazed on the hearth.

Silver-haired Bertrand sat in a high-backed oak chair that faced the fire, its wooden arms worn to a smooth patina. The lines on his face were deeply etched into a permanently severe expression, and he looked every inch the experienced commander that he was.

His wife perched closer to the hearth on a three-legged stool, much like the one Annelise used, although the lady's was cushioned with wool dyed richly red. A mousy woman with almost no color in her complexion, Bertrand's wife bent over her work, her shoulders rounded, her demeanor meek. She wore an expression of permanent exhaustion, and never had Annelise heard her speak a word unbidden.

It was a characteristic rather alien to the outspoken Annelise.

The golden firelight danced over them all and cast what was a tense discussion in a falsely warm glow of intimacy. The light burnished Yves' mail to silver and cast mysterious shadows in the secret corners of the room.

"Annelise wedded?" Yves asked, as though the thought had not occurred to him before.

"Yes." Bertrand nodded. "A man cannot make his way dragging a sister by his side." The older man's silver brows drew together sternly. "You did ask me for advice, after all, and this is the only option that makes good sense."

"Perhaps someone might ask my opinion." Annelise piped up, unable to hold her tongue any longer. "After all, it is my future that you discuss."

Bertrand's wife shot a warning glance in Annelise's direction, but both men acted as though she had not spoken.

Yves tapped his toe in indecision. "Perhaps the Lord de

Tulley should be involved in this match," he mused. "I would not want to offend him by taking delicate matters into my own hands."

Irritation fired through Annelise at his ready assumption of her agreement to this entire idea. Since they had left Sayerne, Yves had changed, and he no longer looked to her for advice.

Not even on this matter closest to her own heart. Indeed, since their sire's demise, Yves had shown a decisive side that Annelise had barely glimpsed before. She did not really care for this aspect of her half brother, for it reminded her too much of her sire's determination. Annelise was forced to acknowledge that she truly did not know Yves that well.

She had returned to Sayerne from the convent only a year before Jerome's death, after all.

"Bah!" Bertrand dismissed Yves' comment. "Tulley has too much on his board these days to trifle with the match of a noblewoman without a dowry."

Annelise felt her color rise at being discussed like some baggage to be rid of.

"But who is this Hildegarde?" Yves asked, only the first of many questions Annelise had.

"Hildegarde de Viandin, an old family friend. Her husband, Millard, and I trained together. Sadly, Millard passed away some years ago."

Annelise licked a thread and fed the floss through the eye of the needle with a herculean effort at control. *A lady should hold her tongue.* She repeated the nuns' admonition to herself with gritted teeth.

Bertrand cleared his throat. "She has written to ask whether I know a suitable young woman to marry her second son. The eldest, of course, is the heir, but Hildegarde might be persuaded to ensure that the younger son be granted a small holding."

Yves said nothing, to Annelise's relief, but Bertrand frowned. "Annelise cannot expect to do much better, you

know, what with her lack of dowry. And everyone knows
about the curse of her forthright manner.'' He fired a glance
at Annelise that kept her from protesting the accusation.

The nuns would have been proud, she thought rebel-
liously, and jabbed the needle into the linen.

''The timing is most opportune, Yves, and the family is
a good one. Their holdings are prosperous, and your sister
would have a most satisfactory life.''

Annelise could keep silent no longer. ''Satisfactory by
whose standards?''

Bertrand visibly gritted his teeth. ''It is a curse,'' he muttered under his breath, and Yves' lips tightened.

''It is not a curse to know one's own mind,'' Annelise
argued. ''I fail to see how my opinion could not be relevant.
You are discussing my future and a man with whom I
would be destined to spend the rest of my life.''

''Annelise, can you not hold your tongue for once?''
Yves said impatiently. ''These matters are delicate. You
know that this decision is not yours to make.''

''I know it, but I do not like it.''

''It does not matter what you like,'' Yves retorted in a
sharp tone he had never used with her before. His rebuttal
stung, and Annelise blinked her tears away furiously as she
stared at her despised needlework.

Her conviction that Yves would do his best for her was
dealt a sharp blow.

Yves paced across the wooden floor in the shadows beyond Bertrand, his hands clasped behind his back, his bright
blond hair catching the light. His expressive amber eyes,
so like her own, were hidden from view, and Annelise felt
that her brother had become a stranger.

He straightened, and before the words even fell from his
mouth, Annelise saw that Yves meant to agree with Bertrand. She tossed the needlework aside, hating Yves for
betraying her treasured hopes.

Yves *knew* what she wanted. They had discussed her

future often since their sire's death. How dare Yves cast her aspirations aside for his own convenience?

Before she could protest, there was a knock on the door.

"The Lord Enguerrand de Roussineau to see his lordship," Bertrand's manservant announced.

Bertrand winced, then composed his features and beckoned with one stately finger. His wife laid aside her embroidery and scurried to summon refreshment. Annelise watched openly as a young man of whom she had heard much—and little of it complimentary—swept into Bertrand's chamber.

Enguerrand was dark haired, and more lavishly dressed than Annelise would have expected he could afford. There was a dusting of snow across the heavy green cloak tossed over his shoulders, and he held his helmet under his arm. His gaze flitted assessingly around the room, and he swallowed a coy smile when he spotted Annelise.

The glimpse of that smile before it was hidden made Annelise dread his mission.

Then Enguerrand smiled with all the charm of the angels, bowing low to Bertrand. The older man tolerated the gesture, although he arched a brow at Yves over the new arrival's head as though he, too, wondered at Enguerrand's purpose. Enguerrand accepted the welcome cup offered by Bertrand's wife, although he took no notice of the woman herself.

His gaze flicked again to Annelise, and she saw his eyes glitter hungrily before he turned away. She bent over her needlework to hide her revulsion.

"It is long since we have had the honor of your company," Bertrand said with a coldness that could not be missed.

Enguerrand chose to ignore the older man's tone. "Bertrand, neighbor of mine, I come for news. Do you know the whereabouts of Annelise de Sayerne? I have just found Sayerne deserted, and Tulley is away at battle."

"Why do you seek my sister?" Yves demanded.

Enguerrand jumped as though he had not seen the younger man, then his eyes narrowed as he stared boldly at Yves. "Sister?" he asked. "I had thought Jerome de Sayerne spawned only two children."

"Two legitimate children," Yves confirmed with the usual bravado he saved for such inquiries. "I am his bastard, although my father spoke of recognizing me legally as his own."

"But he did not?"

"No."

"Ah!" There was no mistaking the relief that swept over Enguerrand's saturnine features. His gaze slid to Annelise once more. "And might this then be the fair Annelise herself?"

Annelise rose to her feet and cast her handwork aside. "I am Annelise de Sayerne," she said flatly. "Why do you seek me?"

Enguerrand sank to his knee before Annelise and lifted her hand to his lips. "Fairest Annelise," he purred. "I am most charmed to make your acquaintance."

"Indeed?" Annelise should have returned the compliment and she knew it.

"Indeed," Enguerrand confirmed, undeterred. "Your beauty is more than I might have hoped for when I set out to seek your hand in marriage."

"Marriage?"

That the subject should come up twice in such short order was beyond belief. Annelise had always been told how unsuitable she was for marriage, both by her miserable father and by the cursed nuns. Too outspoken, too poorly skilled in household tasks, too tall. And without a dowry, as Bertrand had so admirably reminded her just moments past.

Yet two offers for her hand were to be heard on the same day.

It defied explanation. Unfortunately for both offers, Annelise had decided long ago that a match rooted in love would be the only one for her.

She was about to refuse, when Enguerrand's dark gaze darted to meet hers. Annelise fell silent when she saw avarice gleam there.

*He thinks Quinn will not come home,* she realized in that instant. *And he wants Sayerne for himself.*

Was that also the Lady Hildegarde's motivation? Did she seek a holding for her younger son outside her elder son's legacy of Viandin?

"Yes, lady," Enguerrand cooed. "You will be fairer than fair as my bride."

To be desired for her potential holdings alone was a travesty of Annelise's own dreams. "I will not be your bride!" she snapped. She hauled her hand out of Enguerrand's grip and backed away, knowing her distaste showed on her face.

"Annelise!" Yves chided. Bertrand's wife gasped, and Bertrand fired a reproving glance Annelise's way.

Enguerrand stepped back and fastidiously brushed off his cloak. "Do not worry yourselves," he said in a dangerously low voice, his gaze fixed on Annelise. "I have always enjoyed women of spirit."

Annelise did not flinch from his cold gaze.

"At any rate, you may have come too late," Bertrand interjected.

Enguerrand tossed the weight of his cloak over his shoulder as he turned to Bertrand. "What do you mean?"

"Hildegarde de Viandin seeks a wife for her son. Yves and I were discussing the terms of our agreement."

"So, now it is an agreement!" Annelise protested, but the men ignored her. Bertrand's wife frowned and shook her head, signaling Annelise to be quiet.

"Who is this son?" Enguerrand demanded, the curl of his lip condescending.

Bertrand gave no evidence that he noticed the affront.

"A knight who has taken up the cross—the younger son, name of Rolfe."

"So, he is in the East?" Enguerrand scoffed. "This sweet blossom of a woman has no need of a spouse far away in the Holy Land."

Annelise grimaced at Enguerrand's honeyed words.

"He is expected home by the Yule," Bertrand said firmly.

"Ha!" Enguerrand threw out his hands. "If this Rolfe never returns from the Crusade, then where would our fair Annelise be? Do you imagine Hildegarde would show compassion for a widow of an unconsummated match?"

Bertrand clearly did not appreciate the observation. "How dare you imply that Rolfe will not arrive home?" he demanded. "How dare you imply that Hildegarde's intent is less than honorable?"

"Admit the truth, Bertrand," Enguerrand retorted coolly. "You do not even know whether this knight still draws breath. There have been many casualties in the East, and this man might well have been among them."

"Rolfe is bold in battle!" Bertrand insisted. "He is the son of a noble and esteemed family who will treat his intended bride well!"

But he trots home on his mother's bidding to marry the bride she has chosen for him, Annelise amended. That was no man for her. She would have a man who could make a decision for himself.

"Enguerrand's concern is not without merit," Yves said quietly to Bertrand. At these words, Enguerrand smiled confidently. "My only goal is to see Annelise safe in my absence," Yves continued. "Perhaps it would be best to await this Rolfe's return."

Enguerrand's features contorted with shock. "Are you quite mad?" he demanded. "You already know that the Lord de Tulley has summoned Quinn to claim his holdings. We have all heard the horrible tales of your brother's cruelty. Surely you cannot imagine that Quinn will have any concern for your welfare or that of your sister?'' Enguerrand made an exaggerated bow in Annelise's direction, which she ignored. "With apologies to the lady, of course.''

Yves stiffened. "I had no idea you were so informed as to our family's affairs,'' he said coolly.

Enguerrand had the grace to flush. "It only makes sense, when one seeks a lady's favor, to determine her situation.''

Annelise barely restrained herself from rolling her eyes.

"But to return to the matter at hand,'' Enguerrand continued, so smoothly that no one could easily interrupt him. "In contrast to this possibly deceased man, I am here this very day, bearing gifts for the delightful Annelise. Surely, Yves, my offer bodes better for the future of your lovely sister.''

Annelise eyed Enguerrand and silently named him an opportunist.

"You?'' Bertrand drew himself up in his chair. "We all know the handicap of Roussineau! Even the second son of Viandin would be better situated than the heir of Roussineau!''

Enguerrand flushed, which told Annelise that Bertrand was too close to the truth for comfort.

"Roussineau is a holding of much potential,'' Enguerrand argued stiffly.

Particularly, Annelise concluded, if he could marry into a larger and better situated holding. Sayerne had been badly abused in the last years of her father's life, and certainly had been poorly managed, but at least the fields were fertile.

Unlike Roussineau. Annelise had heard about its setting in the foothills, rife with boulders and stones. There was precious little soil between the rocks, and even less sun, with the mountains surrounding Roussineau to the west and south. She knew that the vein of silver mined there in the past had been depleted and she suspected that tithes must be very low.

They would have to be, to make abused Sayerne look like a prize.

"Has anything changed at Roussineau of late, Enguerrand?" Yves asked.

He could not be considering the man's offer! Annelise fired a glance across the hall that her brother chose to ignore. How dare he not take her own desire into account?

If Yves made this match without her agreement, Annelise would see his heels held to the fire this very night!

Enguerrand smiled silkily. "Roussineau may be a small holding, but it is well outfitted and adequate to see to your sister's needs and safety. I am not without ambition, though, and imagine that your charming sister will be more finely housed within short order."

"Housed like some steed acquired at the market," Annelise muttered. Bertrand's wife was the only one who heard, evidently, and her lips thinned.

More likely Annelise's own potential legacy would see her better "housed," not any ambition of Enguerrand's.

"Adequate?" Bertrand retorted. "Roussineau is hardly adequate for any manner of lady. Yves, do not be a fool! Accept Hildegarde's offer and see Annelise's future assured!"

Yves' manner was thoughtful, and he flicked considering glances at the two older men as he paced.

He did not, Annelise noted with rising anger, even so much as acknowledge that she was in the room.

"Yves!" Enguerrand appealed. "Do not shackle such a lovely flower to a corpse! See her wedded now, to me!"

"I say she should wed Hildegarde's son!" Bertrand bellowed. He rose to his feet and pounded on the arm of his chair, clearly not accustomed to be challenged in his own home. "There can be no other sensible choice!"

"And I say she should wed me!"

Annelise made a vicious stab through the linen with her needle and winced as she jabbed the tip of her finger. She inhaled sharply at the pain and cast her work aside impatiently. Bertrand's wife clucked under her breath, but Annelise was finished with holding her tongue.

She pushed herself to her feet, but the trio of men did not so much as look at her. She cleared her throat pointedly, but to no avail.

"Perhaps we could leave the matter for a few days," Yves suggested.

"No, Yves, there is no need to wait so long," Annelise said firmly. All three men looked at her then, their expressions surprised, as though they had forgotten her very presence.

"There is nothing to decide," she declared. "I shall wed neither of these men and that is final."

"Annelise!" Enguerrand whispered in shock. He clutched at his chest as though she had dealt a lethal blow to his heart. Bertrand's face set in antagonism, and Yves watched her with open curiosity.

At the very least, Annelise had their attention.

"What manner of young woman would show such audacity to her seniors?" Bertrand demanded. "No wonder your sire saw you cloistered for most of your years! It is your place to be silent, woman!"

"As Hildegarde's son's place is beneath her thumb?" Annelise retorted. "I cannot imagine what I should want of a man wrought of such mettle."

"And I cannot imagine how a woman of such sweet countenance could be cursed with a viper's tongue," Bertrand snapped.

"Then we are agreed that the match would not be a wholesome one," Annelise concluded sweetly.

She flicked a glance at Enguerrand. "What do you know of this man, Yves?" Annelise already knew the answer, but she wanted her brother to say the words.

"Only what he says and the rumor I have heard," he admitted reluctantly.

"Consider, then, whether you would grant my hand to a stranger whose repute is somewhat less than ideal." Annelise forced herself to continue in an even tone. "I would not slight another guest of our host, but it could well be that this gentleman's sights are set upon Sayerne itself."

Enguerrand's lips set in a thin line of malice, but Annelise ignored him.

Yves frowned in thought. "Annelise, surely you cannot mean to discard both of these suitors?"

"Surely, I can and do." Annelise folded her hands across her chest in a most unfeminine gesture. "I would have neither of them."

"But you cannot mean to wait for Quinn to make your match?" Enguerrand demanded. "He might find a worse fate for you, if he lives up to his reputation for cruelty."

"I pledged long ago that I would make a match for love or not at all," Annelise admitted proudly. "And I stand by my vow."

"Love?" Bertrand cackled. He settled back in his chair, his temper obviously mitigated by this turn of events. "What has love to do with marriage, child? Yves, your sister is blessed with strange ideas!"

But Annelise had seen only too well the price a woman paid for a match not made in love. Her lips set stubbornly, though she would not tell these fools what she had seen.

That secret had been hers alone for too many years.

"I would make a love match or none at all," she insisted, her throat tight with her vivid memories.

"Love needs only time to grow," Enguerrand purred.

"No, you are mistaken." Annelise's gaze locked with Yves', and she once again willed him to consider her own desires in this. "I shall know the man for me from first glance."

There was a moment's silence in the solar, then Bertrand

coughed and grimaced. He shook his head, dismissing
Annelise's interruption, and turned his bright eyes upon her
brother.

"Come, Yves, make a choice."

Yves' somber gaze danced over the group before colliding with Annelise's own once more. She saw, to her relief,
that he had listened to her words. "It would be churlish to
deny the lady's own request for her future," he said quietly.

Annelise felt her lips curl in a smile. But the taste of
victory was quickly wiped away as the two older men bent
their wills upon Yves in an attempt to see his mind
changed.

"But women do not understand the ways of the world,"
Enguerrand argued.

"If a valiant knight like Hildegarde's Rolfe does not
meet with her favor, then none will satisfy." Bertrand's
tone was clipped, and he pointedly ignored Annelise.

"She only wants to remain here at Beauvoir without ob-
ligations. It is the way of women everywhere." Enguerrand
lent his voice to persuade Yves. "She will undoubtedly find
marriage has much to commend it, once she has a babe or
two and a keep of her own to manage."

"You cannot take Annelise with you while you seek
your fortune, Yves, and I will not have her remain here
unwed," Bertrand stated flatly. "This keep is too full of
warriors and it would be unfitting for me to accept responsibility for a young, unmarried woman. Annelise cannot
return to Sayerne, and Tulley is unavailable to grant you
aid in this, even if he were so inclined."

"Surely you do not desire to see sweet Annelise left
alone, without husband, hearth and protection?" At Enguerrand's whisper, Yves' shoulders sagged.

"Annelise," he appealed. "You must make a choice,
despite your opinion."

"You could take me with you."

Yves shook his head. "No. I must see you safe before I

depart to seek my own fortune." He took a deep breath and held her gaze resolutely. Annelise's heart sank with the certainty of what he would say.

"I must insist that you choose one suitor or the other and wed before Quinn's return. I bid you decide immediately."

"No." Annelise straightened proudly and tossed back her auburn hair, certain that Yves would bow before her determination. Surely, once he saw the strength of her will, he would back down.

Yves knew how much she had loathed the convent. Surely that fact could be used to show him the magnitude of her objection?

"No, there is a third choice," she continued. "If I cannot marry a man I choose, then I will consign myself to become a bride of Christ." Annelise shrugged with a casualness she did not feel. "Maybe in the cloister I will find the love I seek."

Her threat hung in the air like a tangible thing. The fire crackled, and all eyes were fixed upon her in shock. Yves opened his mouth, then closed it again. Annelise waited impatiently, but he did not protest.

He knew! How could he not see her meaning?

To her astonishment, Yves nodded with calm demeanor far beyond his years. "So be it," he said.

No! Annelise's mouth fell open in shock. How could Yves betray her in this? "You would dispatch me to a convent?" Her voice was husky in her astonishment, but Yves held her gaze steadily.

He arched a fair brow, his mind clearly made up. "It was you who named the price," he said firmly. Then his voice dropped slightly. "I would have you safe before Quinn comes home, Annelise, and you have made your choice."

Annelise forced her mouth to close and composed her

features as her anger rose. How *dare* Yves take her at her word? How dare he ignore what she had told him?

Annelise had thought she could trust him!

But she would not beg him to reconsider. Annelise had her pride, after all. Should the convent be the price she was condemned to pay for her convictions, then pay she would.

The sky was gray before the dawn when Annelise appeared expectantly the next morning. The snow was falling thick and fast. The wind was cold enough to chill right to the bone, and she shivered as she accepted aid to mount.

Yves would not be able to consign her to a convent, Annelise was certain. He alone knew how she had loathed her years in the convent. He would realize she had made the claim to show him her determination to avoid these matches.

And Yves had never held out in opposition to her strong will before.

Surely she would be told this morning that she could accompany him, after all.

Annelise's gaze flew to her brother as he stepped out of the hall, apparently preoccupied with donning his gloves. He would come to her, Annelise was certain, and tell her she had won this battle.

But no. Without even glancing at his sister, Yves strode to his destrier, mounted and turned his horse to leave.

Annelise fussed with her reins and refused to acknowledge her budding doubt. Yves only waited until they were upon the road. He simply did not want to back down before all these soldiers and the Lord de Beauvoir.

But there was a newly resolute set to her younger brother's lips that troubled her.

The horses snorted, their breath making puffs of steam in the cold air. Squires blew on their hands to keep warm, and the gatekeeper apparently wore everything he owned.

Another burly man stamped his feet as he paced back

and forth in the tollbooth, although at this early hour, no traveling merchants had yet crested the pass. Annelise was not surprised that Tulley—and Beauvoir—had no intention of missing any coin due.

The portcullis protested with a squeal as it was hauled skyward. Yves cast a stern glance over his party, but did not meet his sister's eyes before leading the group out onto the road.

Bertrand and his wife had not even come to say farewell. Annelise's heart turned as cold as the snow around her.

What if she *was* left at the convent? What if Yves did not back down? Unlike the last time, when she had been sent to the nuns purportedly for her education, Annelise would not be able to leave the cloister.

She would be consigned to a lifetime of silence. She would be alone, entrusted to the care of an abbess who was a complete stranger, surrounded by yet more strangers.

And there would be no hope of respite.

It had been that hope alone that had made the cloister bearable before. That and the dreadful secret Annelise had confided in none, a secret that held no fear for her any longer, yet still left its legacy in her thoughts. The bile rose in Annelise's throat that once again she would be banished for being an inconvenience in the lives of men.

But neither Hildegarde's cowed son nor the avaricious Enguerrand fit Annelise's expectations of a mate.

On that point, she was resolute. She would not back down. Yves had bidden her choose and so she had. She was not one to go back on her word.

Yves would change his mind.

Annelise lifted her chin proudly and eyed the snow-covered road before her. The portcullis dropped behind the little party with a resonant clang that echoed in Annelise's own heart.

Outside the protection of the gates, the height made the wind viciously strong and cold. It shrieked through the pass and burrowed beneath all the layers of clothing Annelise wore.

Pine trees decked in fresh snow flanked the road; rocky cliffs above disappeared into the low clouds. The morning was as gray and cold as a tomb. The party was sullenly silent as the icy wind cavorted about them, and the horses bent their heads as they headed southward.

Curse Yves! Annelise thought as she blinked back angry tears. Curse Quinn! Curse one brother for making her choose and the other for ensuring that she could not remain safely at home! Curse these meddling men who would dictate her fate! And curse these knights for their resentful attitude!

It was Annelise, after all, who might be left behind with the Sisters of Ste. Radegund.

The little party rode in silence throughout the heartlessly gray day. The house of the Sisters of Ste. Radegund was outside Tulley's lands, nestled in the forest on the south face of the mountains. It was a secluded place, well away from the traffic of the secular world.

Once through the pass, the silent party turned away from the fitted stone of the straight Roman road and onto a track that trailed eastward through the woods. The horses' hooves stirred the snow as they proceeded. Annelise took little interest in their direction, although Yves and the men frequently dismounted and conferred over the trail.

The snow had apparently hidden much of it, and Annelise took a grim satisfaction in the inconvenience of delay. She was not in a hurry to begin her life as a bride of Christ, even if it meant spending more time in the cold.

The sky was darkening to twilight when Yves drew his steed to a halt. Annelise, riding directly behind him, slowed her own beast. Although it had been two years since she had ridden this road. It seemed to her that they had traveled far too long.

Nothing but endless snow and dark, leafless trees greeted her sight in every direction. Only the clatter of barren branches in the wind carried to Annelise's ears. She shivered and huddled in her cloak, feeling the cold more deeply now that she knew there might not soon be any relief from its chill.

"We could return to Beauvoir," she suggested. One of the knights snorted and Yves ignored her comment. It seemed he *had* decided to consign her to the cloister. Annelise opened her mouth to argue with him anew.

It was then that the wolves began to howl.

One howled first, far to the left of the path they followed, and Annelise's protest was silenced in fear. The call was chilling, and the men exchanged glances even as they tried to appear unconcerned.

Then another wolf responded from the right side of the trail. Its cry was much closer than the first and made the hair on the back of Annelise's neck prickle.

She looked to Yves in alarm. "Surely the convent cannot be far?" she asked, hearing the anxiety in her tone. "We could at least seek haven there."

"In truth," Yves confessed heavily, "I do not know. The snow upon the path must have led us astray. We should have arrived hours ago."

"Could we have passed the convent by?" one of the other men demanded.

Two more wolves howled. They were even closer, and Annelise could not tell whether they were the same as the first two or not. The sky darkened an increment more.

The autumn had been unseasonably cold, with much early snow, Annelise recalled with dread. The wolves would be hungry.

And night was quickly falling.

"Surely, Yves, you have some plan in mind!" protested a third man. "We cannot take shelter in the woods with wolves abroad!"

"I cannot lead you to a hearth without knowing where we are!" Yves flung out his hands in frustration, and for the first time in months looked his youthful fifteen summers. "Tell me in which direction you would head."

They all looked into the woods about them, and it was then that Annelise saw the shadows of the wolves.

# Chapter Three

Annelise gasped aloud, and the men, seeing the wolves as well, rallied their steeds hastily about her. The horses snorted nervously, well aware of the scent of wolf in the wind.

A wolf howled to its brethren. The horses shied nervously away from the sound. Annelise stroked her mare's ears, but the beast was oblivious to her touch. Its ears flicked, and its dark eyes were wide with fear.

"Surely there must be somewhere we can take shelter," she argued.

The man beside her tightened his lips. "It is too late now." Annelise watched with dawning horror as he drew his blade. "They are all around us, my lady, and hungry at this season, unless I miss my guess."

Annelise looked into the woods, at the pacing shadows of the predators. She caught her breath at the glimmer of pale eyes in the shadows.

The awareness that one of their party—if not more—was doomed to become a meal for these beasts made her heart race.

"We should flee!" she declared.

"And to where?" the sardonic man beside her commented. "Wolves are possessed of an unholy cunning and stamina beyond all. They will separate us and dog our steps until our horses fall from exhaustion."

Yves cleared his throat and gathered his reins in his gloved hands. When he spoke, his voice was grim. "We must flee, even knowing that one of us may fall. I remind you all that you have already given your pledge to protect Annelise."

The men grunted in reluctant assent and slanted hostile glances in her direction again. Annelise could meet the gaze of none of the four at the reminder that one would be compelled to pay a heavy price for the escape of the others.

"Shall we draw lots or allow Dame Fortune to make the choice?" Yves asked.

The men barely glanced at each other before responding.

"Dame Fortune is my choice," the sardonic man replied. "And let our fates fall as they may. May she not be a greedy wench this night and see us all fallen."

The other two men grunted their agreement, drawing their blades as they gazed into the growing shadows under the barren trees.

Yves flicked a glance at Annelise and their gazes clung. "I bid you good fortune, sister of mine," he said softly, "lest I not have the opportunity to do so later."

Annelise's heart leapt at the import of his words. "Yves, I never thought..." she began, but Yves dropped his gloved hand over hers.

"It is not your fault," he murmured. "I erred in being as stubborn as you in this." His grip tightened briefly, his gaze locked with hers, and he was once again the young man she had come to trust. "I wanted only to ensure your safety before I left." The corner of his lip tilted in a smile, making the dimple that graced his chin deepen. "Fare thee well," he whispered.

It was her own stubbornness that saw them in this predicament, and Annelise felt the full weight of her guilt. She should never have made such a threat as she had, regardless of what Yves' foolish ideas about her safety were.

She could have ridden alongside him, but it was too late to argue the matter now. Annelise hoped desperately that neither of them were destined to pay a high price for their stubborn natures.

"And may you fare well, also." Her voice broke, but Yves had already moved away.

"I cannot even count their numbers," whispered one man.

"And they are gaunt from this cursed winter," muttered the third. "Mark my words, they will be bold."

"As shall we!" Yves bellowed. The wolves ceased their pacing and eyed him warily, their eyes glinting silver in the underbrush. "Away to the right! And mind the lady!"

All four men gave spurs to their horses at that instant. Their nervous steeds were only too glad to obey the call to flee. Annelise heard the smack of leather on her mare's rump and the palfrey sprang away, racing in their midst.

The horses ran wildly, virtually unchecked in their desperation to escape. Annelise crouched down as her mare plunged into the forest. A low branch brushed over her hood, but she did not dare to look up. The snow crunched underfoot as the horses broke trail, their breath billowing steam into the air.

The wolves howled in protest at their flight, and the horses hastened their pace at the sound. Several wolves barked, and Annelise glanced back to see them lunge in pursuit.

She clutched her mare's reins, her heart in her mouth. Her heels dug into the horse's side as the wind ripped her hood from her head.

The mare bolted forward and ran alongside Yves' steed at breakneck speed, leaving the other three horses behind.

"Flee, Annelise!" Yves cried when he saw her. "Do not

wait—our mail will be our doom!'' His hand smacked heavily on the mare's rump.

It was all the encouragement that beast needed.

Rolfe heard the party of knights in his woods and his heart leapt with anticipation. He cared little about their mission—it was enough for him that they were here, close enough to aid him in gaining his freedom.

This last month had shown the curse was real indeed. Rolfe's skepticism of jinns and their powers had been eliminated by the very real experience of changing from man to wolf and back to man again with a relentless repetition that echoed the sun's rise and fall each day.

To say that he tired of this adventure would have been an understatement, to say the least.

The other wolves avoided him, although the jinni's acceleration of winter had made them gaunt with hunger. It was as though they knew him to be different, though Rolfe had little desire for their company.

But his life, such as it was, was a lonely business.

The familiar sound of men and mail and horses brought him running, but not before his fellow wolves had attacked. To Rolfe's shock and dismay, the largest and meanest wolf had separated the only woman from the group.

A noblewoman! And on a small palfrey! She had no chance against the wolf's determination, and Rolfe knew it well.

The oath of knighthood he had sworn an eternity ago burned in his mind. Though he might be condemned to don the cloak of a wolf, Rolfe was yet a knight within his heart.

There was only one thing he could do.

He gave chase, hoping that the large wolf would be satisfied with the horse alone. Somehow, Rolfe would save this woman, even if he had to pay the price with his own miserable existence.

There was nothing else a knight of honor could do.

The palfrey ran like the wind, gradually outpacing the other larger beasts with their heavier burdens. The pounding of hoofbeats filled Annelise's ears. The stark silhouettes of the trees danced past her in endless succession as she craned her neck for some sight of a sanctuary ahead.

The carpet of twinkling snow appeared endless. Annelise squeezed her eyes closed against its brightness, illuminated by the setting sun breaking through the scattering clouds.

The sounds of the other horses faded behind her, but she could not have slowed her palfrey to save her life. The beast ran as though it were possessed. When Annelise heard a distant, anguished cry moments later, her mouth went dry.

One of the men had fallen prey to the wolves!

Surely it could not be Yves!

Annelise dared to look, only to find the men had faded from sight, although their cries carried to her ears. She considered trying to turn her horse about, before she saw the lone wolf loping through the forest directly toward her.

It had separated from the pack, its gaze chillingly cold. Annelise's heart stopped. Too late she realized that she had only a very small blade with which she might protect herself.

Small consolation, indeed.

Then she saw that a second wolf dogged the footsteps of the first, and her heart sank to her toes.

Even if she defied the odds and outran the first wolf, the second would still claim her life. Annelise inhaled sharply, remembering only too well the one man's claim. The palfrey ran on, as yet unaware that they were being stalked.

Annelise looked back in fear, but the men-at-arms were too far away to heed any cry she might make for help. She was on her own.

Her grip tightened on the reins. She had done well enough on her own in the past—indeed, Yves had granted her only the impression that he might be relied upon. In truth, Annelise should be used to confronting life's challenges by herself.

She glanced toward the woods, just in time to see the first wolf leap forward and clear the trees. It trotted in the tracks of her horse, not more than ten paces behind. It neither drew closer nor fell farther back.

Just as the knight had said, the beast would follow her until the horse collapsed.

But not if she could outrun the fiend! Annelise dug her heels into her palfrey's ribs. The mare's nostrils quivered in fear and a shudder ran over its flesh. Even as the horse ran with all its might, it was clearly tiring.

And the wolf loped patiently behind, keeping its distance, as though aware that it was only a matter of time.

Annelise was unnerved to know the wolf's intent and be powerless all the same. She urged her mare onward, but the horse stepped suddenly on a patch of ice.

It whinnied in terror as it slipped and lost its balance.

The wolf did not miss a beat.

Annelise glanced back in time to see long white fangs bared. She screamed. The horse fought to regain its footing, but to no avail.

The beast was upon them! The mare shrieked as the wolf's claws dug into its rump. Annelise could feel the heat of the predator's breath as her horse fell to one haunch. The mare writhed and threw Annelise as it struggled to escape.

The wolf growled, the horse made an anguished cry. Annelise fought her way clear of the clutch of snow. She fumbled to her feet and looked back, only to wish she had not.

The snow was stained red, the blood gleaming wetly atop the crusty surface. The wolf snarled and eyed Annelise as it latched its teeth around the trembling horse's neck.

The mare's eyes rolled back and its cries fell silent. Annelise staggered backward, knowing that there was noth-

ing she could do to save her steed. She watched her horse
shudder, then fall curiously still. The wolf ripped open the
mare's belly, its gray fur staining crimson as it began to
eat.

It looked up, its disconcertingly cold gaze filled with
malice and deadly intent.

Annelise's mouth went dry.

She turned and fled wildly. Tears rose to choke her as
she ran. Her breath rasped, her heart pounded, but she could
not risk stopping.

Only when Annelise heard the soft patter of his footfalls
in the snow behind her did she recall the second wolf. She
cast a glance over her shoulder to find him dogging her
footsteps.

She was being hunted! Annelise's breath came in uneven
spurts and she gathered up her skirts in two fistfuls. She
ran as she had never run before, certain the predator behind
waited only for her inevitable exhaustion.

It was a cruel way to die.

The sight of a path ahead gave Annelise new strength.
She cut between the trees, plunging onward despite the
knee-deep snow. She fell once, trapped by her skirts, and
her pulse hammered in her ears. Her auburn hair fell loose
about her face as her veil was ripped away, and she risked
a panicked backward glance.

The wolf, she saw, took a more roundabout path.

Annelise caught her breath that she had gained a bit of
time. She stumbled onto the road on frozen feet and ran
blindly as she shook clumps of snow from the hem of her
kirtle.

Then she saw the walls. Annelise drew in her breath at
the sight. The convent!

But no convent had walls so high and artfully built as
this. She blinked, but still the smooth white walls remained.
A castle, although Annelise could not guess why it was
here in this remote spot. Nor did she care.

Most importantly, it was just a little farther down this road. She might survive! Annelise glanced back to the wolf. By some trick of her mind, he seemed to have slowed his pace slightly.

Annelise sprinted for the gates. The wolf loped leisurely behind, and Annelise stifled the curious thought that he guided her toward the palace.

Foolish whimsy!

Then her heart filled with delight as the gates loomed high above her. They were closed, but at dusk she would have expected nothing else. She had only to awaken the gatekeeper. Determined to do so as quickly as possible, Annelise pounded on the wooden portal with both fists.

"Who knocks?" demanded a genderless voice.

Annelise could not tell where the voice emanated from, but had no time to ponder such oddities.

"Annelise de Sayerne." She spared a leery glance over her shoulder at the pursuing wolf. He drew yet closer, and she pounded again on the door when the gatekeeper did not respond. "I beg you for sanctuary! A wolf pursues me!"

The keeper took ridiculously long to answer, and his words were spoken with a slow precision that seemed inappropriate to the circumstance. "A price must be paid for your entry here."

A price? Surely such matters could be settled once she was inside?

"Anything!" Annelise declared. "I will pay anything if you let me in!"

"The price of your finding sanctuary here," pronounced the voice slowly, "is that you wed the master of this abode."

Wed? Had he said *wed*?

Annelise stepped back from the portal, shocked at the curious request. She frowned, wondering what manner of ogre the master of this fortress must be to gain a wife in such an unconventional manner.

A snarl behind Annelise recalled her to her senses.

Her panicked glance revealed that the wolf was directly behind her and quickly drawing nearer. She would be eaten alive, just as her mare had been! She backed into the gates, unable to tear her gaze away from the wolf.

"I accept! I accept! Open the cursed gates!" The portal abruptly fell open behind her. Annelise found herself sprawled on her rump inside the fortress's gates.

But she was not safe yet! The wolf leapt, as though he, too, would enter.

Or as though he would drive her into the palace. That made no sense. The beast would gobble her up, just as his compatriot had devoured her palfrey!

Annelise screamed and scrambled backward. As she did so, she caught a glimpse of the wolf's eyes, noting that one was blue and one silver-gray. Then the heavy wooden doors abruptly slammed shut—leaving the wolf trapped outside.

Rolfe paced restlessly outside the palace gates, watching the setting sun with even more impatience than usual. He had heard the gates make their request and was shocked at the reminder of the first jinni's curse.

How could he have forgotten those words?

A noblewoman reposed within the walls of the palace that had been granted to his keeping. A noblewoman who had pledged to be his wife. It was incredible to think that Rolfe, the younger son who had never expected to have the right to a wife, should have a woman waiting for him even now.

Who could have imagined that the curse could have brought him such fortune? Rolfe would woo this woman destined to be his bride. He would win her heart. They might have children.

Rolfe's excitement made him pace more and more

quickly. He would build a marriage like the one his parents had had! He would pledge himself to this woman's happiness, and together they might gain his freedom.

But what would happen when this mysterious noblewoman learned of his status? Reality crashed around Rolfe in a cold wave. What would she do when she learned that this palace was nothing but illusion?

She would laugh, as Rosalinde had laughed at Rolfe's attentions. That lady had welcomed his affections until she had learned Rolfe was the younger son. Then her charm had fled and he had seen her character for what it was.

Rolfe abruptly remembered the second jinni's pledge that he could be saved by love. Love. He stared at the gates as he summoned every vestige of his resolution.

Love was a physical act, and one natural between husband and wife. This woman would grant Rolfe the opportunity to win his freedom, but he would never trust her enough to give her the chance to wound him as Rosalinde had done.

Trust, after all, fell in the class of things that a man could not see or hold. Rolfe knew enough of the world to discount that manner of whimsy.

This noblewoman and he would have an arrangement to their mutual benefit. No more than that. Women, like Rosalinde, understood that intimacy was negotiated.

At least Rolfe could thank Rosalinde for teaching him the rules.

Annelise exhaled raggedly and closed her eyes for a moment. Her heart thundered in her ears at her near escape.

She was safe. But what about Yves and the others?

"Gatekeeper!" she cried, and glanced about for the first time. It was only then that she realized she was alone.

She must be mistaken. The gate could not have opened by itself. Surely the gatekeeper who had spoken to her was nearby.

But there was no one in sight.

"Hello?" she called. "Gatekeeper? Are you here?"

Nothing moved. Goose pimples rose over her flesh as the silence echoed eerily in her ears, but Annelise refused to be daunted.

There had to be a gatekeeper. He had talked to her, after all. And he could not have gone very far.

Annelise rose purposefully and brushed off her kirtle as she examined the walls on either side of the heavy gates. They were as smooth as glass, without so much as a nook for a keeper to hide in. She propped her hands on her hips and tipped back her head to eye the height of the walls.

They stretched toward the heavens, smoother than any wall she had seen before. The masons here had been talented, indeed. There was neither a ladder nor a stair, nor so much as a walkway. Nary a lookout along the entire wall, as far as she could see.

What a curious place.

There was not even an opening in the portal to let one peek outside the heavy walls. Did the lord have no interest in seeing who approached his gate? It made no sense at all to need to open the gate to see who came.

Wolf or no, Annelise could see no other way to find Yves. She knocked once more on the solid door. When no one stirred in response, she knocked harder.

"My brother also needs sanctuary!" she shouted in frustration.

Only silence greeted her ears.

Annelise tapped her toe impatiently. She spun around, but the walls surrounding the palace were smooth and featureless as far as she could see. She eyed the empty arched windows in the strangely low-built keep, with its sparkling blue pool.

Those windows were most impractical, without so much as a shutter across them. The hall would be cold as cold could be in these winter months. Obviously that skilled mason had not had a speck of sense.

It was then Annelise realized that the air in the bailey smelled as green as the spring. Indeed, her russet-wool kirtle and emerald cloak with its squirrel-fur lining were so heavy that a trickle of sweat was making its way down her back beneath her chemise.

Annelise looked about herself with wary eyes. What manner of castle had she entered?

And what manner of man would be its lord?

One thing was certain. Annelise was effectively his prisoner, and she did not care for that in the least. Surely the keeper could not have truly meant that she would have to wed the lord? It was all very strange and puzzling.

If nothing else, she and this lord must have a talk.

Annelise strode through the budding garden and under the broadest archway. It was impossible not to notice the richness of her surroundings or the complete absence of any other being.

She quickly decided that the keep was in fact a palace, for never had she seen a keep of such gracious design. And this palace had not been built for defense, as difficult as it had been for her to enter.

The walls were blindingly white, the floors tiled with intricate mosaics of stones in varying shades. Luxuriously thick rugs in shades of red and ochre were scattered across the floors.

The twilight painted the white interior with inviting aubergine and indigo shadows. The rooms were large and uncluttered, the size of the windows indicating that the interior would be bright in the daylight.

As prisons went, this one was exceptional. Annelise could hardly complain.

Her antagonism against this lord had dwindled appreciably by the time she found a room flooded with candlelight.

The room faced onto a small tiled courtyard, where a

fountain splashed playfully in the last glimmer of twilight. The walls were hung with rich tapestries resplendent with exotic flowers she could not name. So many carpets were flung on the floor that they overlapped two and three deep. Annelise's feet sank into their softness when she stepped into the room.

Hundreds of candles covered storage chests and were scattered across the floor right out into the courtyard. The smell of beeswax was inviting, and the flickering golden light picked out the mother-of-pearl inlay on the chests.

In the middle of the room was a low table, evidently set for a meal. An embroidered cloth covered it, tassels wound with gold and as thick as Annelise's wrist hanging from its four corners. Three brass salvers reposed on the table, glinting in the candlelight.

Annelise glanced over her shoulder, but she already knew that the palace was empty. She sniffed the air and caught a delectable whiff that was enough to make her stomach growl.

She could at least see what the meal was.

A waft of steam was released when she lifted the first lid, and Annelise inhaled the rich smell of a savory meat stew. Her stomach growled openly, defying her to believe that the crust of bread she had had at Beauvoir that morning was enough to sustain her.

The meat was venison, the gravy thick and crowded with tiny onions and carrots, the serving the precise amount she could eat comfortably. Annelise felt herself salivate as she eyed her favorite dish.

How had her host known she loved venison stew?

Nonsense. Annelise dismissed the thought. Although, if a man had ever been bent on earning her favor, he would be wise to offer food. More than any women she had met in both convent and Sayerne, Annelise possessed a love of good, hearty fare.

But it was impossible that the lord could have known, let alone that he might have cared to court her approval. Annelise eyed the stew and knew that she was being presumptuous to think this feast was laid out for her.

Of course, there was no one else here to enjoy the meal. And no one here to make such preparations, either. Just as there had been no one to open the gate.

Perhaps Annelise should not be so quick to dismiss the impossible in this unusual place.

She discovered a loaf of fine white bread with a perfect golden crust under the next salver. A knife reposed on the wooden plate beside the bread.

It was enough to drive her mad with hunger.

The third sheltered a cheese of sufficient tang to make her inhale deeply of its scent, as well as a pot of freshly churned butter and a bowl of olives.

There was a single spoon for the stew on the table, Annelise saw now. Fruit, a chalice, and a decanter that proved to contain red wine completed the setting.

A meal laid for one.

As one would greet a guest.

Annelise glanced around the room again, only now noticing the large tub steaming in the corner. Her skin itched at the very idea of a bath, and she immediately investigated. Rounded flower petals the size of her thumb floated across the surface of the water, and their unfamiliar scent was heavenly.

This was no lord's bath, but one prepared for a lady.

A guest who was a lady.

Annelise knew there were not two such as she in this palace on this evening. She dipped a finger into the scented water and decided it was too hot as yet.

But if she ate first, it would be near perfect. She chewed her bottom lip, but made her choice in a heartbeat. If this enigmatic lord planned to keep her prisoner here, she might as well take advantage of his hospitality.

Besides, if she was going to argue with him over his odd condition of marriage, she would do well to be at her best.

Rolfe's sense of purpose deserted him when he rounded a corner in the palace and saw the candlelight pooling on the stone floor ahead.

She was in there.

He swallowed and hesitated. The noblewoman who held his fate in her hands was only a dozen paces away. The wound that Rosalinde had left upon Rolfe's heart twinged as he eyed the doorway.

Only now he realized that he had no neat explanation for this curious situation. At least not one that any sensible person might believe.

But there was nothing for it. The noblewoman had given her agreement, and Rolfe was anxious to proceed.

He was well and truly tired of this incessant shifting between forms. One night of loving might well solve his dilemma—if the second jinni had been right—and he was ready to begin.

Perhaps some wondrous explanation of their entwined fates would pop into Rolfe's mind before he confronted her.

Perhaps. He shrugged and strode onward.

The sight that greeted his eyes brought Rolfe to a halt on the threshold. For the second time this evening, the palace had taken him by surprise.

Rolfe had hoped that the lady's desires would be met, but he had never imagined his will had this kind of power.

The room he had always preferred had been transformed

on this night. It was filled with a glow that contrasted markedly with the rest of the deadened palace. Rolfe felt welcome, warm, at home.

He realized suddenly that it was the presence of another person that made the room seem alive. Rolfe took an appreciative breath and caught the sharp tang of a robust cheese.

The lady, though, was nowhere in sight.

Feeling like an intruder in his own palace, Rolfe stepped quietly into the room. Emboldened by the silence, he continued until he was staring down at the remains of her meal.

The lady had an appetite, that much was clear.

A bowl that looked to have contained stew was empty, the spoon licked clean as though every mouthful had been savored. Crumbs littered the dish, evidence that the lady had wiped up the gravy with bread. The pitcher of wine was empty, though there was still a quantity of bread and a piece of cheese.

Rolfe frowned, certain he had never known a woman to enjoy food more or eat with such enthusiasm. Had this savory meal truly been her heart's desire? Rolfe could not believe a lady would eat so simply if she had the choice. Rosalinde had picked at her food and preferred ornamental fancies that did little to fill a man's belly. Maybe the magic had inflicted Rolfe's own plain but hearty tastes upon this stranger.

He realized that he truly knew nothing about this woman he had decided to take to wife.

Rolfe suddenly heard the soft whisper of her breathing and spun on his heel in alarm.

The lady was blissfully unaware of his presence, however. She slept in her bath, shrouded in flickering shadows as wisps of steam rose around her.

Rolfe exhaled in shaky relief, and the sweet perfume of roses carried to his nostrils. He had never smelled roses of such fragrance before encountering the large red roses of the East. He had never thought to smell them again once he had crossed the Adriatic.

The candlelight caressed the pallor of the woman's bare shoulders, and his pulse began to echo in his ears. Being in attendance while a lady bathed recalled past pleasures with lightning speed. He savored the sense that he had stumbled into some forbidden feminine bower as he inhaled deeply of the heady perfume.

It was his palace, after all.

And the lady had to be nude. Rolfe peered unabashedly through the shadows.

Her head lolled back on the rim of the wooden tub; her lips were parted. One hand hung over the side; the other was lost in the water that rose to her collarbone. Her garments were discarded, not folded, as though she had been impatient to bathe.

Her long auburn hair was twisted up on top of her head, evidence of that same impatience in the loose knot she had actually tied in the tresses. Rolfe found himself smiling, understanding exactly how anxious one could be to bathe after a journey.

Rosalinde would have summoned a maid to pin her hair up prettily, regardless of the time involved, he was certain.

The sense that he could have something in common with this noblewoman emboldened him as nothing else could. Rolfe took a tentative step forward, half expecting her to awaken and cast him out.

Did he dream again? He moved slowly so as not to dispel this fascinating vision. When the lady neither stirred nor vanished in a puff of smoke, he could not resist temptation. Rolfe stepped closer to see his bride-to-be.

Hers was not a conventionally pretty face, he noted with interest—not as Rosalinde's had been. This woman's lips were too ripely curved, her eyes would be too large and wide for her to be a man's ornamental prize.

Yet despite her differences from the woman he had once thought perfection in flesh, Rolfe was intrigued by the voluptuousness of this woman's features. Her cheekbones were prominent and she possessed a dimple in the center of her chin. There was a sensuality about her face that suggested an intriguing beauty of an entirely different sort.

The lashes that swept over her cheeks were luxuriantly thick, tinged with the same reddish tone as her hair. Her complexion was creamy, her lips a rich, ruddy hue, her throat and shoulders as smooth and pale as the finest silk.

It was a face that spoke of passion, of the same zest for life evidenced by the remnants of her meal.

The hand that languished on the side of the tub was long and slender, feminine despite the short, cropped nails. Sadly, a goodly quantity of rose petals floating on the surface of the bathwater obscured everything else and foiled Rolfe's rising curiosity. He folded his arms across his chest and stared down at her.

His bride.

He imagined sealing their vows with a kiss on those enticingly curved lips, and suddenly his breeches seemed rather snug.

For the first time, the ordeal begun by the jinns' curses had a certain promise.

Rolfe wondered what color the woman's eyes would be. He recalled that she was tall and wondered whether she would be slender or as voluptuously curved as her sculpted lips.

The very question did hard and thick things to parts of him that had been neglected rather longer than he usually preferred.

An echo of Rosalinde's laughter when she had heard of his status made Rolfe's ears suddenly burn. What manner of fool was he to be so quick to trust a complete stranger? Who was this Annelise de Sayerne? Why had she been abroad in this forest in the dead of winter? Who had accompanied her? And why would she have so readily agreed to wed a complete stranger?

As tempting as this lady's form might be, Rolfe forced himself to face the fact that he knew precious little about her character.

With the exception that she devoured stew like an overworked villein.

*And let the one in whom he confides, lead a killer to his side.*

The sudden recollection of the curse was a reminder Rolfe should not have needed. He could not risk telling this woman his name, he knew. Sayerne was not that far from Viandin that she might not guess his identity. If she did not know his name, Rolfe reasoned, chances were less that she could betray him.

But she might have already met Adalbert! Or his mother! If so, she might guess Rolfe's identity when she saw his features. He and his brother both favored their dame strongly.

Rolfe's mouth went dry. There was too much at risk.

His wife could not see his face.

He pursed his lips, well aware that she might not be enamored of these conditions. Women could be testy when not given their way, Rolfe knew well enough from Rosalinde. Additionally, there was a determination in the set of this one's lips that forewarned him.

The loving he needed to dissolve the curse must be accomplished as soon as possible. Somehow he would have to wed the lady before she could reconsider the wisdom of her choice, and he had to consummate the match this very night.

He could do it. Rolfe would use every vestige of his charm. Why, even the sought-after Rosalinde had granted him favors! This woman could not have the same experience of having a dozen noblemen doting upon her. She would swoon in Rolfe's arms, fall into his bed, beg him to take her! He would come to her in the darkness and labor all the night to earn his salvation.

Rolfe's pulse began to pound like thunder in his ears at the thought. It was clear, he told himself as he eyed his bride, that he had been without a woman's gentle touch for far too long.

And on the morrow, he would be free.

On the morrow, Rolfe could explain everything to her, if indeed the lady was even remotely interested in the tale. He could not expect as much—certainly Rosalinde had stormed away at the first inkling that there was no luxurious future in his cards.

Rolfe pulled the heavy ring his mother had given him when he departed for the Crusades from within his tabard. A cabochon garnet reposed in the gold setting and winked in the candlelight, still safely secured on its chain.

It was the only piece of jewelry he owned, and his mother had declared it to be a talisman of luck. Rolfe had no faith in such whimsy, but he had to admit that nothing ill had befallen him in the East. He had nearly lost this token when the jinni cursed him, but had sought it out and secured it on the chain on his first night as a man again.

A bride had need of a ring, and on impulse, Rolfe decided to give his bride this one. It was a token of his family, after all, and no indication that he had need of all the good fortune he could find.

He removed the ring purposefully from its chain, but lost

his grip. The jewel danced for an instant on his fingertips as he struggled to catch it, then fell. Rolfe watched in horror as the ring splashed into the lady's bath. The chain dropped to the floor with a clatter.

The woman's eyelashes fluttered in surprise, and Rolfe's heart leapt to his mouth.

No! She could not see his face!

He turned and fled.

# *Chapter Four*

Something warm landed between Annelise's breasts with a solid thump.

The lord was here!

He would see her at her bath! Annelise sat up abruptly. Her eyes opened wide and her hands flew to cover her breasts as she anxiously scanned the room. A small, smooth shape rolled down the middle of her belly, but she was too alarmed to heed it.

The room was as deserted as it had been when Annelise had climbed into the tub, though the candles had burned much lower. It was too dark outside to see the fountain in the courtyard, but she could still hear the water dancing.

Annelise recalled the small splash that had awakened her and fished in the tub for the cause. Her fingers closed on something round, and she hauled it to the surface to see what it was.

A man's ring reposed on the flat of her palm.

Annelise's mouth went dry at the import of that. He had been here and left this token behind, clearly as a reminder of her promise.

But she had not even seen him. How much of her had *he* seen? Annelise shivered. What kind of monster must this man be to seek a wife in such an unconventional manner?

Muted music carried to her ears as though it would summon her to a tryst. Annelise swallowed, knowing instinctively that her betrothed was waiting for her.

Well, she had never been shy, and this was no time to begin. Annelise rose from her bath and hastily set about dressing.

There was no time for hose or headdress, she decided impulsively. It would be false modesty to fret about appearances when the man had already looked upon her while she bathed.

Yes. Annelise pinned up her hair with a vengeance. It was time she met this elusive lord so they could talk.


Annelise followed the sound of the music through the palace, her leather shoes slapping lightly against the marble floor. She ducked through a wide archway and found herself alongside the pool in front of the palace.

The moon painted the garden with an ethereal silver light. The scent of the same unfamiliar flowers that had graced her bath filled the air. The perfect stillness of the pool reflected the scattered stars overhead.

But Annelise had eyes only for the bower of cut flowers arranged beside the pool. Her footsteps faltered when a figure draped in dark wool separated from the shadows under the bower.

Her husband-to-be. It could be none other.

A hood sheltered his features, and the indigo cloak fell to his ankles. Annelise caught the barest glimpse of his boots, which far from satisfied her curiosity. She peered into the shadows under the hood, determined to catch some glimpse of the monster she was doomed to wed, but to no avail.

He was completely concealed from her.

At least he was tall and broad of shoulder, although Annelise would have liked to know a bit more about her prospective spouse. She would have preferred to look him in the eye to explain why she could not possibly wed him. It seemed only fitting.

But she was clearly not to have that chance. She summoned a pert smile and stepped forward with a boldness she was not quite feeling.

"Good evening. I trust that you are the lord of this estate?"

"Indeed, I am," he responded. His voice was deep, and Annelise thought she could hear a smile in his tone. She bristled at the idea that he might be laughing at her, and straightened. "And you are Annelise de Sayerne?"

She colored slightly at the reminder of her lack of manners, but the dim light would certainly hide that. "I am."

"I am most pleased to make your acquaintance." He bowed slightly, but contributed no further information. Annelise felt the weight of his gaze upon her and tried not to show her irritation.

He was a fine one to criticize her manners. "I apologize, but I did not catch your name," she said firmly.

"I did not mention it."

"And you are?" Annelise prompted, not so easily deterred as that.

"A man with no name, as far as you are concerned."

Annelise gasped, not in the least appeased when he chuckled at her consternation. She had no intention of providing his amusement. Annelise stared at the cloaked figure coldly.

"Obviously, this is some sort of game you have chosen to play, but I am not interested in participating." She held out his ring at arm's length. "You may as well take this back. I have no intention of marrying a perfect stranger."

"I am far from perfect, *mademoiselle*." The persistent thread of laughter in his voice weakened Annelise's resolve.

She wondered about his smile.

Annelise deliberately straightened, reminding herself of what she intended to tell him. "You know what I mean."

"That I do." He folded his arms across his chest, showing no inclination to take the ring as he surveyed her silently.

What if he refused to let her leave?

"So, Annelise," he purred finally, and her name was a caress on his tongue, "you would prefer to leave the palace?"

Annelise smiled in sudden relief. It had been almost too easy to gain his agreement. "Certainly," she said with satisfaction. "I shall leave first thing in the morning."

She fingered the ring and looked at the enigmatic lord, but still could catch no glimpse of the features secreted under the hood. Nor did he advance to accept his token.

He must truly be a fearsome sight. Annelise placed the ring on the flagstones, rather than approach him, then turned to leave. But his words halted her in her tracks.

"No, not in the morning."

Annelise looked back in alarm to see him shake his head. Dread filtered through her at the curious certainty in his tone.

"Should you stay the night," he continued, his tone amiable but firm, "you must wed me first. That *was* the condition of your admittance, after all."

"But that is not fair!" Annelise pivoted so quickly that her skirts swung out, and she stalked back toward him. "I cannot leave now!"

"You gave your word when you were admitted," he insisted.

"You cannot force me to leave now!" Annelise gestured to the woods beyond the walls. "There are hungry wolves out there! Are you so barbaric as to send me to a certain death?"

The man before her did not appear to be affected by her appeal in the least. "You assume considerably about a man you do not know," he said in a low voice that made her shiver.

But Annelise was made of sterner stuff than that. She tapped her toe impatiently. "Surely you can see that if I leave now I will not survive until the morning?"

"Surely you can recall that you gave your word when you came here?"

"Well..." Annelise frowned. "That choice was made under duress. It was impulsive. You must see that it would be foolish for us to actually wed." She flicked a glance to the man before her, but he remained as silent as a stone. "I apologize for any inconvenience and greatly appreciate your hospitality thus far."

Still he said nothing. Somehow she had to make him understand.

Annelise stepped closer to him and her voice dropped slightly. "You must not be insulted. This has nothing to do with you personally and even less to do with your disfigurement, however horrific it must be."

He stiffened and inhaled sharply, but she plunged on past the obviously sensitive subject, inadvertently revealing more than she intended. "You may think it foolish, but I promised myself once that I would never marry a man who did not love me."

"Indeed?" There was a stillness about him suddenly, as though he listened too intently to her words, and Annelise took a cautious step backward. "Why?" he demanded with more interest than he had summoned so far.

Here she was, telling a complete stranger things about herself that he had no business knowing. What had gotten into her? Annelise was usually adept at keeping her thoughts—in particular one haunting recollection—securely to herself.

She decided to close the subject before she confessed anything further. "My reasons are my own," she said flatly. "And I made this pledge before giving my word to your gatekeeper, so it naturally has to be given precedence."

Mercifully, he did not question this precarious piece of logic.

"And how, Annelise de Sayerne," he mused, "would you know whether a man loved you to your satisfaction?"

"I would simply know."

"How? Give me a tangible example of a man's love."

"Well…" Annelise thought furiously. "He would take care of me and protect me from harm.…"

"Save you from hungry wolves, perhaps?"

She glared at him, guessing that he was deliberately misunderstanding her. "That was not precisely what I meant."

"But it amounts to the same, does it not?"

Annelise pursed her lips and fired a mutinous glance at the man before her. "Perhaps," she admitted reluctantly.

He took a measured step toward her, but Annelise refused to run. "Perhaps," he continued smoothly, "that love might also be found in the marital bed." He closed the distance between them with deliberate steps, and Annelise swallowed carefully.

Her heart began to pound. Although she was yet inexperienced in such intriguing matters, Annelise had heard women complain mightily about rendering their marital debt.

And they had not been wed to horribly disfigured men.

Annelise took a deep breath and wondered how she could talk her way out of this particular tangle.

"Surely a man who loved you would see to the care of all your earthly needs?" the cloaked man demanded.

"Earthly needs?" Annelise echoed. To her dismay, her voice was no more than a squeak.

"Certainly." He paused a mere pace away, and Annelise risked a glance into the shadows framed by the hood. She spied the gleam of his eyes, but nothing more, although she could feel the heat rising from his skin. She was suddenly aware of how close he stood, although she did not dare step away lest he think her afraid.

"Needs like food, shelter, the comfort of a welcome bath," he continued smoothly.

"But you provided for those needs of mine," Annelise argued. "And we both know that you cannot possibly love me. We are strangers, after all."

"Yet the end result is the same, is it not?" he mused. "Surely love, like all things of merit, manifests in tangible results?"

Annelise found, to her dismay, that she could not argue with that point, much as she sensed its fundamental error.

He dropped to one knee before her, distracting her from her thoughts. Annelise tried unabashedly to catch a glimpse of something beneath the cloak.

The bent knee she spied looked perfectly normal.

In fact, even his woolen chausses could not disguise his leg's muscled strength. As though he felt her scrutiny, he straightened and held the ring out to her, the circle of gold pinched between finger and thumb.

His hand was tanned, the palm broad and fingers strong. There was a dusting of dark hair on its back and the nails were neatly trimmed. There was a callus on the palm at the base of his smallest finger. Annelise recognized the hand of a man who wielded a broadsword.

She saw then the white band on his right hand where he had worn the same ring he now offered to her. The garden suddenly felt impossibly intimate, and Annelise could not draw a full breath.

She had to know more about him. His looks could not be so bad as that, and her curiosity was overwhelming. She flicked a glance at his obscured face, then reached abruptly for his hood, hoping to surprise him.

His other hand escaped from the folds of his cloak with lightning speed and locked around her wrist. Annelise could not help but look, and was surprised at her satisfaction that his other hand matched the first.

His grip was strong and sure, yet he did not hold her so tightly that she was hurt. Annelise's pulse fluttered uncertainly at the press of his flesh against her own.

"Take my ring, Annelise," he murmured.

She took a deep breath. "I told you already," she argued. "I made myself a promise."

"And you made a promise to me," he reminded her. His thumb slid across the inside of her wrist in a gentle caress, and his voice dropped as he continued. "The two are not necessarily incompatible."

The rhythm of his thumb against her skin was more troubling than Annelise thought it should be.

She had never stood so close to a man, never had a man touch her so surely. Certainly she had never stood thus with a man destined to be her husband.

Should she stand by her word, Annelise had no doubt that these same strong, masculine hands would one day run over her bare flesh.

She peered up at him, hating anew that she could not see his eyes. "What do you mean?"

"I mean that the two goals can be as one. Your needs were met before you even stated them. I vow to you that that will continue."

"I was expecting more than a meal and the occasional bath from marriage," Annelise informed him coldly.

"And perhaps you were overly ambitious for that," he chided gently. "Many women are abused or ignored by their spouses, kept in dismal conditions and forced to bear countless children. It is not so uncommon as a sheltered woman like yourself might think."

Annelise fought to keep her features impassive so that he might not guess how close his words hit to the mark.

"You will experience none of that at my hand and will

be better situated than most. Surely this arrangement would not be all bad.''

"There would be no love between us," Annelise argued.

He clucked his tongue. "Are you one who divines the future, my Annelise?" he asked silkily. His intimate address made her heart jump a beat. His thumb began to trace larger circles against the soft inside of her wrist, and Annelise found the rhythmic sensation distracting beyond all. "Who can say what will grow between us over the years?"

"This is madness!" Annelise tore her hand from his grip. "You cannot mean to do this."

"Of course I do," he insisted. "As do you."

"I..." Annelise clapped her mouth shut before she could tell him anything more. "What if I decline your offer?"

He turned and looked pointedly to the portal in the outer wall. As if to emphasize his meaning, the howl of a wolf drifted to Annelise's ears.

Her gaze danced between him and the ring. She stared firmly at where she thought his eyes must be. "Tell me your name," she insisted.

The hood moved slowly as he shook his head.

Annelise gritted her teeth in exasperation. "You expect me to wed you when you will not even tell me your name? That does not bode well for this pretty future you promise."

"It is the best I can offer you at this time."

Annelise did not miss the hint of change in the future. She found herself heartened by the possibilities, despite her lingering reservations. "Then show me your face," she challenged.

He shook his head again. "No, you must not look fully upon me before the morrow."

"What will change by the morrow? It is already late...."

His soft chuckle told Annelise all she needed to know.

"Oh! On *this* night?" she asked in astonishment, and he nodded.

Annelise expelled her breath sharply. "But without my

looking upon you? However could we…'' She flushed with the audacity of her thoughts, then decided to have the matter out in the open. She forced herself to ask, ''Is this to be a consummated match?''

''Yes,'' he purred, and moved in the blink of an eye so that they stood toe-to-toe. Her breasts were but a finger's width from his chest, and his breath fanned against her forehead when he spoke. Annelise was assaulted by the very masculine scent of his skin, and her toes curled in her shoes.

''Yes, Annelise, this match will be complete in every sense of the word. I would not miss the delight of your touch.''

''You looked!'' she accused.

He chuckled and lifted her hand to his lips. ''No, but I wanted to. You are tempting in sleep.''

Annelise strained unsuccessfully to see the mouth that tantalizingly brushed against her palm. Her flesh tingled as it never had before.

She tore her hand from his grip and darted away from him, not knowing quite what to make of these alien sensations. ''Ha! You talk about love, but this match is about lust!''

He fell silent, and Annelise knew he was eyeing her. When he spoke, his voice was resolute and he ignored her accusation. ''We must consummate in darkness so that you are not burdened with the sight of me.''

Annelise bit her lip. His disfigurement must be terrible, and she realized rather late that he must be sensitive about it. Perhaps he had once been a handsome man. She supposed she had been less than gracious in insisting on seeing the horror he had become.

''What about the morrow? Why did you say I could look upon you then?''

''Perhaps my situation will have changed.''

By their coupling? It made no sense, but Annelise was given no further time to ponder.

He lifted the ring before her enticingly. The garnet snared the moonlight and glowed a dull red. "Do we have vows to exchange, Annelise?"

"There is no priest," she objected.

"Marriage is the only sacrament for which one does not need a priest," he retorted, more tersely than he had thus far. He extended the ring a little closer. "Annelise?"

How had she gotten herself into this predicament?

Annelise looked into the fathomless shadows within the hood, knowing that her choices now were this match or the wolf-ridden forest of the night.

She supposed this was a better choice than either Enguerrand or Hildegarde's son. At least this enigmatic lord wished to have her for his wife without regard to her potential inheritance.

"I would feel more comfortable if we could spend time and become better acquainted," she suggested, knowing his answer when he growled with frustration.

"Annelise de Sayerne! You gave me your word—will you stand by it or not? The gates can be opened if you wish to leave!"

"Fine!" Annelise snatched at the ring impatiently. "I stand by my word!" She glared at him. "You have talked me into a corner and I admit defeat. Does that satisfy you?"

He chuckled, his good humor apparently restored. He brushed a warm fingertip across the end of her nose. "Ah, Annelise, why do I suspect that you will never truly admit defeat?"

Annelise had no response to that. If by defeat he meant her submission to him, this mysterious lord would have a long wait for that day.

"I thought we were going to exchange vows," she snapped instead.

He captured her hand and led her to the bower of flowers.

The setting was idyllic and might have been romantic under other circumstances. As it was, Annelise could not believe that this was happening to her.

"I take thee, Annelise de Sayerne, to be my wedded wife, to have and to hold, from this day forward, for better, for worse, for richer, for poorer, in sickness and in health, to love and to cherish until death us do part, and thereto I pledge to thee my troth."

The familiar words gave the moment all the ceremony that was needed. Annelise took a deep breath, closed her eyes and pledged her troth in an echo of his vows.

The lord slid his ring onto the middle finger of her left hand. Annelise glanced up when he kept a grip on her hand, wishing she could see his eyes in this moment.

"With this ring I thee wed," he said huskily. "With my body I thee worship and with all my worldly goods I thee endow."

It was done. Annelise stared at the ring in disbelief and missed her husband's quick movement.

He caught her nape with one warm palm and enfolded her in his embrace. The hood of his cloak shrouded her face from even the light of the moon before his lips locked on hers.

His kiss was gentle, cajoling, yet resolute. His other hand grasped the back of her waist and coaxed Annelise against his very solid chest. She could feel no imperfections in his form, although something decidedly hard pressed against her hip.

And the taste of him was heady indeed. A strange longing was awakened within her, its embers stoked to a flame as his lips leisurely explored hers. She grew dizzy beneath his expert caress and barely managed to wonder what the night might have in store.

He pulled away and cupped her face in his hands. "Well, wife of mine," he whispered. "Shall we retire to our nuptial bed?"

It was futile to object.

Worse, Annelise did not want to object. Her flesh tingled in the aftermath of his touch, and though she knew not what was before her, she was anxious to learn more.

She was a wanton of the first order.

And she did not care.

Annelise nodded simply, not trusting herself to speak. Her heart began to pound in anticipation. Her husband captured her hand in his strong one and led her toward the palace.

Toward consummation and the irrevocability of their match.

Rolfe had sorely underestimated the lady's potential effect upon him.

He had never expected her vivacity, although he supposed he should have after witnessing the remains of her meal. Her amber eyes flashed with every argument she made, her mind darted like quicksilver, her slender hands moved with a definite grace. Her laced, russet kirtle revealed ripe curves that his mind was quick to imagine filling his hands.

And those lips. Rolfe was certain they caressed each word she spoke. The moonlight seemed similarly entranced, for it toyed with their luscious curves so artfully that he was driven to distraction.

Her fleeting kiss had inflamed his blood. His lips burned with the faint imprint of her touch, and the softness of her hand within his made him anxious to further his exploration.

She would bewitch him if he were not cautious.

Rolfe could think of nothing but the consummation before them as they headed back to his favorite chamber. The sparkling fountain and candlelight would make a fine setting for romance. He wished heartily that they might have had a solid bed for the deed.

There was nothing in his opinion that could compete with the comfort of a massive bed, rooted to floor and ceiling with four oaken pillars and hung with heavy draperies to block the cold. His parents had had such a bed, and he had not seen the like since he had left for the East.

It was at a moment like this that Rolfe disliked the exotic tendencies of the palace. Likely they would have to make do with cushions and such, leaving them with aching backs on the morrow.

Even the promise of that could not dampen his ardor. One night of loving—one night of loving a woman whose attraction grew on him by the moment—and he would be free of the curse that bound him. Finally, it seemed that Rolfe's usual good fortune had reappeared!

To his complete astonishment, a bed precisely as he had imagined reposed against one wall of the room. The tub and the low table where Annelise had eaten were both gone, although the fountain still danced in the moonlit courtyard beyond.

He gaped at the bed, but Annelise strode directly to it and gave one post a poke, as though she doubted the evidence of her own eyes.

"How did you do this?" she demanded. She gave the bed a hearty shove, then glanced back to Rolfe. "It is fixed to the floor as solidly as though they were made together. This was not here earlier. Is this the same room?"

"Yes."

"Then how can this be?"

Yet again, it seemed that Rolfe's will had an incredible effect upon the palace.

Still he was not quite ready to confide in Annelise. Only too well did he recall the heavy price placed on his confidence. In the morning, in the wake of the curse, he could safely confide all to this intriguingly curious woman.

"Servants," he prevaricated with a cavalier wave of his hand. "I am fortunate to have some gifted ones here."

"Ha!" Annelise folded her arms across her chest skeptically. "No servant, however gifted, could have built this bed in the scant time I was gone."

"Never underestimate the skill of a craftsman," Rolfe insisted, and felt the weakness of the argument.

Annelise's lips twisted, and he knew she would not abandon the issue so readily. By the saints above, the woman was far too clever for her own good! Rolfe had never discussed matters with a woman before, let alone matched wits with one so quick to see through him.

"I have not noticed anyone here since I arrived."

Rolfe was well aware of the assessing light in his wife's eye. "Perhaps you have not looked in the right places," he retorted crisply. Unable to hold her gaze—even though he knew she could not see his own eyes—Rolfe turned away and deliberately snuffed the candles.

As invigorating as it was to verbally battle with Annelise, at this particular moment Rolfe wished she would simply be quiet and get to bed. There was a matter requiring their immediate attention, a matter that had consumed all of his awareness since he had first spied her in her bath.

Annelise did not move, Rolfe noted. Nor did she undress, and he had no intention of fumbling for her beneath her clothes. He paused before snuffing the last candle. "Do you need assistance?"

A gleam lit Annelise's eye. "Will you summon one of your talented servants for me?"

"No. It is too late to trouble them." The lie, to Rolfe's relief, appeared to slide past his astute companion without question.

She folded her arms across her chest, and he suddenly doubted his own conclusion. Annelise cocked her head to one side. "But evidently not too late for them to build a bed."

That was enough. He was not going to argue all night about the presence of this bed. Rolfe propped his hands on his hips, not at all unaccustomed to this sense that he was rapidly losing ground in a discussion with a woman. "Perhaps I should help you disrobe," he said deliberately.

The lady flushed scarlet. "I shall manage on my own," she retorted.

Rolfe waited, but she did not make any move to begin. "Are you coming to bed?" he asked impatiently.

She lifted her chin stubbornly. "Must I?"

God's wounds, but had he ever met anyone so stubborn? Her lips twisted, and Rolfe caught his breath as he remembered their sweet pressure beneath his own.

"Have I not made the situation clear?"

"Oh, most clear," she snapped, and Rolfe wondered if she were nervous. "Well. Snuff the candle and come to bed yourself."

Rolfe was loath to extinguish the last candle and deprive himself of the sight of her. He eyed her full garb pointedly, but was forced to ask when she ignored him, "Are you going to disrobe or not?"

Annelise lifted her chin proudly. "If I cannot see you, then you can be sure that you are not going to see me."

Rolfe grinned despite himself as he pinched the last wick. He cast his cloak aside, discarding boots and shirt in record time. The garments fell audibly to the floor.

Annelise's voice was breathless when she spoke. "Are you certain that this is necessary?"

"Quite certain," Rolfe replied. He crossed the floor, gauging her position by the sound of her breathing.

The darkness pressed against his skin, amplifying each small sound. The room seemed more intimate than it had even with the candlelight. Rolfe's very flesh tingled in anticipation. He paused beside her and dropped his voice to a whisper. "Are you afraid?"

"Of course not!" Annelise snapped. Rolfe said nothing, sensing that this was not the fullness of the tale.

When the silence stretched between them, she sighed.

"Well, perhaps a little uncertain. What *exactly* should I expect to happen this night?" Rolfe imagined that she had tilted her head to look where she thought he was, and he could easily picture her amber eyes bright with curiosity.

"Will it hurt?" she added in a much smaller voice.

Despite her bravado, there was a slight tremor in her tone that dissolved Rolfe's impatience with her. In that moment, he could think of nothing but reassuring her.

He reached out and found Annelise's shoulder, slid his fingers up her throat and cupped her face in his hands. Her skin was softer than the finest silk.

Rolfe could feel her racing pulse under his thumb and wished he could attribute its pace to his personal charisma.

"It may hurt," he acknowledged. "But only for a moment if it does, and only this first time." He felt Annelise swallow. "I vow to you that I shall be gentle."

There was silence between them for a long moment, and Rolfe feared that she would change her mind. What should he do? What else could he say to convince her?

"Yes," she whispered finally. "I believe you."

The simple statement stole the breath from his lungs. Her confidence touched him as Rosalinde's impassioned whispers never had. Rolfe vowed silently that he would do his utmost to please the lady.

If nothing else, he would show her all that lovemaking might be.

"I do not know what to do," Annelise admitted impatiently when Rolfe did not move.

He brushed his lips across hers and she stiffened in surprise. "Nothing," he murmured against her cheek. Her skin was unbelievably soft, and he was seized by a desire to kiss her from head to toe. "Simply relax."

Annelise took a deep breath and released it slowly, the tension easing out of her shoulders. "Very good." Rolfe whispered the words into her ear, and Annelise shivered as she giggled.

"That tickles!"

"And this?" Rolfe expertly pressed a languorous kiss into her ear. The lady shivered again, as he had guessed she would, and he ran his teeth across her earlobe.

Annelise gasped. "That...*that*. I do not know what to call how that feels."

"Good or bad?"

"Oh..." Her laugh was throaty. "Definitely good."

Her enthusiasm made Rolfe chuckle again. "Then perhaps we should try the other ear." He took his time with that kiss, savoring the way she melted against his chest.

"Oh!" Before Rolfe knew what she was about, Annelise had locked her hands around his neck and was mimicking his kiss with an expertise he would never have expected.

He groaned. The night promised to be even more delightful than he could have imagined. Annelise giggled and her breath tickled as it fanned his ear.

"Good or bad?" she whispered pertly.

"Definitely good," Rolfe growled. He ran his hands down her sides and began to untie the laces of her gown. "Not fair," he accused softly. "You are still fully garbed."

As though she had just realized the same fact, Annelise's slender hands slid down from Rolfe's neck to touch his bare skin. Her fingers fanned out as she tentatively ran her hands across his shoulders. Rolfe let her explore, sensing that she needed to know something about him before their intimacy.

He heard Annelise take a deep breath as she let her hands slide downward. When she found the springy mat of his chest hair, she bounced her fingers playfully upon it, then slid them through its tangle.

"Furry," she pronounced, then skimmed her fingertips over his nipples. Rolfe caught his breath at her light touch, and Annelise caressed him until his nipples tightened.

Rolfe leaned back his head and closed his eyes, awash with pleasure as she touched him. He felt her fingertips on his flesh where the hair thinned near his waist, then she halted at the drawstring of his chausses.

She hesitated. Rolfe did not dare leave her time to reconsider.

"My turn," he whispered mischievously.

Before Annelise could protest, he bent and rapidly unlaced the sides of her kirtle. The heat of her skin greeted his exploring fingertips, and unfastening the garment released the soft perfume of roses from her bath.

"Your hair," he whispered, knowing that he would never find all the pins in the darkness. Rolfe heard pins tinkle on the floor as Annelise cast them aside, then the heavy mass of her hair fell over her shoulders and his hands.

It was thick and almost straight. Rolfe could readily picture the satiny shimmer of it and remembered its rich auburn color. He buried his hands in its thickness, then pulled her against his chest.

With those amber eyes, she should be garbed in emerald green, in samite and satin lavish with golden embroidery. She needed veils of the finest cloth of gold to highlight the richness of her coloring.

Indeed, her worn travel garments scarcely did her credit. With such vivacity and life, Annelise dressed richly would be a stunning sight.

The wool of her kirtle brushed against his chest, then the fullness of her breasts was pressed against him. Her waist was delightfully narrow under his hands, her curves ripe enough to fill his hands. Rolfe's heart leapt when she tilted back her head and offered those tempting lips to him.

Her mouth was soft. Rolfe ran his tongue around her curvaceous lips as though he would memorize their outline. He felt Annelise catch her breath, then caressed her bottom lip with his tongue. She parted her lips and Rolfe sampled her deeply, loving the taste of wine mingled with her own honeyed sweetness.

Curves. She was all sweet curves and femininity, her skin soft no matter where he touched her. Rolfe kissed her languidly, reveling in her scent. Annelise was his wife and his salvation both. He could give her no less than his all.

Rolfe's hand moved in her hair, cupping her nape, caressing her jaw, tracing the curve of her ear. Annelise shuddered and her hands locked around his neck. He lifted her to her toes, cupping her buttocks with one hand and pulling her against the heat of his arousal. She moaned softly and rolled her hips against him in a most unsettling matter.

Rolfe caught his breath and closed his eyes as desire washed over him. He kissed her anew, knowing he would spill his seed early if she rolled her hips again, but he could not step away. Rolfe felt her gaze even as he tried to see some vestige of her silhouette.

But the darkness was complete.

"Oh," Annelise whispered as her lips moved against his throat. Her voice was unsteady. Rolfe heard the quick rhythm of her breathing over the rasp of his own.

It amused him that this woman of so many words could only conjure that one small exclamation to describe this. "Oh?" he asked with a smile.

"I…I had no idea."

Rolfe could not help but chuckle at the wonder in her voice. The affection he felt suddenly for this woman he had taken to wife surprised him with its intensity.

No matter. It was just the promise of release that heightened his emotions, no doubt, though Rolfe could not recall ever being so aware of a woman so quickly before.

"And still you have not, wife of mine," he murmured. "We have only begun."

Rolfe bent quickly and took one of her feet in his hands. It was so slender and small that he halted for a moment in silent appreciation.

Her foot was so much more delicate than his own solidly built ones. So different was she. Annelise's hands landed on his shoulders, and Rolfe quickly unlaced her shoe. He discarded it, noting with interest that she did not wear hose.

The delicacy of her foot fit perfectly in his palm, and Rolfe could not resist caressing its curves. The darkness served only to heighten his awareness of her.

If nothing else, his wife was well made.

The other shoe was shed with similar thoroughness, and Rolfe paused with both hands wrapped around the lady's graceful ankles. He glanced up, wishing he could see her, and her fingers dug slightly into his shoulders.

"There must be more," she whispered, her impatience urging him on.

Rolfe swallowed his smile as he slid his hands slowly up her calves. Had he ever imagined a woman could mate with such passion? To coax a cool kiss from Rosalinde had been labor indeed, and Annelise's evident desire fired Rolfe's blood.

Slowly, he let his hands slide up her legs, exploring each increment of flesh. His lips followed suit, tasting and caressing as he progressed.

Annelise caught her breath but did not protest. Her kirtle and chemise caught on Rolfe's wrists, the weight of the cloth lifting away from her as he continued his exploration. The scent of her skin enfolded him; the perfume of roses inundated him.

Annelise's thighs were slender, and when he approached her hips, the sweet perfume of her privacy tempted him. Rolfe filled his lungs with the heady scent and cupped her buttocks in his hands as his lips meandered onward.

She gasped when he drew near to her secret pearl, and Rolfe impulsively buried his nose in the nest of curls. His tongue danced, and he knew he had found the spot he sought when Annelise gripped his shoulders convulsively.

"Oh!" she cried.

Rolfe pulled her resolutely closer, one of his fingers joining the fray as he teased and tasted her. She was sweeter than the richest honey and more intoxicating than the heartiest wine.

Her enthusiasm fed his own passion as nothing else could. Rolfe wanted more of Annelise, all of her. He wanted to make her collapse on top of him, wrap herself around him and cry out as she found her release. Annelise twisted, but he gripped her slender waist, loving how his hand spanned her back at that narrow indentation.

The woman would drive him mad with desire. She writhed against him, her fingers digging into his flesh, her wet sweetness flooding his senses.

When her hips began to buck, Rolfe gripped her more resolutely. Suddenly, Annelise arched back convulsively. She gave a strangled little cry as she strained for the heavens, but Rolfe was not finished pleasuring his bride as yet.

# Chapter Five

"Is that...?" Annelise began breathlessly.

"That, wife of mine, is only the beginning," Rolfe murmured, and he ran his tongue over her tenderness once more.

"Oh!"

He tore himself away from the gem he had discovered and continued his trail of kisses as she sagged against him. Rolfe ran his nose through the tight nest of curls that graced the apex of her thighs, then tickled her navel with his tongue. Annelise giggled as she cupped his head in her hands. She pulled him upward, and Rolfe found his face suddenly buried between the silken orbs of her breasts.

His blood heated and his hands followed suit, cupping their ripeness. He could not resist laving those nipples. He suckled and caressed, his hands sliding over her endless curves, doubting that he would ever tire of the touch of her satiny skin.

Annelise shuddered and moaned softly as she rocked on her feet. Her thighs brushed against his arousal, and Rolfe knew he could wait no longer.

He swept her garments over her head, his lips tracing a line of kisses from nipple to earlobe. Annelise wavered toward him and he swung her into his arms, feeling every inch the conquering hero as he strode to the bed. They tumbled to the mattress that was every bit as luxurious as he had imagined a bed should be.

And his bride was no less perfect. Annelise fit against his side when he rolled across the bed as though she were made to mate with him. Rolfe leaned over her, his fingers seeking the treasure he had already sampled.

She gasped when he found what he sought. Rolfe plunged one knee between hers, and she wrapped herself around him with a thoroughness that took his breath away.

Then she was arching against him, moaning, stretching, pressing kisses to his shoulder, biting him. Her wetness inundated his fingers; her every move increased his own torment.

The scent of her alone was enough to drive Rolfe wild. She shifted beneath his weight, her breath coming in short spurts, her skin emanating a heat that he wanted to lose himself in.

Annelise writhed, and he suddenly found himself between the soft warmth of her thighs. She undulated beneath him and he could resist her siren's call no longer.

Rolfe eased into her portal, and Annelise did not hesitate. She lifted her hips against him, caught her breath, then gave a satisfied sigh when he was securely nestled within her.

Rolfe's pulse thundered in his ears as he began to move inside her. She gasped, then locked her knees around his waist. Her arms folded around his neck; her breasts were crushed against his chest; her breath whispered in his ear. He was surrounded by sweet femininity, and when she groaned at his first thrust, Rolfe knew he would not last long.

He moved as slowly as he could, but the heat built quickly to a crescendo beyond his control. He was lost, buried within Annelise more deeply than he might have thought possible, and helpless to escape her allure.

Suddenly he felt heat flash through his veins. Annelise

cried out and her nails tore into his back as she arched against him.

Rolfe heard himself bellow an instant later. He reared back, clutching her buttocks convulsively as his seed poured into her. Every fiber of his being was taut, every thought he had was of Annelise.

"Oh!" Annelise's exclamation perfectly matched Rolfe's own feelings. She dropped back onto the bed and the mattress bounced.

He closed his eyes as he rolled slightly to one side and held her fast against his side. The slight whisper of her breathing filled his ears, and he felt so empty that he was slightly dizzy.

What a coupling! What a woman! What a wife he had! Rolfe was exultant that they had sent his curse on its way in such a resounding fashion.

But he could almost hear Annelise's mind working in the darkness. When she propped herself up on one elbow and tentatively touched his shoulder, he found himself smiling in anticipation of whatever she might ask.

The woman was irrepressible. He rather liked that.

"Is that how other people consummate their marriages?" There was an awe in her voice that Rolfe certainly shared.

"That has always been my understanding," he confirmed, hearing the thread of amusement in his tone.

"Oh."

Annelise leaned closer, pressing the sweet heat of her breast against Rolfe's ribs. The silken tumble of her hair landed on his chest and his blood quickened.

"Can we do it again?" she asked breathlessly.

Rolfe laughed aloud. "It would be my pleasure," he growled, and rolled his enthusiastic new wife beneath him.

Rolfe awakened early, perhaps in anticipation of his first day of again being a man. Annelise burrowed against his side, her breath fanning his chest. The fountain tinkled merrily in the darkness before dawn.

Rolfe smiled, well satisfied with his fortune. Never would he have anticipated finding a woman of such passion as Annelise simply by chance, much less having such a woman as his wife.

And this morning he would eliminate the faint niggle of guilt lodged within him. It was true he had been less than completely honest with Annelise, but now that the spell was eliminated, he could confess all at no risk to his hide.

Although it was possible that the lady might hold a small grudge. He might do well to ensure she was in a receptive mood.

And flowers were a well-established path to a woman's heart. Reluctantly, Rolfe slipped from the bed, though the palace was flushed with the warm air of a summer morn.

He padded nude to the garden and clipped more of the same red roses that had perfumed her bath. Already their scent evoked the sight of Annelise's smile, the taste of her skin, and Rolfe found himself anticipating the aftermath of his confession.

If the woman had been passionate before she knew the truth, her response afterward might be an exhausting proposition.

Rolfe could hardly wait. Even the memory of Rosalinde's scorn could not color his optimism this morn. Annelise was different, Rolfe was certain.

He hurried about his task, determined to surprise Annelise on awakening, and trotted back and forth between garden and bedroom. Rolfe could make out the silhouette of his slumbering wife as the dawn drew nearer, and he hastened back out to the garden one more time.

The first rays of the sun reached over the roof of the palace, and Rolfe threw back his head to watch the sky lighten. For the first time in over a month, he could savor the sight of the sunrise without the threat of the curse hanging over him.

To say Rolfe was astonished to feel the morning breeze finger his tail would not begin to describe his response.

This could not be! He spun around, and his heart sank when he caught sight of the truth.

No!

An unseen force propelled him across the garden toward the gate, though Rolfe fought against it every step of the way. He was not permitted within these walls in wolf form, but he should not have become a wolf this day!

He had satisfied the conditions! He was being cheated! Rolfe and Annelise had loved. Love was supposed to be his salvation.

What had gone awry?

The clang of the gate—not to mention the sight of his four furry paws—told Rolfe clearly enough that the curse had not been lifted by his efforts.

Had the second jinni been wrong? Or had Rolfe misunderstood her terms? Or had she deceived him with a promise of reward that she stole away when he had rightfully earned it? There was a lesson there on the deceptiveness of women, mortal or jinni, of which Rolfe should not have needed a reminder.

He was a fool to have trusted the jinni and a worse fool for beginning to trust Annelise! And now he would have considerable time to consider his folly.

Alone.

And in the winter snow outside the walls.

He lifted his head and howled in mighty frustration.

Annelise awoke feeling warmly cosseted. She snuggled beneath the coverlet in the great bed and let her fingers dance playfully between the linens in search of her new husband.

He was gone. She sat up with a start, her hair falling over her shoulder as the linens dropped to her waist.

Annelise was alone.

She propped her hands on her hips and scowled at the merrily tinkling fountain, wondering how her spouse could have left her after the night they had spent together.

It was then she noticed the flowers. They were scattered all over the bed and cast across the floor surrounding it.

Annelise smiled with the certainty that he had left them for her. Their scent was becoming familiar, both from her bath and from the garden last evening, but still she did not recognize the blossoms.

For an ogre who used unusual means to find a wife, Annelise's new husband had a surprising quantity of charm.

She rather liked that.

Annelise picked up one bloodred bloom and fingered the soft curve of its petals. Its vibrant color appealed to her. She buried her nose in it and closed her eyes in recollection of the night before.

Just a day ago she had left Beauvoir's bailey. Had she truly wed the lord of this place? It was not preposterous to imagine herself being so impulsive, but this palace and her husband's loving were another matter entirely.

The garnet winked in the ring on Annelise's left hand as though it would confirm the truth to her. She turned it in the light, touched the ring, knocked on the solid wood pillars of the bed, eyed the merry fountain.

She glanced down and noticed the dried stain on the linens. Annelise stared at the mark for a long moment, well aware of its meaning even though she had not seen its like before.

Clearly, she had not dreamed what she recalled of last night. She was wed. And the match was consummated.

And her husband had promised to reveal himself to her this morning. That she knew for a fact. Annelise was more than ready to learn the worst about her charming spouse.

But where was he? Annelise considered the empty room for only an instant before she knew.

Obviously, he had let her sleep and was simply waiting for her to join him. That was all the encouragement she needed to bounce out of bed.

Draped across a chest opposite was another surprise. A new kirtle of emerald green so dark that Annelise had never seen the like awaited her. She touched it tentatively, knowing it must be a gift for her. There were fine ochre shoes of smooth leather fit for a queen, a sheer chemise embellished with fine embroidery, a cloud of cloth of gold for wimple and fillet.

Annelise donned her new garments with delight and spun merrily in the middle of the room. She could become accustomed to her husband's generous hand.

It seemed she had not made such a bad match, after all.

But there was a great deal Annelise wanted to ask her spouse. She certainly had not felt any evidence of disfigurement the night before—at least once she discovered the reason for that unfamiliar hardness!—and she thought she had made a fairly thorough investigation.

Clearly, this morning he would have to concoct some better answers for her questions, for Annelise would no longer accept his evasiveness.

The palace was as deserted as it had been when she arrived. No matter how loudly she called, only the echo of her own voice sounded in response.

She scowled and shook her head as she recalled her husband's talk of servants. Ha!

But where had *he* gone? The pleasure of her surprises dissipated when she could not immediately find another living soul.

She did find a simple meal, evidently left for one. The scent of fresh bread drew her to a room alongside the chamber they had shared. As before, there was sweet butter and cheese, as well as a rosy apple and a cup of golden ale.

The sun was high when Annelise discovered a door she had not noticed before. It led behind the palace. The wall on this side rose relentlessly toward the clear blue sky, in exactly the same manner as it did at the gates.

Annelise wondered whether there was only one portal in the wall's circumference. Or there might be a watchtower at some point where she could overlook the grounds. She decided to explore the entire circle of the wall and headed off at a stiff march.

Hidden along one side of the palace were the stables. The wooden doors were cast open, straw was strewn on the ground inside and out. The pungency of the smell left no doubt as to the building's use, and Annelise's footsteps hastened with the hope that she would find her spouse there.

Or at least an ostler. A stable boy might even offer directions.

"Hello?"

She peered into the cool shadows of the stables, and a horse nickered. Annelise stepped into the darkness. Her eyes adjusted enough so that she could make out a pair of low-built stalls and she made her way toward them.

The first was occupied by a chestnut palfrey so similar to the one Annelise had lost that she burst suddenly into tears. The bile rose in her throat as her mare's dying scream echoed in her ears.

She had never seen the horse before the morning ride, for it was one of Bertrand's, but still Annelise felt guilty for its loss. She leaned against the stall and sobbed for the unfortunate creature.

And what of Yves? Had he been taken by wolves, as well? Only too readily could Annelise recall hearing one man's scream, although she could not have identified the voice.

Had she led her brother to his destruction? Her tears

scattered across her new kirtle with renewed vigor. It was too easy to see the price that her stubbornness had extolled from those around her, and she cursed herself for being so blind.

She should have been more wary of the change in Yves before she defied him, should have guessed that Bernard would be only too willing to consign a difficult woman to a convent. She should have played her cards more cleverly.

What had been in her mind? Only that she had not wanted to wed either Enguerrand or Hildegarde's son...

This palfrey nuzzled her hair as though to console her, and Annelise took a shaky breath. She had been right in that, at least. She could not believe that either of those suitors would have made her first mating as pleasing as her husband had. They had been men with their own objectives—or their mother's—who cared nothing for Annelise herself.

Whereas the husband that fate had given to Annelise wanted her only for herself. Annelise felt her cheeks stain pink with the recollection of his touch, and she forced her composure to return.

She was not solely responsible, after all. If nothing else, Yves and Bertrand had played a role in what had happened. Both could have listened to her. And Yves had admitted that he should not have been so stubborn.

Although in the future, she might do well to curb her impulsiveness. Annelise doubted that she would manage that, but she could at least pledge to try.

She scratched the palfrey's nose and peeked into the other stall. The largest destrier she had ever seen occupied it, his coat blacker than midnight. He flicked an expressive glance her way.

"Well, hello to you, sir," she said cheerfully, giving him a pat, as well. She could still not summon the heart to talk casually to the palfrey.

The stallion's ears flicked, and he nosed the contents of

his feed box impatiently. It was not empty, Annelise noticed with surprise. Indeed, it looked to be filled with oats, as was the palfrey's. They could not be hungry, although she wondered if the stallion might be as bored as she. He snorted and scattered oats about the stall, then glanced back at Annelise.

He might well be used to activity. As though to reinforce her thought, the destrier stomped his feet restlessly in the spotless stall.

Annelise folded her arms across the top of the rail and dropped her chin on them. She watched the horse toss his head. "You seem rather anxious for a run. Does my husband not ride you daily?"

The horse granted her a sidelong glance that seemed almost human in its skepticism. Annelise stifled the urge to laugh.

"You know," she confided to the apparently interested destrier, "my father oft said that a good steed should be ridden frequently."

The beast nickered and tossed his head as though approving of the sentiment. Memory sobered Annelise and she stepped away from the stall.

"Before you decide that my father was a wise man, you should know that he applied the same axiom to women, good or bad."

She frowned at the straw on the floor, determined not to recall another troubling incident so quickly after her tears had dried. It would not do for her to weep all day.

Annelise took a deep breath and looked about herself to distract her thoughts. The stable was as neat as could be, especially since there was not a soul to be seen. A knight's trap was neatly stored along the opposite side of the stable, and her gaze danced over the familiar gear.

She refused to think about Yves.

If this was her husband's horse and his equipment, she reasoned deliberately, certainly there was nothing about the saddle to indicate any deformity. The stirrups were hung at precisely the same length.

A glint caught her eye and she ventured deeper into the stables. A knight's mail was carefully stored there. Annelise laid it out and squinted at it, trying to envision the height of the man to whom it had been fitted.

It could readily belong to her spouse, she guessed, wondering wryly who else she might expect to wear such expensive armor. He was, after all, lord of the keep, and this mail was finely wrought. It was the armor of a nobleman.

Annelise knew well enough that there were not two noblemen inhabiting this place.

Feeling as though she was prying, but continuing nonetheless, she examined the mail. There were a few nicks and scratches, as one might expect from equipment used in battle. On one shoulder it looked to have been remeshed.

But the silhouette it made was that of a perfectly normal man.

Remembering her earlier theory that he might have a scarred but previously handsome face, Annelise examined his helmet with considerable interest.

She frowned. It was without blemish beyond the usual scratches and minor dents. There was evidence of nothing that could have granted him a major disfigurement.

Was it possible that there was nothing amiss with her spouse?

Why then would he hide his identity from her?

Annelise drummed her fingers on his helmet and rocked on her feet as she thought. He could be a villain, an outlaw wanted for some heinous crime. That would explain his reluctance to reveal himself until after the match was consummated.

No. Her lips twisted and she shook her head firmly. Not the man who had treated her so kindly.

He could be falsely accused of a crime. Yes, that made sense! But who might bring a false charge against a man evidently so honorable? Why, a woman spurned. Oh, Annelise was certain she had the truth by the tail!

And her spouse knew not what side she would take in the fray.

Well, she was his wife, was she not? And he had ensured that she had no grounds for an annulment. Annelise's skin tingled with the memory of his heated touch. Her spouse had seen to her "earthly needs" in a way far beyond what she might have anticipated, and had given her hope for a marital future blessed with love.

Annelise was wed, for better or for worse, yet she was not about to abandon her hope of love in marriage.

His battle could be hers. What better way to earn his love than to banish whatever demon haunted him? She would aid him, clear his name, appeal to the king, do whatever was necessary to have him fully as her spouse.

But first she must discover precisely who her husband was.

Annelise examined the remainder of his belongings, telling herself that the greater cause justified the intrusion. His tunic was rich indigo and trimmed with white silk that looked somewhat the worse for wear, as were the caparisons that appeared of a size to garb the destrier.

Annelise recalled the callus on his hand. Clearly her spouse was a man who rode to war and actually engaged in battle. As she ran a fingertip over the scarred leather scabbard of his sword, she wondered where he had fought.

His shield was emblazoned with a white griffin perched on the navy ground. One of the beast's claws was extended as though the talons would shred an attacker. Its wings were spread high, its scowl fierce.

A silver branch that Annelise thought might have borne oak leaves hung from the griffin's beak. A row of tiny silver-and-white fleurs-de-lis ran along both top and bottom edges of the crest.

She traced the emblems with her finger, noting the nicks

and scratches upon them. She did not recognize his insignia, but that said little, for Annelise paid scant attention to such matters of war. If nothing else, she recognized that the fleurs-de-lis signified his family's pledge to the king of France.

It was precious little.

His packs were empty, with the exception of various masculine miscellany. She touched the dagger and spare shirt, found his comb, his flint, his razor, a coil of rope, then grimaced when she discovered some cheese that he had evidently forgotten.

Annelise disposed of the cheese and surveyed the stables critically. Clearly she would have need of her ingenuity to discover the identity of her enigmatic spouse.

"Would you like to go for a ride?" she demanded suddenly of the destrier.

His ears flicked with what Annelise chose to regard as interest. She hefted the saddle with some difficulty and harnessed the large beast, for once glad of the days she had hidden out in Sayerne's stables to avoid her sire.

"We shall check the wall," she informed the horse, knowing that her curiosity about gates and towers was much abated.

What Annelise really wanted to do was concoct a plan.

Rolfe's day of solitude had granted him only one conclusion: it was clear he had not loved Annelise thoroughly enough.

He would never have believed it if the truth had not been so painfully evident. Perhaps his month of transformations had weakened his skills of seduction. Perhaps the lady had not been as pleased as he believed. Perhaps he had not given as much as he had thought he had. Perhaps they had not adequately explored the range of lovemaking possibilities.

Whichever way, it was clear the only possible recourse

was to return to the great bed and approach the issue with renewed vigor.

The conclusion made him anxious for the day to end.

Annelise, Rolfe was certain, would approach the problem with the passionate intent that he was already beginning to associate with her.

Of course, his growing anticipation could only be due to the promise of freedom that dangled before him like a lure. It had nothing to do with Annelise personally, for this day had been the sole reminder he needed of the caprices of women.

Their marriage was a bargain. On Rolfe's side, there was freedom to be gained. On Annelise's side, comfort, security and a spouse who would treat her well.

Trust had nothing to do with any of this.

Rolfe was impatient to cross paths with Annelise again by the time the sun finally had the grace to dip below the horizon. It was simply an urge to be free that drove him; he knew that well. He was determined to put every moment of the night to effective use.

As soon as he became transformed, Rolfe stormed nude through the gates, raced across the garden and discovered Annelise in the shadowed foyer. Mercifully, her back was to him, for the darkness here was not complete.

Rolfe took advantage of the opportunity to creep up behind her on silent feet. He wished suddenly that he had a silken handkerchief and immediately spied one upon the floor.

Her kirtle was new, he noticed—by some strange coincidence the same deep green Rolfe had envisioned upon her. It clung to her curves in a bewitching way that made him all the more urgent to embark upon his nocturnal quest.

Annelise gasped as Rolfe snapped the handkerchief over her eyes. "You!"

"Yes, it is I, wife," Rolfe growled.

"Where are you? And where have you been today?"
Annelise reached for the knot in the handkerchief, but Rolfe
gently grabbed her wrists.

"No peeking!" He spun her around and around before
she could protest, easily evading her searching hands, yet
taking advantage of every opportunity to caress her curves.

"You will make me dizzy!" Annelise accused as she
laughed. The bright sparkle of her laughter made Rolfe
smile himself, and he could not recall when he had last felt
so lighthearted.

She came to a halt before him and wavered unsteadily
on her feet. Watching as her lips parted, Rolfe could not
resist her any longer.

He kissed her thoroughly, then darted away. Annelise
tried to grab him, but her hands closed on empty air. Rolfe
chuckled at her antics, and she spun to face him. "Aha!"

Rolfe stepped silently around her as she walked toward
the place he had been.

"Catch me if you can," he whispered wickedly.

"Devil!" Annelise pivoted and headed directly for his
voice. Rolfe slid sideways, knowing that her hearing would
be sharpened.

"Over here!" he murmured, darting the other way when
she turned. "No, here!"

"You tease me!" Annelise accused. She propped her
hands on her hips impatiently and pursed her lips in a most
intriguing manner. "Though I should not be surprised that
you evade me. Have you not done as much all this day?"
She tapped her toe, and Rolfe recalled having the succulent
weight of her small foot in his hand. "I should have
guessed as much when you promised me an explanation
this morning!"

He crept up behind her, captured her waist in his hands
and bent to kiss her ear. "And what have I done to earn
such skepticism from you?" he murmured.

Annelise shivered, and Rolfe let his hands meander toward her breasts. When her nipples hardened beneath his touch and she leaned back against him, he could not help but smile.

"Miss me?" he demanded impishly.

"Oh! You!" Annelise spun out of his grip and snatched the handkerchief from her head. "You tell sweet lies just to seduce me!"

Rolfe ran for the bedroom before she could look upon him, ducking around a bend in the corridor just in time. "And you fought my touch every time!" he accused playfully.

Annelise chuckled far behind him as he stepped back into the shadows with a smile. It was dark here, and she would not be able to glimpse his features.

"Well, perhaps not *every* time," she conceded before warming to her theme again. "But you are beyond terrible! Not a dozen words of explanation before you try to seduce me again!" Rolfe could not help but grin in anticipation as her tirade carried to his ears.

"Can you think of nothing else between us?" she demanded, the light patter of her footsteps rapidly drawing near. Rolfe flattened himself against the wall, but she strode closer, evidently assuming that he had continued down the hall. "Straight to the bedroom, as though there was nothing else of import in this match—"

Annelise rounded the corner and Rolfe swept her into his arms. Her mouth had barely dropped open in surprise before he kissed her and poured all his desire into his embrace.

When he paused to take a breath, Annelise leaned weakly back against his shoulder. "You protest too much, wife of mine," Rolfe whispered, and his hand crept up to caress the soft curve of her cheek. "At least I am not too proud to confess that I sorely missed your touch this day."

He punctuated his words with another dizzying kiss.

Annelise sighed with delight, and Rolfe wished he could

see her expression. "I must admit the same," she conceded huskily. "It was beyond disappointing to find you gone this morn."

Her words were all the encouragement Rolfe needed. Before she could ask for an explanation again, he kissed her, scooped her up in his arms and continued his route to the bedroom.

Annelise, to his delight, twined her arms around his neck and made a little sound of pleasure deep in her throat.

To Rolfe's good fortune, it seemed the lady had no argument with his plan.

Much later, as Rolfe lay back against the linens to catch his breath, the mattress gave slightly and his heart filled with dread.

Annelise had propped herself up on her elbow to stare down at him, Rolfe guessed, though he could barely see her silhouette. He hoped against hope that she would make a lovemaking suggestion, as she had the night before.

In but a few moments, he would be ready to comply. Rolfe reached out and found the tempting curve of her hip in the darkness, then danced his fingertips along it.

"Who are you?" she demanded.

Rolfe froze in shock. His heart lunged to a halt, then raced at breakneck pace. Her tone was so conversational that he thought for a moment that he might have misunderstood her words.

"I beg your pardon?" His voice croaked like a poorly oiled door.

Annelise dropped her chin onto his chest, her fingers tapping against his shoulder. "Who *are* you?" she asked again, her tone lightly insistent.

There was no mistaking her question. In the wake of the intimacy they had just shared, Rolfe found it difficult to be evasive. "Lord of this palace," he offered, feeling the response was hopelessly feeble.

Annelise snorted with disgust and gave his shoulder a playful swat. "Not that. Your name. I want to know your name."

Rolfe licked his lips. "I told you that I could not share that with you."

"You told me you would explain matters this morning, then evaded me all day."

Rolfe swallowed carefully. "I was mistaken. I am sorry, Annelise. I cannot confide in you as yet."

He felt the intensity of her gaze as she peered at him, and he fought not to flinch from her regard. When she spoke, her tone was thoughtful. "Why do you hide from me? What are you afraid of?"

"I am not hiding."

"No? Then why will you not let me see you?"

Rolfe thought as quickly as he could and mercifully recalled something Annelise herself had said. "You guessed it yourself. I do not wish to distress you with my disfigurement."

It sounded well enough, but Annelise's hair brushed across his chest as she shook her head. "I was wrong," she said flatly. "There is nothing amiss with you that I can feel." She ran her fingertips over his body in a most distracting way. "And I can see nothing amiss with your mail."

"My mail?" Rolfe's blood went cold. "You have found my mail?"

"Well, what else would you have me do here?" she retorted, dropping back to the mattress. "A prisoner can at least explore her cell. I took your destrier for a ride today, by the way."

Rolfe supposed he should have become accustomed to the sense that he was an intruder in his own home by now, but he had not. "You rode Mephistopheles?"

"Mephistopheles?" She sat up again. "You gave that fine creature such a dreadful name?"

Rolfe would have shuffled his feet sheepishly, if he had been standing. "It was the breeder that named him—he named all his black foals after demons, it seemed—and I saw no reason to change his name."

"No reason?" Annelise snorted with disgust. "Honestly, that could bring you the worst fortune! How long have you had him?"

"Six years."

"And your luck?"

Rolfe struggled to keep from revealing anything to his wife under this concerted assault. "No worse than any other's," he admitted warily.

He felt her assessing stare upon him for a long moment and did not dare to fidget.

Then Annelise fell back on the mattress with a dissatisfied bounce. "Well, you should ride him more often, you know, for he was terribly restless." She poked Rolfe in the chest, and he could not dismiss the sense that he had lost control of his universe. "It is not good to treat a steed thus, and I can only guess that you have a sizable investment in such a fine beast."

Rolfe blinked at the canopy above, which he could not see, and tried not to panic as he fought his impulse to respond. How was he going to protect his privacy from such an inquisitive creature? And what could he say to dissipate her curiosity?

The mattress rocked as Annelise waved to the room around them. "And this place. What is it called? Why are you here? Why is *it* here, for that matter? It is miles from the road and there seems no good reason to locate a keep here."

Rolfe licked his lips, but said nothing as his panic rose to a crescendo. He could not risk confiding in her. That was all he had to remember. He could tell Annelise nothing.

And tomorrow, if they loved with singular intensity, he

might be free of his curse. Then he could confess all. Then it would be safe to tell her everything.

Annelise would simply have to wait for her explanation.

She rolled closer, setting her chin against his shoulder. Her breath fanned across his flesh in a most unsettling way, and Rolfe acknowledged that she was probably not the best at waiting.

"And where were you this day?" she asked. "By the saints above, I have explored every mouse hole in this keep and found no sign of you anywhere." She chuckled under her breath. "Nor of those servants you pledged to have. How is everything accomplished in this place?"

*Let the one in whom he confides, lead a killer to his side.*

A cold hand closed around Rolfe's gut and he knew he had to do something to halt her rampant enthusiasm for investigation. It was bad enough to live under this curse without dying under it.

He took a deep breath and rolled toward his expectant wife. He caught her chin unerringly in his palm and leaned toward her, noting the way she inhaled with pleasure. Those tantalizing lips were just a finger's breadth from his and Rolfe knew it, just as he knew that he had to avoid temptation for a moment.

"You have erred seriously this day," he informed her in his most formal and forbidding tone. Annelise stiffened within his grip, but Rolfe at least knew that he had her attention. "Do not question what is around you."

"Well, why not? What kind of a person could come to this place and have no questions? Surely you ask—"

Rolfe gave Annelise's chin a little shake to silence her and did not miss the way she shrank back as he did so. He made his tone deliberately resolute. "Look only at what you are shown, Annelise."

The words hung between them for just a heartbeat before she protested. "But—"

"But *nothing*," Rolfe whispered, dropping his thumb

over her soft lips. "It is imperative that you follow my dictate on this."

Feeling her hesitation, he leaned closer, knowing he loomed over her in the darkness. He could feel her breasts beneath his chest, and her legs entwined with his seemingly of their own accord. God's wounds, but she had to know how readily she fired his blood!

"Give me your word," he growled, and he heard the threat in his own tone.

When Annelise parted her lips, he lifted his thumb an increment. "Yes, husband," she whispered with uncharacteristic meekness. "I do."

Rolfe had only a fleeting awareness that her compliance came too easily before she had rolled him to his back and leapt atop his chest. He fleetingly realized that Annelise had never initiated their coupling and that this rare delight was one to which he could easily become accustomed.

Then her lips closed demandingly over his own and obliterated all such logical thought from his mind.

# Chapter Six

It was a week before Annelise managed to make her husband doze off in bed. She was more than ready to doze herself, she was so exhausted by their enthusiastic lovemaking.

But before she indulged herself, there was something she must do. She would go mad if she learned nothing more about her spouse. As though to confound her curiosity, he had become even more taciturn as the week progressed.

Annelise needed some answers.

It was true that she had pledged only to look upon what she was shown, but her enigmatic spouse had made no conditions dictating how things were shown. Anything within Annelise's view was fair game, from her perspective.

She guessed that her husband would have a rather different view of the situation. But surely, once he knew she meant to aid him in his quest, any foul temper would be soothed. How could she help to clear his name without knowing what it was?

Surely he was only testing her ingenuity by setting this condition.

All the same, Annelise's fingers faltered as she found the candle she had secreted beneath the bed. She hesitated guiltily, and her husband's hand fell heavily on her hip. Annelise jumped, certain he had guessed her plan, but he nuzzled sleepily against her.

"Rosalinde," he mumbled, then stroked her flesh.

Rosalinde? *Rosalinde!* Who was Rosalinde? Was he loving another woman in his mind while he caressed *her?*

That was all the encouragement Annelise needed to strike the flint. The wick sputtered unwillingly to life. She caught her breath and rolled to face her spouse with her hands cupped protectively around the flame.

She had only a fleeting glimpse of his features before he awakened with a bellow. He glared furiously at her, his eyes bright with accusation.

Annelise's heart stopped cold. Only now did she realize what she risked, the cold light in his eyes reminding her all too well of an incident she had struggled to forget. Annelise was once again a little girl who had unwittingly ventured too far.

"Annelise!" he roared. She flinched as he raised his arm.

But her spouse merely snatched the candle from her hands. He pinched the wick between his fingers and cast the candle against the wall.

It fell with a resounding clatter. Annelise blinked like an owl as the darkness dropped suddenly around them again.

Now he would beat her.

In the darkness, where she could not see his face.

Annelise's heart raced so wildly she was certain it would burst. She could hear the angry rasp of his breathing and carefully put as much mattress between the two of them as possible.

Her palms went damp as she struggled to reconcile the harsh visage she had glimpsed with the laughter she often heard in her husband's tone.

Annelise wished, too late, that she had curbed this particular impulse.

"How dare you deceive me?" The words sounded as

though they had been torn from his lips. His voice was low, and Annelise shivered at the danger in his tone. "How *dare* you break your word? You gave me your solemn promise!"

How could Annelise have forgotten what it meant to risk the ire of a man?

His demand hung between them, but she could not summon an excuse for her behavior. She had known he would see this as a breach of trust, but her curiosity had compelled her onward.

When Annelise failed to respond, her spouse shoved himself to his feet. She caught her breath, uncertain how or why he meant to punish her, but heard him snatching up his garments. She was certain he would turn upon her, beat her senseless and leave her weeping on the floor.

But he simply stalked out of the room.

Annelise's mouth fell open in shock. He would come back. Certainly. He only fetched a switch; she knew it must be so.

But the retreating echo of his steps showed Annelise wrong. His footfalls faded, and she exhaled shakily.

He had simply turned away. Words alone had been his weapon of choice.

What manner of man had she wed?

A man who was gone. Annelise dropped back on the bed. Her pulse was racing and her mouth was dry.

He had left her. She was safe.

As her pulse slowed, Annelise questioned what had just happened. Certainly her spouse appeared to be of a different ilk than her father.

But enough of that. Annelise closed her eyes and let herself recall what she had seen of her husband. Indeed, the image of him was burned into her eyelids.

He was admittedly a handsome man even in fury, his wavy hair as black as jet, his brows darkly etched against his tanned visage. Those brows had been drawn tightly to-

gether and his glare had been fierce. His jaw was square
with determination, his nose straight and narrow.

Despite the cold anger in his eyes, Annelise guessed he
was not a cruel man.

No, he had been far from cruel to her. Even when she
had defied his specific demand.

Indeed, Annelise could think of no one who had ever
treated her with such kindness. She had been fed, sheltered,
cosseted, introduced to lovemaking with a tenderness unexpected in marriage to a stranger.

And how had she rewarded his kindness? A lump rose
in Annelise's throat and she curled into a ball on the bed
as she faced the ugly truth. She had deceived him! She had
deliberately defied the single demand he had made of her.

And now he was gone. Perhaps for good. And certainly
due to her own impetuous move.

The tears spilled over Annelise's cheeks and she bit into
her fist to silence her sobs. What had she done? What had
she lost? When would she ever learn not to be impulsive?

And what would be her fate now?


Betrayed!

Rolfe was furious as he had never been before, though
his anger was directed as much at himself as his wife. He
stalked the length of the stable and railed at Mephistopheles.

"Seven kinds of fool!" he roared. "How could I have
trusted her? I *never* should have trusted her! I never should
have trusted *anyone!* Have I learned *nothing* in this life?"

Mephistopheles rummaged in his feed bin. Rolfe
stomped to the side of the stall and leaned over in an effort
to catch the beast's attention. He had to talk to someone or
go mad, but Mephistopheles retained his attitude of studied
indifference.

"Was it not enough for me to be cursed with this shifting?" Rolfe demanded. "No, I had to insult a jinni and

have the curse redoubled. It is one thing to not believe in the unseen, quite another to tell a jinni as much!''

He snorted in self-disgust. ''And was that enough? No, even once warned, I had to trust Annelise that I might be deceived!'' Rolfe flung his hands skyward in frustration, but Mephistopheles continued to chew complacently.

Rolfe wagged a finger at the disinterested destrier. ''One would think that I had a good reason to trust her.'' He folded his arms across his chest and his lips thinned to a harsh line. ''Oh, yes, it was a fine reason, and I shall share it with you. The lady is attractive and possesses a rare enthusiasm for mating!''

Rolfe spat out the words and turned on his heel to pace the length of the stable again. ''Is that not adequate reason to entrust my life to her keeping?''

He waved a hand. ''Oh, yes, lest I forget, she also appreciates a venison stew.'' Rolfe shoved his hand through his hair, sick with the knowledge that he had been his own worst enemy in this.

The sad truth was that he knew virtually nothing about Annelise, even a week after wedding her. He could unerringly find every mole upon her flesh in the darkest of nights, he knew precisely how to caress her to send her scaling the highest cliffs of pleasure, but he knew little about her personally beyond her name.

To be sure, the lady had a passion for life and a sharpness of wit that captivated him. Rolfe liked how she laughed and appreciated that she was the first woman with whom he had ever been able to talk. But who was she in truth?

Annelise de Sayerne. Rolfe had heard of the estate, but he knew little about it. And he knew even less of Annelise's relationship to the knight from there whom he had met in the East.

Why *had* Annelise been in these woods at this time of year? Rolfe had never even asked her, so enamored had he been of her maidenly charms, so convinced had he been that lovemaking would win his freedom.

Yet that had proved ineffective in the end. Although Rolfe could not fathom why, still he changed shape with relentless precision each time the sun rose and sank.

It made no sense. Trust the second jinni to have fouled up the one spell that might save him from an existence of such dismal routine.

Women.

And now, if the *first* curse came true, Rolfe might pay for this week of passion with his life. He had trusted Annelise, at least enough to fall asleep at her side.

He shook his head self-deprecatingly. Perhaps he deserved to die for his stupidity.

But the worst was that all he could recall was the hurt in Annelise's lovely amber eyes just moments past. He wanted to return to the bedroom, to console her and make her smile.

Ridiculous. The beguiling creature had tied him up in knots.

Just as Rosalinde had done.

That reminder was less than welcome. One would think that Rolfe could manage to remember at this point just how deceptive women were. One would think that he could manage to recall that Annelise had deliberately tricked him just moments past.

"But what happens now?" Rolfe muttered to himself. "What exactly was that foul curse?" He halted and scowled at the straw-strewn stone floor for long moments as he tried to recall the precise wording.

"And let the one in whom he confides, lead a killer to his side." Rolfe's soft words faded away, then he raised agonized eyes to Mephistopheles.

"God's wounds! There is a promise a man does not need to tempt! It is true enough that *I* told her nothing, but now she has seen my face. She could send a killer to hunt me down!''

Mephistopheles returned Rolfe's gaze unflinchingly. His ears flicked as though he, too, struggled to understand. The matter then apparently lost his attention, for he began, once again, to chew.

Rolfe's mind worked like quicksilver. What if Annelise had met one of his family? She might readily figure out his identity. The woman was not a fool, after all.

Rolfe caught his breath in alarm. ''A killer, a killer to my side,'' he muttered. He scowled as he paced the floor. ''But who? And why?'' He looked to his destrier in alarm as he made a panicked conclusion. ''What if she desires nothing but this palace? What if she was parted in the woods from a lover and schemes now to see them both living in comfort? Rosalinde would have done anything to see to her own interests. Is Annelise truly any different?''

Rolfe knew the answer to that well enough. He drove his fist into his other hand in annoyance. ''Fool that I am, I have played right into her hands! A quiet wedding of which none know! No one but she knows where I sleep each night!''

Fear tripped through Rolfe's veins and he gripped the sides of the stall. He knew better at this point than to question whether the curse would come true.

The issue was how to protect himself from an unseen foe.

''I must leave this place,'' Rolfe muttered as he glanced over his shoulder. Mephistopheles calmly ignored his master's agitation, continuing to eat leisurely. ''It is the only place an assassin would know to find me.''

Rolfe reached out and scratched his destrier's ears, knowing he did not dare spare the time to pack his belongings. And what would become of the destrier when Rolfe changed form the next day?

''Farewell, my friend,'' he said. ''I shall return for you

if I can." Mephistopheles, however, seemed markedly disinterested in whatever he might or might not do.

Rolfe crept out of the stables, half convinced he would meet some foe while he escaped. Surprisingly, he hesitated before the great gates to look back over his shoulder. The palace reposed serenely in the glimmer of the moon, the light making it appear no more than an ethereal illusion.

Rolfe's breath caught when he heard the faint but quite real sound of a woman sobbing. His heart wrenched, but he knew he had no choice. Annelise had deceived him, as Rosalinde had done—undoubtedly also for her own gain. He should not have needed either the jinni's warning or Annelise's prank to see the truth.

It was no reassurance that turning away from that plaintive sound was the hardest deed he had yet done.

The light of dawn brought a semblance of reason to a sleepless Annelise. Her spouse's anger seemed much less fearsome when the bright sunlight slanted into the bedroom.

Annelise considered the fact that her husband had never treated her poorly. He had not lifted a hand to her the night before, despite her transgression, and she could not believe he would do so now.

That fear put to rest, Annelise considered how she might ease his anger against her. She sat up in bed and frowned thoughtfully.

Surely what she had done could not have been unexpected. He knew that she was curious beyond all, and he must have anticipated that she would find a way around his demand.

Why, any fool could see that her intentions had been honorable!

And Annelise had already seen evidence of her spouse's agile thinking, as well as his keen sense of humor. Surely a night of solitude would have calmed him enough to listen to her explanation.

After all, harmony could be found between two people only by discussion and compromise. Annelise was certain he would understand as soon as he heard her explanation.

She shivered in the chill air of the morning and hastily donned her travel-worn russet kirtle. It seemed unfitting to seek him out in the fine new garb he had supplied, and she donned her old, heavy wool stockings, as well. Annelise wished too late that she had thought to close the doors to the courtyard the night before.

Intent on finding her husband, she tossed her fur-lined cloak over her shoulders and darted down the corridor, realizing only after she left the room what had been different.

The fountain had not made its magical music this morn.

Annelise shrugged, too impatient to present her case to return to the room to investigate. She dashed out the front of the palace, and the first wet snowflake hit her nose with a splat.

Annelise stopped and stared at the garden in amazement.

The courtyard of the palace had been transformed. The summer garden was rapidly disappearing under fat flakes of snow. There was a thin sheen of ice crinkling the surface of the pond, and the red flowers she had grown to love had shriveled up at the change in the weather.

It was colder than it had been since she arrived here. Indeed, the weather seemed to be precisely the same as that *outside* the palace walls.

What did this mean?

A lump rose in Annelise's throat. There could be only one explanation.

He was truly gone.

Her heart began to pound with the certainty that her spouse had left her. She would have no chance to explain!

Annelise rushed to the stables. Relief made her knees shake when she saw both horses still in their stalls, and she gripped the door frame unsteadily.

"Good morning, Mephistopheles," she said unevenly. "Have you seen your lord this morn?"

Mephistopheles fixed her with an accusing eye, his breath making an emphatic white plume in the chilly air. Annelise spotted horse blankets folded with the rest of her spouse's equipment and hastily covered the two beasts.

Her spouse's equipment. Annelise eyed his armor, wishing she knew more about all the various bits and pieces. There was nothing missing, as far as she could determine.

Did this mean that her husband had not abandoned her?

Annelise could not be certain, but she would check every inch of the palace to find out.

"It is time for our daily ride, Mephistopheles," she informed the destrier, and reached purposefully for his saddle. If her husband was still here, Annelise would find him within the extensive grounds.

And if he were not, she would somehow find a way to open that cursed gate and pursue him.

No husband was going to condemn her without Annelise first having her say!

Annelise quickly confirmed what she had suspected all along.

She was alone.

And she was trapped inside the palace.

The gates, she decided, would bear the brunt of her efforts. If her husband had left, she would have to leave as well in order to find him and explain.

Where exactly she would seek him once she did manage to leave the palace was an issue she would confront when necessary. First, she had to discover how to open the gates.

And Annelise had never met anything or anyone more stubborn than she once she had set her mind upon an achievement.

The gates were doomed to lose.

These gates, though, had no visible means of being

opened or closed. There were no handles or bars, no latches or hooks. The gates were simply two perfectly matched and perfectly smooth planes of wood. Annelise knew that the gates opened in the middle, swinging into the courtyard. Each individual portal was both higher than she could reach and wider than she could stretch, but she was undeterred.

Annelise propped her hands on her hips. Words had worked before. She cleared her throat and began in the most authoritarian tone she could manage. "I demand the gates to open immediately."

There was not so much as a rustle in the courtyard in response. She tried again, with no result. She changed her tone and her wording, but nothing worked.

Finally, Annelise knocked on one panel door and raised her voice. "Let me out!" she demanded. "I wedded your lord, as I promised, and now would leave!"

She pounded upon the gate, but to no avail. Snow continued to settle leisurely over the ground and along the top of the wall, turning the palace and garden into a whimsical confection of winter white.

Annelise kicked the heavy oak, cursing whoever had seen fit to design such a solid gate. "My promise is fulfilled! I demand to be released!"

No voice came to her ears this time, despite her efforts. "He is not even here!" Annelise wailed in frustration. "There is no reason to keep me here alone!"

The gates stubbornly held their silence.

"All right," she growled. She brushed her hands and backed away, glaring at the door as she assessed it. "If I must submit to force, then I shall do so." She shook a warning finger. "Do not insist that you were not warned."

It was midday by the time Annelise had gathered everything she deemed useful and hauled it through the snow to the gates. The sun was obscured by the gray blanket of cloud overhead and she shivered in her cloak as she eyed the motley assembly of goods.

First she would try to force the lock, Annelise decided. She snatched up a dagger and turned on the gates, as though she might surprise them with her tactic.

Of course, there was no sign of a lock.

Annelise squinted and tried to stare into the seam where the two doors met, hoping to get a glimpse of the catch. Either the space was too narrow or the doors fitted too well to give her any clues.

She decided that halfway up, at about shoulder level, would be the most logical place for whatever kind of latch these odd gates might have. Annelise jammed her blade into the space as far as she could.

The tip of the dagger snapped off.

The point did not even remain wedged in the door, but fell to the snowy ground so suddenly that Annelise imagined the gates had spit it out.

No matter. She had a bigger blade.

Her husband's quillon dagger was her next tool of choice. Annelise refused to be daunted when it met with the same fate as the first dagger.

Obviously, she needed a sturdier weapon.

Annelise struggled under the weight of her spouse's broadsword, making no small effort to brace it on her shoulder. She peered down the blade, took aim and dove at the gate.

To her delight, the blade slid neatly into the minute space between the doors. Annelise leaned forward to drive it even farther and savored a moment of elation before she heard the sharp crack of metal.

Then she pitched forward as the blade snapped off at the hilt. Annelise lost her balance and twisted her ankle slightly. Her spouse's sword fell in the snow, and she was momentarily glad that he was not present when she saw the mangled state of the blade.

Judging from all the nicks and scratches, it had been a trusty and sturdy weapon for him. Annelise rubbed her ankle as she thought.

Clearly, these were no ordinary gates.

The power of Mephistopheles was added to the task of escape. But being a creature of moderate sense, he refused to participate in Annelise's last, direct assault on the gates. She had the idea that she might ride the destrier at full attack and break them down by throwing their combined weight against them.

Mephistopheles stopped dead an arm's length from the gate on every try. Faced with such stubborn uncooperativeness, Annelise was forced to attempt another method of escape.

The destrier was put to work dragging furniture through the rapidly increasing snowfall to the wall. Annelise, at times less easily than others, stacked furniture chaotically in an effort to reach the top of the wall.

When she deemed the stack high enough, she dropped Mephistopheles' reins and scaled the unsteady pile. A chest rocked precariously when she put her weight on it, but she scrambled onward.

She gained the summit with a triumphant smile. "I will let you out from the other side," she declared confidently as she waved to Mephistopheles—who was quickly gathering a blanket of snow—and reached for the top of the wall.

It was just beyond her fingertips. Annelise stretched to her toes and strained with all her might, but to no avail.

She could not reach the top.

But she was close. So close.

"One more!" she cried to the destrier. "We need just one more thing!" Annelise scurried down the side of the piled furnishings and tugged Mephistopheles back toward the palace.

A quick scan of the palace showed the perfect choice, a

table carved of some rosy wood. It was rife with ornamentation, tall and probably quite light.

Annelise hauled the table out into the garden, rolled it onto its back and tied a rope around it. Mephistopheles flicked his ears, but obediently hauled it over to the wall.

"Almost, almost, almost," Annelise chanted.

Annelise's breathing was labored by the time she reached the top. Grunting, she hauled the table up the last stage, smiling despite the trickle of sweat running down the middle of her back.

She was almost free.

Annelise stood up and took one last look over the snow-clad palace and its environs. It was pretty in its own way, but a prison all the same. She pivoted determinedly to face the wall.

Annelise reached up, but the summit was still just beyond the tips of her fingers. She scowled and stretched, but it made no difference.

She could not reach the top.

How could this be?

The table she had added to the pile came to the height of her hip. How could it not have brought her closer to the top? Annelise stretched again and was forced to confront the illogical truth.

She was no closer than she had been on the last try. How *could* the top of the wall always be just beyond the reach of her fingertips?

How had the portal opened without a keeper?

Where had the voice that had hailed her originally come from, if there was no keeper? And if there was a gate-keeper, where was he hidden?

Annelise sat on the table, crossed her arms and planted her chin in her palm. The snow landed on her lashes, her shoulders, and tangled in her loosened hair. She stared out over the garden and watched the glittering snowflakes meander out of the sky.

For that matter, how could the weather here change over-night from midsummer to the dead of winter?

It was clear that this was some kind of bewitched place. And Annelise, curse her luck, was stuck within it.

She glanced up and the top of the wall taunted her with its apparent nearness. Annelise took a deep breath, then squared her shoulders determinedly.

Maybe she had misjudged the distance. Maybe one more item would make all the difference in the world.

Mephistopheles trailed behind her with even less than his usual low level of enthusiasm. He ambled into the foyer as Annelise sought another piece of furniture that would not be too heavy to haul up the side of the growing pile, yet would give her much-coveted height.

She decided upon a chair and made to pull it away from the wall. It resisted. Annelise pulled harder, and it slipped free so suddenly that she sprawled ungraciously on her rump.

That was quite enough.

"Curse this place!" she bellowed in frustration, pound-ing her fists on the inlaid floor. "Curse the wolves and curse the gates and curse my husband and curse this ridicu-lous wall! Curse each and every one!"

Mephistopheles nickered. Annelise looked at the horse just as he lifted his glossy black tail and relieved himself in the middle of the artfully tiled foyer.

Annelise could have sworn there was a mischievous glint in his eye. She laughed aloud, forgetting her own anger to see the destrier's gesture so accurately reflect her own re-sponse.

Annelise might have stopped laughing, but Mephistophe-les snorted as though he had suddenly caught scent of something foul. He glanced about, as though gravely of-fended by what he found upon the tiles behind himself, then stalked proudly back through the archway to the garden.

And abandoned his fragrant souvenir.

The sight of the steaming manure on the inlaid floor, surrounded by tastefully understated opulence—in the wake of her trying day—reduced Annelise to hysterics. Out of the blue, she pictured the look of horror that the fastidious Enguerrand would don if he were here.

A tear rolled down Annelise's cheek as she laughed.

She imagined Bertrand de Beauvoir's lips puckering in the disapproval that characteristically drew a white line around his mouth. Annelise guffawed.

She pictured Bertrand's mousy wife, desperately anxious to please, scurrying in to remove anything offensive to her husband. Likely that woman would try to cover the mess with her embroidery, rather than burden her husband with the sight.

Annelise sprawled back on the floor and laughed until her ribs hurt.

And Tulley? Ah, the overlord would be priceless. Imagine such a thing happening within the vaulted halls of Château Tulley! She could see the lord's eyes shooting sparks and his neck turning red as he pointed to the offense with a quivering finger. He would bellow a demand to know who was responsible, setting both servants and tableware to quaking.

Annelise thought of the conspiratorial glint that would light Yves' eye at the sight and sobered immediately.

Yves was probably dead.

Annelise sat up, her laughter dismissed. She hugged her knees to her chest and acknowledged the ache of loneliness within her heart.

If nothing else, she and Yves had had each other these last two years. Now she was alone again, as she had been for most of her life. Tears welled up in Annelise's eyes and she glanced about for her discarded veil.

It was then she saw the book.

Bound in dark green leather, adorned with elaborate gold filigree, it was unlike any book Annelise had ever had the good fortune to examine before. It lay on the floor, behind the chair near the wall. From its position and the disturbance of dust, she guessed it might have been the reason the chair had been difficult to move.

Annelise crawled over and picked it up.

It was a weighty tome, as thick as her hand was wide, and layered with dust. Annelise turned it over, blew the dust off the cover and sneezed as the resulting cloud enveloped her.

She opened the book cautiously, then grimaced in dissatisfaction. Its contents were inscribed in a beautiful but unfamiliar script. With heartfelt regret that she could not read its pages, Annelise touched the foreign text.

The letters shimmered for a moment, as though slightly out of focus, then settled into the Latin script with which Annelise was familiar. She blinked, but the legible writing remained. Annelise closed the book and opened it again, only to find that the script had not changed back to its original form.

She supposed that nothing should surprise her any longer in this place. Annelise carefully turned the fragile leaves to the first page and began to read.

There was, there was not, in the oldness of time, twin daughters born to a jinni and his wife. Herein lies the tale of Leila and Kira, twins born to Azima and Azzam. They were matched in looks but not in manner.

Annelise grimaced. This was a fable for children, undoubtedly a light tale of spells and sorcery.

Spells.

Annelise blinked as she thought. Spells. She closed the book and set it firmly upon the chair. She had no time for fables now, but the book had given her another idea.

If this was a bewitched palace, maybe a spell of some

kind would open its gates. Indeed, the more she considered the idea, the greater its appeal.

She spared a fleeting glance to the darkening sky as she hustled into the garden. Mephistopheles was grazing placidly in the flower beds, nudging the snow away from the hidden plants.

She would have time to try a few incantations this day— and likely plenty of time this night to conjure a few more. That was, *after* she cleaned up after Mephistopheles and hauled the furniture back into the palace.

Suddenly, her empty life seemed positively demanding, and Annelise ran to her tasks so she might have more time to cast her amateur spells.

It took Rolfe a fortnight to acknowledge that no killer dogged his footsteps. It seemed he was not going to die, after all.

Although he had certainly entered a special kind of hell. That it was one of his own creation did little to reassure him.

Solitude, he discovered, tormented him as it never had before. He told himself it was the bite of the winter wind that troubled him, when he knew the clime was temperate within the palace.

But deep in Rolfe's heart, a seed of doubt took root.

He had found a ruined tower not overly far from the palace. It was here that he stayed at night, although he did not often sleep.

Instead, he paced relentlessly. It seemed he would wear a trough in the stone floor before he tired of walking.

The rustle of the wind irritated him as never before, let alone the lonely wail of it in the stairwell of the tower. Rolfe hated that no human sound carried to his ears by day or by night. He ached to hear just one peal of Annelise's merry laughter or the soft tread of her foot upon the stair.

Of course, his loneliness had nothing to do with Annelise herself. No, it would have been deeply unnatural for a woman to hold such sway over him after a mere week in her company. It would not have been logical.

Nor would it have been wise. Rolfe berated himself with the memory of his misbegotten adulation of Rosalinde. Had she not given him clear evidence of how women were selfish and cruel?

No, Rolfe certainly did not need the company of women generally, or of Annelise specifically. It was simply human contact of any type that he craved. Rolfe was certain that Annelise herself was not at the root of his sleeplessness.

So he paced the floor, night after night, and struggled to make sense of the change within him. Perhaps as a man grew older he had greater need for companionship. Perhaps there came a time when a man was ready to set down roots, start a family, claim a hearth for his own.

Certainly, Rolfe had looked for a home of his own in bringing his cursed gift to Adalbert.

But Annelise had awakened an entirely new dimension to this. Perhaps it was simply a desire for progeny that fed his need for her touch.

A *woman's* touch, Rolfe corrected himself savagely.

Only too readily could he recall the smooth, warm satin of Annelise's skin beneath his hand. And remember her swelling curves, so different from the hard contours of his own body. In his mind's eye, he saw her eyes sparkle, her voluptuous lips curl mischievously as they did directly before she laughed aloud.

And when he closed his eyes, Rolfe could smell the honeyed perfume of her skin. It was all too easy to remember the taste of her kiss—and long to sample it again.

When Rolfe did sleep, he was tormented by amorous dreams and would reach for Annelise as he awakened, only to have his hand close on emptiness. The shock of finding himself alone in the chill of the stone tower with the winter wind whistling through the bare windows convinced him to sleep even less.

One night his footsteps took him, seemingly of their own accord, to the high white walls that marked the perimeter of his palace.

Rolfe stared at the top of the wall, outlined against the starry sky. He found himself straining his ears for some sound that might reveal Annelise's presence, and instantly his neck heated with embarrassment.

Yet he felt more alone than he had in all his days. Rolfe leaned his forehead against the wall and silently admitted that he was confused.

What had the good jinni promised him? *Finally, by grace of the powers above, let this curse be broken by the blessing of love.*

Love, Rolfe had learned, was purely physical. Not only did the delights of the bedroom seem worthy of the minstrel's honeyed odes, but Rosalinde had expected concrete gains from the granting of her favors.

But Annelise had declared herself unwilling to marry a man who did not love her. She had seemed confused when Rolfe talked about material comforts in the same breath as love. Was it possible that she had not meant the same thing as he?

Was it possible that Annelise was not like Rosalinde?

Could he have misjudged his wife?

As the cold of the stone wall chilled his skin, Rolfe acknowledged a niggling doubt that there might be more to this "love" issue than he had imagined.

Annelise, at least, seemed to know more of it than he.

Or was he making excuses to see her once more?

Rolfe frowned and decided that marriage might be a reasonable place to start a search for love, whatever it was. His mother had professed love for his sire, as he recalled, although Rolfe had always assumed she meant the act that begot children. Looking back, he admitted that he might have been wrong.

And Annelise did seem to possess an unexpected affection for both Rolfe and his touch. Perhaps he could convince her to love him. His heart skipped a beat at the promise of that.

And why not? She laughed at his jests. She arched to his touch, and he had already taken her flowers. In fact, they were wed, and *she* had been the one to insist that love belonged in marriage.

It was almost too perfect.

If nothing else, it was certainly worth a try.

# Chapter Seven

Fourteen days of shouting spells and thirteen nights of conjuring up new ones had made no discernible difference in the gates' interest in opening for Annelise.

As the sky darkened at the end of the fortnight, Annelise was hoarse from her efforts. She had racked her mind for recollections of every childhood tale she had ever heard. She had stared at the canopy of the bed all night while she struggled to remember every rhyme she had ever read, on the off chance that they might have something to do with opening stubborn wooden portals.

Annelise had tried them all. She had danced and stomped, threatened and cajoled, tossed substances in the air and at the gates and ground them under her feet. She had even turned her back and spun around quickly, as though to surprise the uncooperative entryway.

All to no avail.

But every puzzle had a key. She had only to find it.

The palace had grown steadily colder as the days passed, and winter settled in with a vengeance. As Annelise had originally thought, the broad arching windows were ridiculous. The chilly wind ripped through them with delight, danced within, cavorted among the drifts of snow that had built up in the corridors. The great bed was cursedly cold without her husband's warmth, and Annelise was rapidly losing patience with her elegant prison.

But that made little difference. She passed a tired hand over her brow and frowned, knowing that she had not another single idea on this day. A few errant flakes of snow wandered out of the sky as she glared one last time at her most worthy opponent.

"On the morrow," Annelise threatened, "I shall return with more."

She spun on her heel and stalked toward the palace. In her mind, the gates had taken on a life of their own as she battled against them, and Annelise was determined not to let them guess how exhausted she was from this ordeal.

A subtle creak of hinges brought her to an abrupt halt. Annelise caught her breath before she dared to turn.

It could not be! She turned back warily, fearing the gates would snap shut as soon as she glanced at them.

But slowly, almost reluctantly, the great wooden gates yawned wider and wider.

Annelise cried out with delight and ran for the opening. She did not care when they stopped; she could squeeze through the space even now and then she would be free! She would flee this palace, seek her husband, even return to Beauvoir if she must. It only mattered that she was free!

She was between the opening gates, one foot straining toward the forest, when she saw the wolf. Annelise's giddy thoughts died an abrupt death.

She had forgotten about the hungry wolves. This one paced restlessly, as though he waited for something. When Annelise inhaled sharply and stumbled to a halt, the wolf fixed his cold glare upon her.

She knew with sudden and dreadful certainty that he was waiting for her.

It made no sense. He was just a wolf, a beast incapable of reason, but his steadfast stare made shivers run down her spine. She recalled only too well the wolf that had chased her toward these cursed walls.

Her heart stopped when she saw that this wolf also had one blue eye and one silver-gray.

It was the same beast that had chased her to the palace!

Wolf and woman stared at each other for a moment that stretched to eternity. Annelise's mouth went dry. She did not dare to move beneath his regard, even as her heart began to thunder in her chest.

She had to escape before he attacked!

Annelise took a cautious step backward toward safety.

The wolf snarled, and Annelise's heart leapt to her throat. He would consume her now! She danced backward, tripping over her own feet as the wolf bounded closer. Annelise gasped, turned and fled into the palace.

"Close, gates, *close!*" she shouted. "Keep out the wolf!"

The gates, curse them, remained ajar.

Annelise ran through the garden as quickly as she could. She could hide behind something in the palace, climb atop a chest, barricade the stables, *anything* to save her life.

When she reached the palace, she was surprised at how far she had gotten before the wolf attacked. Annelise paused and looked back.

Only her own footprints graced the snow in the garden. To her astonishment, there was no sign whatsoever of pursuit.

She glimpsed the wolf pacing impatiently back and forth outside the open gates. He snarled at them, as though agitated, and Annelise grew curious as she watched.

Why had he not pursued her?

Perhaps he did not want to devour her. What then could he want?

Curiosity roared to life and Annelise tapped her toe indecisively. The wolf ceased his pacing, as though he felt the weight of her gaze. He turned to face her and, though he was some distance away, Annelise felt pinned to the spot by his regard. She swallowed carefully, half convinced that he would lunge through the portal now and gobble her up.

Unexpectedly, he wagged his tail.

Perhaps the beast did want something of her. Had she been anywhere else, Annelise might have questioned the sense of this thought, but it was clear this palace ran by rules of its own.

Perhaps he merely tried to lure her out into the forest because he could not enter the palace. Suspicion received its due as she recalled the man-at-arms' assertion that wolves were wily.

But, Annelise thought furiously, if the wolf could not or would not enter the palace, she could simply ensure that she remained inside the gates. She could approach him, discover whether he wanted anything of her, yet remain safe.

Her decision made, Annelise strode purposefully out of the wolf's view. When she reached the encircling stone wall, one wooden door hid her from the creature. She would surprise him and perhaps learn more about his plan.

Annelise crept silently back to the gate, sidled along the wall and peeked around the edge of one heavy wooden door. She caught her breath when the wolf's unsettling gaze fixed upon her as though he had known all along where she would appear.

"Do you desire something from me?" she demanded with a boldness she was far from feeling.

The wolf's ears pricked up, then he trotted a dozen paces away. He turned and pranced back to the gate, then repeated the motion.

Annelise folded her arms across her chest. "You expect me to follow you? You must think me mad." She spared a telling glance at the darkening sky. "Night is coming and

I do not fancy being alone in the forest with a wolf when it arrives."

The wolf trotted away and back once more, his feet marking a trail in the snow. Annelise chewed her lip indecisively. Every instinct within her demanded that she follow the beast, although she knew it was folly of the worst kind.

Curse her curiosity.

"Why should I trust you?"

The wolf opened his mouth in what looked disarmingly like a smile. Annelise could have sworn he winked.

That was it. Her mind was playing tricks upon her of the most cruel nature. How could she even consider following a wolf into the forest at night? How could she imagine such a beast could smile or wink?

Evidently, contesting the gates had dismissed any scrap of sense she might have had.

"This is madness." She could not help but explain herself to the animal. "You are a wolf, a brute beast. You cannot possibly be urging me to accompany you, and I cannot be considering doing precisely that. Go away and leave me alone."

Annelise stalked back into the courtyard, but the wolf let out a mournful howl from behind her.

"I will not be able to sleep if you insist on making that noise!" she cried.

The wolf barked sharply, then howled louder.

"Cursed creature!" Annelise stormed back to the gates and pushed upon one heavy wooden door. "Cursed gate! Close out this creature that I might spend the night in peace!"

She pushed and strained, but the gate was as immovable open as closed. The wolf ceased his howling when she drew nearer, and Annelise spared him a skeptical glance.

He wagged his tail as disarmingly as the pups the ostler

had once kept in Sayerne's stables. Who would have imagined a wolf might have a certain charm?

Clearly, the cold was addling her wits. Annelise shoved desperately at the door without success.

"A plague on this palace!" she muttered, then stepped through the portal to try to pull it closed.

Too late Annelise realized she had stepped over the line the gates made when closed. The wolf barked, and the portal slammed closed so quickly that Annelise almost had her finger caught between the doors.

And she was locked outside the palace's gates.

Reluctantly, she turned to face the wolf and propped her hands on her hips. "You did that," she accused coldly.

The wolf wagged his tail as though readily conceding his guilt, then trotted toward the forest. He glanced back expectantly to Annelise.

"You truly expect me to follow you."

He ran back to her, nuzzled her kirtle so quickly that she had no time to pull away, wagged his tail, then bounced along the increasingly well-trodden path once more. He waited patiently on a small rise of snow ahead.

Annelise gritted her teeth and gave the gates a shove, already knowing that nothing would happen. They did not budge.

"It seems that I hardly have a choice."

The wolf barked and trotted purposefully into the woods. If she was going to keep sight of him and not find herself lost in the forest at night, Annelise would do well to pursue him quickly. She gathered up her skirts, muttering under her breath in dissatisfaction, and did precisely that.

The wolf set a killing pace through the forest, yet his path was unerringly straight. It was evident he had a definite destination in mind, and had Annelise not known it was ridiculous, she would have sworn his manner was anxious. He glanced repeatedly at the darkening sky, which Annelise eyed with no small trepidation herself.

It was twilight. Her shoes quickly filled with snow and her fingertips became chilled. The cold was growing more intense, and in only a matter of moments the light would fail completely.

And Annelise, fool that she was, would be lost in the forest in the company of a wolf.

She wondered if he were as hungry as he had been weeks before.

Annelise called herself every manner of idiot as she struggled to keep up with the wolf. What had possessed her to step out through the gates?

It was with no small measure of relief that Annelise saw the outline of a tower separate itself from the silhouetted trees ahead. It loomed in the shadows, a tall fortification glorious to her eyes.

Her spirits lifted and her step lightened. If nothing else, she would have shelter this night. And hopefully, could bar the entrance against intruders of the four-footed sort.

The wolf ran back and forth excitedly at the door, sitting to one side as Annelise drew near. It was clear he intended for her to enter, and her hopes plummeted as she noted the tower's advanced state of disrepair.

Would she be safer within or without? Annelise looked dubiously at the crumbling tower, the rapidly darkening sky, then down to the wolf.

Those eyes of differing shades were disconcerting, to say the least.

"Is this where you wanted me to come? Why?"

The wolf barked with marked enthusiasm. He ran in a tight circle around her, then went back to the door, sitting beside it once more. His alert gaze never wavered from her face.

Annelise pursed her lips. "You mean for me to go inside? This place does not look solid enough to last the

night.'' Just saying the words fed her fears. Was this some
elaborate way for the wolf to see his belly filled this night?

"What is in there?" she demanded, her voice rising in
uncertainty. "*Who* is in there?"

Some of her fear must have been audible, for the wolf
trotted purposefully through the open doorway. He disappeared into the shadows within, reappearing moments later
with snow on his snout. He barked and wagged his tail,
standing to one side as though inviting her onward. The
snow made him look even less threatening and more like
the ostler's adorable pups.

Annelise frowned. The sunlight was fading on the horizon, the forest seized by the encroaching shadows of the
night sky. One last finger of light framed the doorway in
gold as though it, too, would invite her to enter. Annelise
shivered and wondered whether she would live to see the
morn.

"It is evident I have nothing to lose," she grumbled.

The tower was made of heavy, square-cut stones, reminding Annelise of the Roman road that passed through
Beauvoir. It was clear from the skill of the masonry that it
had once been grand, if splendidly isolated. She wondered
how old it was and what its purpose might have been.

Annelise took a deep breath and stepped into the interior's murky shadows. Silence buffeted her ears, and as her
eyes adjusted, she made out the steps of a staircase. It must
curve along the wall to the summit. Having little choice
and an anxious wolf at her heels, Annelise climbed the
stairs.

The single room at the top was round and possessed four
small windows. The dying light stretched over the forest
and fanned through one window. The floor was illuminated
with its golden gleam, and a sharp line was drawn between
light and darkness. What Annelise could see of the room
was unfurnished, save for a small lump of textiles beneath
the west-facing window.

She crossed the room to examine the pile, lifting the first garment into the light. They were men's breeches, made of a dark wool, and they looked vaguely familiar.

Annelise knew well enough that she had only seen one man's breeches of late. She flicked a glance to the wolf, who settled on his haunches in the doorway, and her skin crept to find his gaze fixed knowingly upon her. The shadows had claimed that side of the room, and only the gleam of his eyes and teeth were clearly visible.

The hairs on the back of Annelise's neck prickled. There was something about the weight of the wolf's stare, something not canine in his expression, something that made it easy to believe he might be capable of a wink.

He looked almost smug, as though he knew something she did not and dared her to discover it.

Solitude was clearly making her fey. Annelise shivered all the same, but turned her back on the unsettling creature. Her hands shook as she lifted a white linen shirt from the pile, then stopped midgesture at the scent that surrounded her.

It was the aroma of a man's skin, of a particular man's skin, and Annelise's heart skipped a beat in recognition. The achingly familiar scent left no doubt in her mind, for Annelise would have recognized it anywhere in Christendom.

It was her spouse's flesh she smelled.

"Mother of God," Annelise whispered. Tears blurred her vision as she touched the boots resting beneath the shirt.

These were her husband's clothes.

And he evidently had no need of them any longer.

Annelise remembered only too well the creature behind her, not to mention his great teeth. It was all too easy to imagine how her spouse had found his end. She spun on her heel, clutching her husband's garments to her chest. She had been a fool of the worst order to trust this engaging wolf!

The wolf's silver fur glistened in the dying light and his long canine teeth flashed evilly. He sat motionless and stared hungrily at her.

It seemed that he did not even blink.

Was she destined to share her spouse's fate? Annelise's gaze danced over the small room in a panic.

There was no means of escape. The doorway was effectively blocked; the windows were too small for her to squirm through.

Annelise caught her breath. She hugged her husband's garments, hating that he had been stolen away from her so cruelly. She had not even had the chance to make amends!

And now she would meet the same end, caught by the wiles of this wolf. Why had she been so foolish as to leave the palace?

The wolf did not move. Would that he would do his worst and be done with it!

"If you mean to gobble me up, then do not make me wait!" Annelise snapped. She backed against the wall as the wolf displayed his teeth once more in that unsettling grin.

The last finger of sunlight slipped below the horizon, and the room was suddenly plunged into evening shadows. Annelise blinked furiously, frustrated by her inability to see her surroundings.

Or her predator.

But the sound of a familiar masculine chuckle made her breath catch in her throat.

"I shall gobble you up with pleasure, wife of mine, but not in the way you are imagining."

It could not be! Annelise's knees gave out beneath her in relief and she collapsed in an ungraceful heap.

"You. *You!* How? Where?" Never had Annelise felt so inarticulate in her life. She could not believe that her spouse was here.

She would not believe it, although her senses told her differently.

"Do not tell me that you of all people are speechless, Annelise?" her husband said with all the warm affection she recalled. She blinked back a tear as he chuckled. "You will leave me doubting that you are my feisty wife at all."

Annelise heard a man's tread as he crossed the room, felt the warmth of him looming over her, shivered as his hand closed over her clutch on his breeches.

It was true. Annelise shuddered as she exhaled unsteadily.

"I shall need these if I am to be decent in the presence of a lady," her husband murmured.

The low thread of amusement in his tone nearly undid her, so certain had Annelise been that she would never hear it again.

He was here!

"You are alive!" Her voice was uneven, but Annelise did not care. She threw her arms around his neck and rained kisses against the solid warmth of his chest. His arms closed tightly around her, holding her close with the care she had missed, and Annelise dissolved against his heat.

"Yes, Annelise. I am alive," he murmured into her hair. "Surely you did not imagine otherwise?"

"But you have been gone all this time. And there was the wolf!" She started at the recollection and tried to stare past her husband's shoulder as she dropped her voice to a whisper. "Is he gone? Will he tear us both limb from limb? I saw one kill my horse, that first night that I came to the palace, and it was dreadful beyond belief...."

"Hush." He stroked her neck with a tenderness that made Annelise tremble with the memory of other ways he had touched her. "The wolf will not trouble you."

"But—but he was just there, right inside the door! You must have seen him when you came in."

"But nothing, Annelise." His thumb slid reassuringly

across her lips, silencing her. He cupped her chin in his hand and tipped her face up to his. Annelise could barely see the silhouette of his features. "Whenever I am with you, Annelise, I vow that you will be safe."

The simple words reassured Annelise as nothing else could have. She realized in that instant that no one had ever made such a promise to her before. Certainly she had always been more or less safe, but the men in her life had ensured that primarily by isolating her.

In one way or another, she had always been alone. She had always ached for a tenderness she had never known. Maybe that was why her husband's touch affected her as strongly as it did.

In his presence, she would be safe. It was a promise that spoke of togetherness, not solitude. That was all Annelise had ever wanted and more.

To her dismay, she began to cry and could not stop.

"Oh! I am so sorry about the candle," she confessed brokenly. "I never dreamed that you would be so angry."

"Annelise," he whispered. "No harm came of it in the end." He massaged her nape, one gentle fingertip wiping away the result of a fortnight of running the emotional gamut. "Why these tears?"

"I never cry," she managed to mumble, though the evidence to the contrary streamed down her cheeks.

Her husband stifled a chuckle unsuccessfully and rocked her in the warmth of his arms. "Of course not," he agreed amiably, then his voice hardened slightly. "But perhaps you would have been happier not to see me again?"

How could he even say such a thing?

How could he be surprised by her response? How could he make such promises, touch her so gently, yet act as though his disappearance had barely been worthy of note?

"I thought you were dead!" Annelise deliberately stepped out of his embrace.

"And that concerned you?" His evident surprise served only to fuel her temper.

Annelise stamped her foot. "You addlepated fool! Of course, I was concerned! At best, I thought you had left me! At worst, that wolves had devoured you. Where have you been all this time?" He folded his arms across his chest, and Annelise could feel the weight of his gaze.

"Why did you deceive me?" he asked in a low voice. "You knew that I did not want you to look upon me."

Annelise echoed his posture and raised her chin defiantly. "You had to know that I would be curious. A woman has every right to know exactly what kind of man she has married, and I certainly felt no disfigurement...."

To Annelise's astonishment, he laughed. "Truly? This was why you made such a scheme? Curiosity alone?"

His response infuriated Annelise. "And what is the matter with that? A little curiosity is a healthy thing! You had looked upon me to your satisfaction—I refuse to see why my desire to do the same should come as such a surprise."

He said nothing to that, but Annelise had plenty more to say. It seemed that once her questions began to flow, she could not halt their course.

"And why did you leave? How *could* you leave? Why did you not tell me where you had gone? Have you any idea how *worried* I have been?"

Annelise glared up at her spouse and caught a faint glint of a twinkle in his eyes.

"And what do you think, my Annelise, now that you have looked fully upon me?" His voice resonated with a confidence in his looks that prompted her to make a thorough study.

There was enough light from the moon's reflection on the snow that she could see her spouse fully. He was well wrought, to say the least, and her cheeks heated with the awareness that he watched her perusal.

It was unnatural for a man to be blessed with such handsome features.

"And what of this supposed deformity?" she demanded, trying to hide her awe with argumentativeness. "You led me to believe that you were a twisted monster, but I see nothing wrong with you at all! In fact..."

Here she stopped, her cheeks burning.

"In fact?" he prompted mischievously. He arched a dark brow, the very image of a rogue bent on making trouble.

And one well used to having matters turn his way.

Curse him! He knew precisely what she had been going to say! The man had no illusions about his charms, and Annelise guessed he was only too adept at using them to his own advantage.

She felt suddenly that she had been a tremendous fool. Why had he married her? It helped matters little that his smile of amusement only increased his masculine appeal.

"You scarcely need me to tell you that you are not foul to look upon! From the expression on your face, you know it well enough. Likely you have enjoyed making sport of me!"

That last eliminated his smile, and he regarded her with a slight frown. Annelise slipped a cautious step backward, seeing in his abruptly stern visage the evidence of the warrior he must be.

Too late, she recalled that she had deceived this man and that he had not been pleased. She inched backward, wagging a warning finger.

"Do not imagine that I will permit you to lay a hand upon me now!" she declared wildly. "You may beat me senseless, but I will not readily succumb to your charms again!"

He looked so astonished that Annelise fell silent. "Beat you?" he asked, with what appeared to be genuine doubt.

"Do not imagine that I know nothing of men using their

fists to achieve their desire,'' Annelise persisted, despite her increasing doubt.

Her husband cleared his throat and folded his arms across his chest. "May I say something?" His gaze was assessing, and Annelise regretted having revealed so much of herself in her accusations.

Her emotions were tangled. She was relieved to see him whole, yet disappointed that he had not trusted her enough to tell her where he had gone. She was embarrassed that he should have so easily had his way with her, yet was afraid that he would punish her for her outspoken criticism.

And beneath it all, the scent and touch of him had set her desire to simmering once more. Annelise felt a fool for craving his touch when he could obviously have any woman he desired. She had revealed so much of herself, while he had revealed only his face, and that unwillingly.

"Say something?" She jabbed her finger into her husband's chest, ignoring the tears that blocked her vision. He backed across the floor, Annelise in hot pursuit as he stepped into a stray moonbeam.

"Yes, you may say something, and I shall tell you what that will be. You owe me an explanation, sir! I demand to know who you are and where you were and…''

The silvery light arched through the window from the low disk of the moon and fell full across her spouse's face. Annelise caught her breath at what she saw, and her hand fell limply to her side.

He had one blue eye and one silver-gray.

She swallowed carefully, only too aware of when she had last seen eyes like that. She knew with sudden certainty where the wolf had gone, even though all logic fought against it.

It was only too clear the nature of man she had wed.

Her stomach churned. Snippets of childhood tales about those who changed form tore through her mind in rapid succession. They were chilling tales, told on windswept winter nights and designed to make children huddle in their beds.

Annelise was wed to a demon who shifted shape. She had pledged to remain by his side until death parted them.

He returned her gaze impassively, and Annelise struggled to quell her fear. What would be *her* fate? As well as she could recall, those who tangled with such creatures either killed the fiend or were devoured themselves.

Did her spouse intend to devour her? Or would she have to kill him first?

Annelise wanted the truth. Immediately and regardless of how unattractive it might be. Her voice dropped as she squared her shoulders, holding her husband's gaze unswervingly.

"And *what* you are," she said deliberately. "I want to know what you are."

He held her gaze for a long moment, as though assessing the strength of her will, before he looked away. "And if I refuse to tell you?"

"I will leave." Simply saying the words caused a lump to lodge in Annelise's throat.

His bright gaze locked abruptly with hers and she could not turn away. Although he did not come nearer, she felt as aware of him as when he held her in his arms. He scanned her features, and she caught a glimmer of anxiety in his eyes that she found oddly reassuring.

"Do you want to leave, Annelise?"

She was shocked that she had no doubts, even knowing what she already did about her spouse. And the full tale might be even worse. But still, her answer resonated in her mind with frightening clarity.

Despite the oddities of their match, this man treated her with more respect and tenderness than anyone she had ever known. And she had vowed to help him find a solution to his woes, though she had not guessed their full extent at the time.

She shook her head. "No, I do not want to leave," she confessed quietly. "Tell me the truth."

He stared at the floor for a long moment, then flicked a glance toward her. Annelise struggled not to flinch before the telling gleam of his eyes.

"I was afraid you might ask as much," he admitted. "In truth, Annelise, I would have lost much of my admiration for you if you had asked for less."

Admiration?

He propped his hands on his hips as he frowned with consideration, and she was aware once more of his potent masculinity. Annelise watched his features hungrily while his attention was diverted and hated that she could not guess his thoughts.

The corner of his mouth quirked when he finally turned back to her, and only now could she see evidence of the humor she had often heard in his voice. When he spoke, his voice was as smooth as velvet.

"Perhaps we could make a bargain, Annelise de Sayerne."

Annelise found that her mouth had gone dry. Where had she learned that bargains were a demon's stock-in-trade? She lifted her chin, determined not to let him see her fear. "What kind of bargain?"

A fleeting frown creased her spouse's brow. "It seems to me that we know very little about each other for people who have been wed almost a month."

"That is no fault of mine."

His gaze hardened slightly, and Annelise was embarrassed that she had taken such a challenging tone. He spoke softly now and his gaze was intense. "I shall trade you a story of me for a story of you."

"Oh, no," Annelise argued. "You will not pacify me with the tale of some hunting romp in the past."

"I doubt that you could ever be pacified." She barely

glimpsed his smile, it was so fleeting. "Nor would I want you to be."

His import was obvious, and Annelise struggled not to blush at the reference to her enthusiasm for their mating. "I told you what I want to know," she insisted.

His gaze burned into hers as he sobered. "That is no small tale."

"I want to know."

"Then your tale must be of equal worth. I will not stand for some confession that you have always had a weakness for apple tart."

Annelise eyed her spouse, knowing precisely the stakes he raised. Only one tale of her past would suffice, and she had never shared it with another living being. Did she dare to trust him with the telling?

Annelise watched him for a moment and knew she had little choice. If he meant to tell her what she feared he would, she owed him no less.

They could go no further without trust between them. Perhaps if she made the first show of trust, he would be encouraged to tell her more of himself.

He was her husband, after all.

It was time Annelise shared the weight of the burden that haunted her. Perhaps the time for such secrets had passed with her sire's demise.

Perhaps she would feel less alone if someone else knew her secret.

Annelise took a deep breath. "I agree," she said firmly, and handed him his clothes. "But you had best be dressed, husband. The telling of this will not be short."

It was chilling to watch Annelise as she settled in to tell her tale. Rolfe could see that she had taken his demand seriously, for she composed her features with a care that revealed the importance of what she meant to confess. He granted her the time she seemed to need, kindling a fire in the middle of the stone floor so they might be warmer this night.

He shot surreptitious glances in her direction, intrigued by the way she had turned inward. Her face was an expressionless mask, her eyes blank, and Rolfe guessed she was lost in some painful recollection.

It humbled him to realize that she intended to trust him with a tale of such import to her. She could not be giving a performance, as Rosalinde would have done. Rolfe could see that this telling would be painful for Annelise.

Indeed, there was much about his wife that fed the awe he had originally felt for her. He admired her boldness, her outright bravery, the plucky way she lifted her chin when she did not want him to guess at her fear. He liked the passion with which she greeted life, the way she threw her heart into everything she did.

Perhaps Annelise was someone worthy of his trust.

The fire grew beneath his hands, and Rolfe swallowed a smile as he recalled the sweet press of Annelise against him. She had been relieved to see him. She had been glad, until she had guessed the truth, and the certainty of that launched a warm glow within him. And she had tricked him only to satisfy her curiosity.

Yes, he had been right to hope to make her love him. Although the telling of his tale would test her acceptance of him in truth. Even now Rolfe did not know how he would tell her enough to satisfy her curiosity without endangering his own safety.

*Let the one in whom he confides, lead a killer to his side.*

Rolfe shied away from his impulsive thought once he remembered the jinni's curse. Despite his growing urge to confide in Annelise, the threat of his own demise was one worth keeping in mind.

But first, her own tale. Sensing that she needed her privacy, he sat on the opposite side of the fire.

Annelise never looked at him, her gaze fixed on the

dancing flames. As soon as Rolfe was settled, though, she began her tale.

"Once upon a time, not that far from where we sit, a woman was given as bride to a lord. I do not know whether she was happy with the match or whether it was simply the arrangement of her parents. Perhaps she did not particularly care where she wed as long as she would be kept in comfort. It matters little what she thought, for the reality was destined to be vastly different than any woman might expect from marriage."

Annelise frowned slightly and clasped her hands tightly together. Rolfe knew well enough that this was no abstract tale, but was content to let her tell it in her own way.

"The lord, it seemed, was possessed of a rare temper. When he did not have his way, he beat anyone he could, and his wife, since she was convenient to his hand, was destined to bear the brunt of his anger.

"At first, it was undoubtedly an infrequent occurrence, and almost certainly when she bore him a son in short order, she escaped his wrath for a goodly time. It was said the lord was in uncommonly good spirits for several years.

"But those years passed, and the lady did not ripen with the lord's seed again. Matters did not go well even with his own son, and the boy defied him openly. It was said they were two of a kind, though some insisted the son was more cruel than his sire. The lord was furious, however, at the boy's defiance, but the overlord intervened and took the son's side.

"This enraged the lord, who had to bow to the overlord's will or risk losing his holding. I have little doubt that the lady bore the brunt of her spouse's frustration. Ultimately, the legitimate heir of the estate, the lord's only son, left his home.

"This was more than the lord could bear, despite the troubles that had been between himself and his son, for now he was without issue. The overlord refused to tell him where the son had gone, so the lord's heir was effectively lost. Perhaps the overlord did not even know. At any rate, the lord wanted another son, but the lady's womb did not play to his tune.

"When the lord drank—and he did so often—his displeasure made itself known, and the servants would hear the lady cry out in the night. In the morn, she would sport bruises, usually artfully hidden but always noted by her maids. No one dared to interfere, however, for fear that they would bear the weight of their lord's fists themselves.

"The lord accused his wife of all manner of evil, even in front of the servants. She was a witch, she was a sinner, she was an adulteress, she deliberately denied him his sole desire, and on and on. The lady bore his abuses silently, probably because she did not dare incur yet more of his wrath by denying his accusations.

"Remarkably, despite all this abuse, or perhaps because she knew there was only one way to make it stop, the lady bore fruit once more. The lord, needless to say, was delighted, and made great plans for this son."

Annelise swallowed, and Rolfe watched the light play over her strained features. Her voice, when she continued, echoed that strain.

"The son, sadly, showed the poor grace to be born a daughter."

And Rolfe had a very good idea who that daughter might have been.

# Chapter Eight

Annelise fell silent for a long moment.

Rolfe knew his guess made good sense, for he knew of one Quinn de Sayerne. That must be the older brother who had left home young, but Rolfe knew nothing of his being cruel.

Annelise cleared her throat to continue, and Rolfe abandoned his speculative thoughts.

"The lord, of course, was enraged. The overlord, though, had feared this response and, out of necessity of protecting the only heir to the estate whose whereabouts were known, had sent an armed guard to watch over the lady while she nursed the babe. The lord took out his vengeance upon his villeins, and the land soon abounded with his bastards.

"None were good enough, though, for none bore the stamp of legitimacy."

Annelise flicked a glance at Rolfe, and he did not look away from the pain in her amber eyes. She turned aside first, frowning into the flames once more before she continued.

"The armed guard, of course, could not stay forever. When the child was weaned at two years of age, the soldiers left." Her brows arched and her voice broke slightly, though she did not look up. Her fingers traced a pattern on the stone floor. "They left the lady and her child alone in that keep with a lord who was good at saving his anger."

Annelise flicked a glance around the barren tower as though seeing it for the first time. Rolfe saw tears gleam on her lashes, and she cleared her throat.

"They say a small child cannot recall events." Her gaze locked with Rolfe's as though she dared him to challenge her. "They are wrong," she said bitterly. "I recall every moment of that night."

Confession made, she continued with increasing speed. "I remember the fear on my mother's face when he knocked on the door. I remember the sweet cajoling of his voice as he lied, to convince her to unlock the door. I recall every heartbeat of the eternal moment that it took her to lift the latch. Even then, I sensed the doubt in her mind."

Annelise sighed. "But I suppose she did not feel she had the right to refuse her rightful husband entry to his own solar. And perhaps she believed he would not harm her in front of me."

Annelise shook her head. "She erred."

The fire crackled before them, and even without knowing the entire tale, Rolfe felt an echo of his wife's pain. She had been but a child! "I can see him still as he leapt through that doorway, as drunken and disheveled as ever he was. She shrank back, while he bellowed that she had shirked her debt to grant him a son.

"And then he began to beat her. It was horrifying to watch, for he clearly derived great pleasure from making the pain last and last. My mother bled, she wept, she screamed, she cried, she begged, but nothing could turn him from his path. His eyes glowed, I swear to you he laughed, his curses falling unabated until my mother fell bonelessly to the floor."

Tears streamed unchecked down Annelise's cheeks, but Rolfe did not dare to touch her. She seemed to need to purge herself of this tale, and he would not risk interrupting her, though his heart ached for what she had endured.

"The solar was silent then as the blood seeped from her limp body. I do not know whether she was dead or whether she lingered in a haze of pain.

"It was odd then, the change I saw in him. He whispered her name, but she made not a sound. He bent over her, touched her throat, straightened. The anger melted from his face, leaving a much smaller man in its wake. He looked suddenly like the child I was, lost and certainly confused. Then fear flickered across his face, fear that he would be caught at what he had unwittingly done.

"He glanced guiltily around the solar, and I remember well the cold dread that clutched my spine when he saw me standing in my cradle."

Annelise's hands grasped fistfuls of her kirtle and her face drained of color. Her eyes were out of focus, and Rolfe knew she was reliving that moment. He wished mightily there might have been something he could do to reassure her, yet knew the best salve was to let her talk.

He wondered if she had ever shared this painful tale with another.

"His eyes blazed with anger again and I knew he would kill me, too. Even at that age, I knew that I had seen something I should not, and I feared the consequences. I flinched, I tried to hide in my cradle as I heard him start across the room. I even tried to climb out of the small bed to save myself.

"Then there was a knock at the door. He halted, I froze, we both stared at the wooden panel. The chatelain had brought the warmed goat's milk my mother had begun to give me at night in lieu of her own milk. 'For the heiress,' the chatelain said from the corridor outside, and the blood-lust faded from my father's eyes."

Annelise exhaled shakily. When she continued, her voice was flat and matter-of-fact. "He had no heir without me, and the chatelain had unwittingly reminded him in the nick of time. I knew then that he would not kill me, but it was only much later that I understood why.''

She fell silent and toyed with her fingers, looking bruised and much younger than her years.

"Did he beat you then?" Rolfe asked gently.

Annelise shook her head. "Never. I was always afraid that he would. Although truly, I wonder now whether he would have risked that I might tell my tale out of spite if he had beaten me.''

She shrugged. "It ended up that he had not the chance. You see,'' she said, her voice turning hard, "my mother had an unfortunate accident when she was riding alone with my father early the next morn, at least that was the explanation offered of her death. Only my sire and I knew the truth. The overlord, when he heard—and I do not know exactly how much he heard, for even my father could not have silenced all of his servants' gossip—insisted that a young lady had need of feminine influence in her upbringing. I was consigned to a convent shortly thereafter and spent my childhood in the nuns' fine care.''

The stress Annelise laid on the word *fine* told Rolfe her true opinion of the convent life. He was not surprised, though it astonished him that such an experience should have left so few scars upon her. It seemed that survival of hardship had only forged Annelise into yet a stronger woman than she might have been otherwise. She had a rare determination to savor life in all its wonder, a determination he could only admire.

A weaker soul might have become bitter and manipulative.

Not unlike Rosalinde.

But in the wake of Annelise's sad tale, it was time enough to make her smile. Rolfe deliberately made his tone teasing. "Now, there is a difficult image for me to conjure,'' he said softly.

Annelise fired a glance his way, and Rolfe smiled encouragingly. "You in a convent. Silent. Biddable. Spending hours at embroidery." He rolled his eyes to demonstrate his skepticism.

Her lips twisted unwillingly and broke into a tentative smile before she checked herself. "You should not have wed me if that was the kind of woman you wanted," she said stiffly.

"On the contrary." Rolfe held her tear-filled gaze and hoped some of his admiration showed in his own eyes. It was only too easy in this moment to recall his determination to win her love. "I should find such a woman insufferably boring."

Annelise flushed scarlet, and to Rolfe's amazement, appeared to be uncertain what to say. "Well," she mumbled awkwardly. "The nuns were glad enough to be rid of me when my father summoned me home. Their switch was fair worn out, after all."

Rolfe did not miss the fleeting reference to her sire and latched onto it like a hunting hound to a scent. "And why did he summon you?"

Annelise's gaze was sharp once more. "He was toying with the idea of recognizing a bastard son several years younger than me. Perhaps he wanted to see what kind of woman I had become."

"And whether you had forgotten what you had seen," Rolfe guessed shrewdly.

"In all likelihood." Annelise took a deep breath and frowned. "I tried to evade him, but once or twice in that year before he died, without meaning to do so—" she shrugged and looked into the distance "—I flinched when he approached me, and I fear he guessed the truth. He was unresolved as to what to do about Yves when he died."

"I hope your father died as befitted a man of his deeds," Rolfe said, and heard the anger in his own voice.

Annelise glanced up, her expression sober. "He died

alone in his sleep, abandoned by his villeins, his property sliding into ruin about him. You see, he had taken to abusing the holding and the tenants, for lack of any family to bear the brunt of his anger.''

Her voice was toneless, but Rolfe felt a curious satisfaction in her words. A man who raised his hand against his wife deserved no less, to his mind.

"What happened to Yves? And your older brother? What was his name? Did he ever return?"

Annelise's glance turned cold as she held up a single finger. "One tale. Need I remind you that we agreed to trade tales, one for each? I have not heard yours, husband, yet you demand another from me. Are you implying that the tale I told you did not have enough meat on the bone to satisfy your curiosity?"

The lady's opinion of that was more than clear, and Rolfe felt guilty for pressing her. How many others could have approached marriage to a stranger with as little reticence as Annelise, after having lived the tale she had? Rolfe was astonished that she had not been more cruelly scarred by her father's actions.

He met her gaze steadily and saw an uncommon resilience in that amber gaze. He suddenly felt a glow with pride that this woman was his wife.

"No, Annelise," he said quietly, willing her to believe him. "Your tale but entranced me." Rolfe reached around the small blaze and captured her hand within his own. She was trembling, ever so slightly. "I wanted only to know more of what made you the fascinating woman you have become."

"Do not say what you do not mean," she objected. Tears shimmered on her lashes, and Rolfe moved to sit beside her.

"I never say what I do not mean," he said in a low voice. Annelise stared at him as though she did not dare to believe him. Rolfe could not deny the impulse to press a kiss into her palm.

"I have never met a woman like you." As soon as the words had left his mouth, Rolfe recognized the resonance of truth within them.

"Not even Rosalinde?" she asked bitterly.

Rolfe regarded his wife with alarm. "Rosalinde?" he repeated as innocently as he could manage. How could Annelise know about Rosalinde?

"Oh, do not play games with me!" she retorted. She shook a finger at him in warning. "Do not imagine that I am so naive to not know the import of a man calling a woman's name in his sleep!" Annelise's lip trembled despite her anger, and Rolfe could think only of reassuring her.

He reached for her, but she evaded his touch. "Who was she?" she demanded, hurt echoing in her tone. "Do you love her?"

"It was something that happened long ago," Rolfe said curtly.

Annelise eyed him warily as she folded her arms across her chest. "Perhaps so. But you do not answer my question. Do you love her still?" She tilted her chin proudly. "And to whom do you make love when you touch me?"

Rolfe stared at her in amazement. "How can you ask such a thing? What manner of base knave do you think I am?"

Annelise never flinched. "That, I believe, is what you are going to tell me. But first answer this—would you rather it was Rosalinde in your arms when you touch me?"

"Annelise!" Rolfe tried again to embrace her, but his wife danced out of his way, her expression hostile. Rolfe chased her for an instant, then stopped and propped his hands on his hips in frustration.

"Trust a woman to make much of little," he growled. "Here, then, is the tale. Rosalinde was a woman—yes, a *beautiful* woman—who deceived me with her charms, then cast me aside. It was long in the past and has nothing to do with what is between us.''

Annelise cocked her head to one side, and to Rolfe's relief, the shimmer of her tears seemed to have disappeared. ''Why did she cast you aside?'' she asked with more characteristic curiosity.

Rolfe sighed with exasperation at her inconsistencies. ''If I am to have but one tale of yours, then you may have only one of mine,'' he reminded her firmly. ''Choose which it shall be.''

Annelise, evidently reassured, smiled engagingly, and Rolfe did not know what to think.

''You try to distract me so that you can avoid telling the other tale,'' she accused with all her usual spirit, and her full lips twitched with laughter.

Rolfe shook his head. ''You are madly unpredictable.''

Annelise smiled and playfully shook a finger at him. ''And you will simply have to become accustomed to that, husband of mine,'' she declared with a certainty that sent a sudden chill through him.

What was he thinking?

Rolfe reminded himself that he could not risk trusting Annelise as instinct urged him to do. As painful as her tale had appeared to be, he knew little else about her.

He forced himself to consider that he had no way of knowing whether her tale had been true or not. He eyed his wife and admitted that Rosalinde had not been above deception in achieving her desires. And Annelise was more clever by far than Rosalinde had been.

Clearly, her charm was blinding his sense.

Annelise jabbed her finger into his chest impatiently and her eyes danced. ''Now, begin. Surely I do not have to ask you for this tale again?''

Rolfe eyed her warily. His wife wanted answers, that much was clear, but Annelise had provided few answers of her own. She demanded that he reveal himself to her, that he risk his own safety, without revealing much of herself.

Perhaps he would be wise to confess as little as he could.

If Annelise turned her copious charms upon him, Rolfe knew he would be as malleable as butter in her hands. He stepped past her with the excuse that the fire needed rebuilding. A man could only try to steer clear of a woman's enchanting touch.

A man could only try to avoid repeating his mistakes.

It was an unexpected delight to be able to watch her husband as he composed his thoughts. Annelise crossed her legs and folded her arms about her knees as he built up the fire. His brows tightened with concern and it was clear he was thinking deeply about how to present his story.

Annelise took advantage of his diverted attention to study him. He was as finely wrought as her fingers had told her during those nights at the palace, and she tingled with the awareness that this man had touched her so intimately.

Annelise's toes curled within her shoes. Who would have guessed that she might have gained so fine a mate by chance alone? And it was more than looks, for her spouse was tender and kind. He treated her well, he spoke to her with respect, he promised her safety in his presence.

And now, apparently, he intended to explain himself to her, in a manner completely unprecedented by men Annelise had known.

She could easily become accustomed to such indulgence.

"Well." He crouched on the opposite side of the fire and rocked on the balls of his feet, his hands loosely locked before him and his gaze fixed on the small blaze. "Well, I shall tell you what happened, although you may not believe it to be true."

He frowned and cleared his throat without meeting Annelise's gaze. "These past years I have been in the East, at Crusade, and on my return purchased a gift in the market there. It was a bottle of unusual design.''

He hesitated, and Annelise, ever helpful, interjected a question to urge him along. ''A gift for who? And what was inside it?''

Her spouse flicked a telling glance her way. ''I could not know what was inside, for it was sealed, and I did not understand the speech of the old merchant who sold it to me.'' He shrugged one shoulder. ''I also was curious about its contents, but as it was a gift, I felt it would be unfitting to open it.

''At any rate, as I traveled northward and it grew colder, I noticed that the wax seal had popped open. I decided to satisfy my curiosity, as none would be the wiser, and I opened the bottle.'' His gaze fell to the floor and his voice dropped. ''Little did I expect that there would be a jinni inside.''

''A jinni?'' Suddenly the entire nature of the palace made sense to Annelise. ''How exciting! What did she look like?''

Her spouse seemed surprised at her questions. ''I would not blame you if you thought my tale a lie, for I was skeptical of her claim myself.''

''Why would you doubt her? Did she not come from the bottle itself?''

He glanced Annelise's way. ''Yes.''

''Then why were you skeptical?''

He scowled, though Annelise could not imagine what troubled him. His tale was most intriguing. ''Well, that she was a jinni! One does not expect childish tales of fancy to come to life before one's eyes!''

''But why ever not? You said already that the bottle was unusual. You could not have expected it to contain something mundane, like perfume or some eau-de-vie!''

Her spouse's lips thinned to a hard line of what might have been disapproval. ''How can you so readily believe such nonsense? I scarcely can give it credit now.''

"It is not nonsense!" Annelise retorted. "It happened to you!"

He leaned forward and his eyes gleamed with purpose. "Do you not see that it is illogical for something invisible to drastically change my life?"

Annelise snorted. "Surely you would not insist that nothing invisible could have any effect upon you?"

"Of course I would!"

"Then what of faith?" Annelise demanded. "You were in the East, you said, which likely means you were on a Crusade. What drove the Crusade other than faith?"

Her spouse grimaced. "You are naive, my Annelise. Greed and a hunger for power are the greater forces there. Otherwise, why would knight and bishop both grasp all that they could in the Holy City itself?"

"You will not convince me," Annelise said with a toss of her hair. "Things unseen can be powerful indeed."

Her spouse snorted with self-deprecation. "I should need no reminder of that," he muttered, and Annelise leaned forward in anticipation.

"Do cease your stalling! What happened when the jinni was freed?"

He fired a glance at her, then frowned in thought. "The jinni who came out of the bottle was of particularly foul temperament and did not take kindly to my skepticism. The palace is hers, and she was apparently condemned to grant it to me, but she had her own way of revenge."

Revenge? "What did she do?"

"She cursed me." Her spouse's disconcerting gaze locked with hers again. "She condemned me to become a wolf."

Annelise's mind leapt over the confession she had foreseen to more pressing details. "But you are not a wolf now."

"That is due only to the intervention of the second jinni."

"A second jinni? There were *two* in the bottle?"

"Yes, but fortunately, the second possessed a more kindly manner." He paused and gazed thoughtfully at Annelise. "You truly believe this tale I am telling you," he commented, as though amazed.

She shrugged. "Of course. It makes perfect sense."

"Perfect sense?" he echoed in evident disgust, then flung out his hands. "There is nothing that makes sense about it! Whoever heard of a jinni changing a man to a wolf because he uncorked a bottle? Whoever heard of a man changing to a wolf at all?"

"One hears it all the time," Annelise said matter-of-factly.

"In children's tales alone," he snorted.

"Well," she said carefully, "you did admit that you were less than charming to her. Surely you could expect some retaliation."

"Of course, I was less than charming! I could not believe what she was telling me!"

"It only makes sense that if you insulted her, she would take offense."

"Are you not listening to me?" her spouse demanded impatiently. "The woman claimed to be a magical, often invisible being who had been trapped in that bottle for several centuries. Clearly, this tale is far from logical."

"But you saw her come out of the bottle."

He shifted uncomfortably and averted his gaze. "Yes," he admitted with obvious reluctance.

"And you *did* become a wolf?"

"Yes," he acknowledged awkwardly.

"And the palace exists where there was none before? Meals are served by invisible hands? Gates open by force of some unknown will alone?" Annelise settled back and folded her arms across her chest as she eyed her spouse. "What greater evidence do you need of enchantment at work?"

"But it makes no sense!"

"It makes perfect sense, once you acknowledge that it has occurred." Annelise shrugged. "Frankly, I cannot imagine how you could *logically* insist otherwise."

He shoved one hand through his dark hair and pushed to his feet to pace. "It is mad," he muttered.

"And evidently done. Now tell me what happened, if you please."

Her husband tossed Annelise a mutinous glance, though as he continued pacing, he began once more to recount his tale. "I must admit that my manners were somewhat less than they might have been when the second jinni arrived. You see, the first jinni's curse had begun to take effect."

"You were changing to a wolf?"

"Before my own eyes." He shook his head, but Annelise interjected a question before he could insist once more that it was not logical.

"What did you do?"

His firm lips twisted in a self-deprecating smile. "She reprimanded me, and in the end, I begged shamelessly for her aid." He winked across the fire in an abrupt change of mood that made Annelise's heart flutter. She knew that, in that jinni's place, she would have been hard-pressed to deny him. "I have been told that I am not without charm."

Annelise could hardly argue with that, but she was not about to reinforce her husband's opinion of himself, either.

"So many women easily succumb to shameless begging," she said instead.

Her husband laughed suddenly, as though she had surprised him. "But not you?" he asked with a warm smile.

Annelise returned his smile coyly as she lied. "Not me."

Their gazes locked and held over the dancing flames. Annelise noted the crinkles around his eyes as he grinned, and realized she liked that her husband smiled often. His smile transformed him, giving his otherwise stern visage a surprisingly boyish look.

Annelise was not fooled that his had been an easy life. She could see in the firelight the evidence of his livelihood in the few faded scars that marked his flesh. She recalled the well-used but meticulously maintained spurs and armor in the stables, as well as the fine warhorse. It was easy to imagine that her spouse would be a formidable foe in battle.

But he smiled for her. And he had given her his guarantee of protection.

It was enough to tempt a woman to lose her heart.

The errant thought made Annelise blink. Lose her heart to a man cursed to change shape?

"And what did the second jinni do?" she asked crisply. Her tone effectively dismissed the cozy moment that had stretched between them.

"She changed the curse slightly and made me a wolf only by day."

"That seems somewhat less than desirable."

Her spouse snorted a laugh. "I was less than enamored of her solution."

"And you had already begged shamelessly."

His quick glance revealed that the twinkle was still resident in his eye. "But that did not stop me from trying again."

"Yet she resisted you?" Annelise could not help but tease him a little. "Perhaps your charm is less compelling than you think."

"Perhaps." His eyes glowed with sudden intent, and his voice dropped to a sultry murmur. "Can *you* resist me, Annelise?"

Annelise stared into his eyes for a long moment before she gave herself a shake. "The question truly is," she said as pertly as she could manage, "whether the jinni could resist you."

"No. She only granted me some hope of reprieve." Her spouse frowned, but Annelise was delighted with his confession.

"Reprieve?" she repeated. "She offered you a reprieve? You can eliminate the first curse? You are not condemned to always spend days as a wolf?"

His eyes narrowed consideringly, and Annelise guessed he knew more than he intended to tell her. He watched her as though assessing her motives, though she could not imagine what doubt he could have. Obviously, she would rather have a man for a spouse than a wolf!

"She granted me terms that might lead to a reprieve," he admitted carefully.

Annelise rose and brushed off her kirtle purposefully. "Well, what are they? What must we do? How do we start?"

He eyed her for a long moment, then stepped away. "*We* are not going to start anything."

She regarded him in astonishment. "Well, you are not going to spend the rest of your life changing to a wolf every day if I have anything to say about it!"

"That is precisely the point, Annelise," he said tightly. "You do not have anything to say about it. This is my problem, my curse and my burden. It will be resolved with my efforts alone."

"Then why did you wed me? Are we not partners in this ordeal?"

He looked left and right, his suave charm slipping under her concerted assault. He looked as though he would have preferred to escape the question, which intrigued Annelise. But she was not about to let him slip away without a full explanation. "Tell me!"

"It matters little," he said with a shrug.

Annelise was not fooled by his casual manner. There was something of import here, otherwise he would not have become so nervous about confiding in her. "You were the wolf that chased me to the palace," she charged.

Her spouse shifted his weight from foot to foot. "I, too, saw the other wolf take your steed," he admitted. He swallowed, his gaze colliding with hers for the barest instant before he continued. "I could not let you perish like that."

Her heart skipped a beat. "You did not even know me."

His jaw set resolutely and he stared straight into her eyes. "I am a knight, Annelise. I have pledged to protect those in danger, and I fulfill that pledge regardless of my own circumstance. Do not make more of the matter than is there."

If the man had not been burdened with such a curse, Annelise knew she could have abandoned her heart to him this very moment. A man of honor was not readily found in these times, let alone one who stood by his vows, treated his wife as a thinking creature—as his equal!—and who had shown her nothing but kindness.

Even if he did try to dismiss her admiration for his deed.

"I simply forgot that one of the jinni's curses insisted that the first to cross the palace's threshold would be condemned to wed me." He shrugged. "I must apologize for so meddling in your life."

Annelise's spirits sank momentarily at his confession and his manner of delivering it before she was encouraged again. Undoubtedly, he was simply dismayed by this changing of form.

But he had already admitted that there was an opportunity to remove the curse. She set her lips with determination. If this man could be her husband in truth, for all of the day and the night, then she would certainly lend her hand to the task of gaining his freedom.

Annelise closed the distance between them and was reassured that her spouse did not bolt. She let her fingers meander over his shoulders and around his neck. She pressed herself closer and was gratified to feel the accelerated beat of his heart.

It emboldened her to know that he was not immune to her own brand of charm. She stretched up, nibbling a path of kisses up his neck until she reached his ear. He caught his breath, but his hands closed surely on her waist.

"What must you do to earn your reprieve?" she whispered, deliberately letting her breath fan across his skin. Her husband shivered and buried his face in her neck.

"Do not trouble yourself with the details. It is my task." His voice was strained, and Annelise felt the evidence of his interest in her touch pressing against her belly.

"Tell me just one thing," she urged before she kissed him full on the lips. His tongue plunged into her as though he could not stop himself, and Annelise hastily ripped open the laces on her kirtle. Her spouse tore his lips from hers and stepped away.

"No. No, Annelise. Ask me no more."

But she bared her flesh to his view, and it seemed he could not help but look. He inhaled sharply at the sight of her breast, and his eyes brightened with fascination as the nipple tightened to a peak.

Then he was kissing her with an ardor that set her aflame. Annelise arched her back and closed her eyes with pleasure. She clutched a fistful of his hair and returned his embrace.

With an effort, she recalled the one thing she wanted to know most of all.

"Tell me just your name then," she murmured.

He stiffened at her suggestion, then tried to hide his response. Instantly, Annelise knew that she had inadvertently found an issue.

"No."

"You will not tell me?"

"No, I cannot." He released Annelise abruptly and backed away, his eyes wary.

This was no good at all. Annelise wanted to know every demon that haunted him and was determined to find a way to dismiss his curse. It was promising that he had confided as much as he had this night.

But she would have more.

Well, there was one deed for which her spouse clearly had a weakness. Annelise was not above using the tools that she had.

She shook off her chemise and kirtle, tossing her shoes and hose recklessly aside. When she stood nude before him, she could not help but notice the way his heated gaze danced over her.

He wanted her. It was a start, but Annelise needed more from marriage. She wanted this man to love her.

And she was going to ensure that he did. She walked slowly toward him, pulling the pins from her hair and shaking the tresses out, and let a smile slide over her lips.

"Then I shall guess your name, husband of mine," she threatened in a cajoling voice.

He inhaled sharply. "You cannot."

Annelise savored how sharply his gaze burned when she stopped directly before him. She immediately set to unlacing the front of the shirt he had hastily donned.

"But I can." She kissed his chest and smiled when he caught his breath. "And I will," she vowed, punctuating her assertion with another flurry of kisses until he sighed. His hands found their way around her waist and he lifted her against her. "I am very good at solving puzzles," she whispered against his flesh.

Her spouse chuckled reluctantly. Annelise glanced up as he slowly smiled, and the intent that gleamed in his eyes made her heart beat faster. "I cannot dissuade you, can I?" he murmured.

Annelise smiled back. "No." His shirt was discarded in short order and she set upon his breeches.

"But Annelise..." he began to argue, until her busy fingers made him gasp aloud.

Annelise sensed that he had lost the thread of their conversation. Which suited her rather well. She intended to know the man's name, despite his protest. What could it hurt for her to guess, after all?

"Is it Michel? Antoine? Richard? Gautier? Christophe?"

"No, Annelise, no, no, no..." His voice faded when her nimble fingers dove into his breeches.

"Didier? Bayard? Edouard?"

"Annelise!" he protested when her fingers closed around him and his breeches dropped around his ankles. He groaned as she caressed him, and Annelise pulled his head down for a soul-shattering kiss.

And it was many hours before her husband had enough breath to argue again.

Annelise grumbled when her husband woke her just before the dawn. She reached for him, but he evaded her touch with an alertness she was far from feeling.

"It is time to leave," he said, his voice flat and determined.

Annelise opened one eye at his jarring tone. She propped herself up on her elbows and gazed around the small tower room. As romantic as their tryst here had been, visions of the palace's previous luxury danced in her head.

"This place lacks somewhat in comfort. Could we sleep at the palace tonight?"

Her spouse's lips thinned as he dressed with disconcerting purpose. "No. I will not return there."

That statement captured Annelise's attention and she sat up, fully awake. "Am I not to see you again?"

"Annelise, I do not know."

"You do not know? What manner of answer is that? And why not go back to the palace? If it is granted to you, why not stay within its walls? It is markedly more comfortable than this place—at least it used to be before it became so cursedly cold. And if we were together, we might manage to warm the bed."

He turned with sudden interest. "It is cold there now?"

"Yes, just like here. Snowing and all." It seemed he had no intention of changing his mind about their departure, so

Annelise donned her hose in poor temper. "The temperate clime of the garden there is fully gone."

"Would you prefer it was warm?" His question might have passed as idle conversation had there not been a keen note of curiosity underlying his tone.

Annelise glanced up at him. "Of course. There is not a shutter in the place and the snow drifts inside. For all its discomfort, I might as well remain here with you." She fought with the knotted string in her chemise for a moment, then flicked a glance in his direction. "I could stay here, you know. Indeed, I would rather remain with you."

"You cannot stay here." His tone was that of a man used to making firm decisions and standing behind them. "You will return to the palace."

Annelise folded her arms across her chest. "What if I refuse?"

Exasperation danced across his features and he glanced pointedly to the window. "Then you will not be safe. Already I have told you that I take my vows seriously, and I pledged to keep you safe. Get dressed, Annelise, and hasten. We must be back at the palace before the dawn."

"Why?"

"Make haste!"

Fine! Annelise spun on her heel, hauled on her kirtle and shoes. She stomped down the stairs without looking back and plunged into the woods, even though she did not precisely know which direction to head.

Her husband's warm grip closed around her elbow and he turned her completely around. "This way."

The man at least had the grace—or the wisdom—to refrain from teasing her about her poor sense of direction.

He marched her through the woods without another word, and Annelise kept mutinously silent. If she thought he could push her about without an explanation, then he had another thought coming!

The palace gates loomed out of the shadows ahead of

them, and Annelise briefly considered fleeing the prospect of being imprisoned there again.

Then her husband turned to face her, lifting her chin with one finger when she refused to look to him. She knew he would kiss her, and her anger melted at that possibility.

"Annelise, how would you prefer it to be in the palace?" he asked softly.

She rolled her eyes impatiently even as she told herself not to be disappointed that she had been denied her kiss. "In all honesty, I cannot see how or why it matters. There are many more important issues that we might discuss, were you not so evasive all of the time—"

His finger landed firmly over her lips, and—curse him—his eyes twinkled.

"Warm like summer?" he asked, as though she had said nothing.

Despite herself, Annelise had to smile at his determination, but she smothered the smile as soon as she could. "Not too warm. Like late spring, as it was just after I arrived."

He turned to glare pointedly at the gates and Annelise followed his glance uncomprehendingly. "I wish that it was so," he said—rather loudly, to Annelise's way of thinking.

Then he looked back at her and smiled with devastating charm. "Take Mephistopheles for a ride for me, if you will, and give him my regrets for my inattention. He takes such matters quite seriously, you know."

Before Annelise could argue, he kissed her with lazy thoroughness. She was breathless when he broke his kiss, but he knocked firmly on the gates.

"Open and admit the lady!" he demanded.

The gates, to Annelise's astonishment, did precisely that. She gaped at them as they opened, but her spouse simply squeezed her shoulders and pressed a kiss to her brow.

"Be good," he murmured, and gave her a little shove.

Annelise stepped forward, marveling that the gates did his will, then she looked back.

He was gone already, and with such completeness that she was suddenly afraid he had never been there at all. The gates creaked and she darted forward, fearful they would leave her locked out in the cold and alone.

Only when they slammed shut behind her did she realize the scent of the air inside had changed.

Rivulets ran across the damp ground, all that remained of the snow that had drifted here when she left. The air was mild and humming with the sounds of insects.

It was incredible. Annelise strolled forward in wonderment, touching the flowers that only the night before had been bent beneath the weight of the snow. The sky was flawlessly blue overhead and a bird swooped low over her.

Suddenly, she recalled her husband's questions and his odd wish. He had done this for her! She spun back to face the gate, even as she tossed the weight of her heavy cloak aside.

"How did you do this?" she shouted joyfully.

There was no response, but then, Annelise had not really expected one. She laughed and danced through the garden, certain she was wed to a wonderful, if enigmatic, man.

Not only did he attend to her needs, but he cared about her discomfort. He had somehow changed the weather within the palace walls purely to please her.

And that could only be a good omen for the future. The man had a weakness for her, Annelise was certain, and she was determined to see that affection ripen into something more.

She gathered up her discarded cloak and made her way purposefully to the stables, a merry and unfeminine whistle on her lips.

She would guess her husband's name. She would convince him to trust her. And along the way, she would win his reprieve from the jinni's curse.

Annelise was certain that, in the end, this match would be precisely as she had always hoped marriage would be.

# Chapter Nine

Rolfe had no intention of seeking out his wife that night. Surely the ceaseless pacing of a day had exhausted him enough that he might readily sleep. Alone. He returned to the tower after his change, determined to spend the night in solitude.

And he had already decided to avoid that enchanted palace. That was a place where a man could not even believe in what was before his eyes. Rolfe climbed the falling stairs of the tower and reveled in its solid predictability.

But as he crossed the threshold of the tower room, he was struck by a memory of Annelise bathed in the last rays of the sun, just across the floor from where he stood. The dying light, he recalled, had turned her auburn hair to a glorious halo of amber.

He had come so close to confiding in her, he reminded himself savagely and purely for the purpose of soliciting a tiny jolt of fear within his heart.

The jolt did not come. He could not risk seeing Annelise again so soon, Rolfe told himself sternly.

His heart traitorously longed for her.

He crossed the room, unable to resist the allure of the window where she had stood. The ashes from the fire he had kindled for her stirred around his boots as he walked.

He stood on the same spot that she had graced and stared out over the snow, which glowed faintly in the evening light.

Rolfe imagined that he caught the faintest whiff of her scent.

But no. Annelise was safe within the walls of the palace, comfortable in the clime she favored.

The clime he had changed. Rolfe frowned. What had possessed him to do that? A shadow of dread passed over his heart as he acknowledged that he had simply wanted to please his wife.

Not a bad impulse in itself, but one dangerously close to becoming the trust he did not dare indulge.

Was he becoming the same smitten suitor who had brought gifts to Rosalinde like a hapless pup? Rolfe had sworn he would never play the fool again, especially for a woman. Women were deceitful. Women thought only of their own ends. Rosalinde had deceived him, as had the first jinni and possibly the second, as well.

As might Annelise. Again.

Rolfe's gaze lifted of its own accord to peer into the darkness in the direction of the palace. Despite it all, he could not bring himself to believe that Annelise meant him ill, much less that she might share Rosalinde's disregard for all others beside herself.

Surely, Annelise's every thought showed in her expressive eyes?

Rolfe gazed across the snow-clad forest and wondered. What was Annelise doing now? Did she expect him? Was she waiting for him to return? Rolfe's gut twisted as he imagined the spark dying in those magnificent amber eyes when she finally turned away from the gates in disappointment.

Truly, she seemed to hold him in some regard.

Indeed, Rolfe had never met another like her.

He propped his hands on his hips in indecision. Every

instinct within him told him to go to Annelise, to make
love with her in that tantalizing way she had, to talk to her,
to confess the full tale to her.

But he should not risk it.

He could not risk it.

Experience had taught Rolfe not to trust women and their
charms. The jinni's curse told him the price he would pay
for trusting anyone. What manner of fool was he to entertain any uncertainty in what he should do?

And, in addition, Annelise was determined to guess his
name. What would happen if she discovered his identity in
his absence? She had already found his horse and might
have seen his shield with his family's insignia.

Would permitting her within the palace's walls be adequate trust for her to betray him? Could anything she divined there put him at equal risk as what he told her directly?

Rolfe's heart chilled. This was no childish game they
played. It was charming of Annelise to insist on guessing
his name—not to mention the way she had distracted him
from his objections—but he could not risk her actually doing so.

If she knew his name, she could go to his family and
tell them of his fate. If she knew his name, he could not
hide from her anywhere.

Nor from the killer the jinni threatened would seek him
out.

Rolfe gathered his cloak about his shoulders and took
the stairs three at a time in his haste to return to the palace.
He must somehow convince Annelise to abandon her determination to know more about him.

Surely it was only the awareness of what was at stake
that made his pulse race as he drew near the palace and
Annelise.

That explanation was proven false as soon as Rolfe entered the gates. Annelise was cavorting in the long pool

lined with blue tiles and was gloriously nude and singing as clearly as a lark in springtime. Rolfe's footsteps halted of their own accord as he swallowed and stared.

Her skin was as creamy and smooth as he had guessed it to be, her curves as ripe as his hands already knew. Water sluiced over her breasts and splashed on her belly as she emptied an urn over herself. The moonlight played with her curves, and Rolfe hungrily watched the falling water shimmer as it slipped over her form.

He wanted her. And in that instant, Rolfe realized that he had never wanted Rosalinde the way he wanted Annelise. It was not enough to possess Annelise physically; he wanted to talk to her, to confide in her, to learn every secret that hid within her mind.

Annelise must have heard his approach, for she turned abruptly. Her eyes widened slightly when she saw him, though she said nothing. Their gazes locked for a moment in which Rolfe forgot to breathe, then she smiled a welcome that warmed him right to his toes.

When she crooked her finger and beckoned to him, Rolfe knew he was lost.

He strode, fully clothed, into the shallow pool, with an uncharacteristic abandon for his boots. He could not help but grin triumphantly when he finally captured Annelise in his arms.

"Waiting for someone?" he teased.

Annelise smiled up at him, her arms slid around his neck and her eyelids closed. The slick length of her nudity was pressed against him and the fragrance of her skin rose to tease his nostrils.

"Only you, husband," she whispered. A twinkle glimmered in her eye as her fingers locked into the hair at his nape. "I guessed that you would come." Before Rolfe could respond to her terrifying certainty, Annelise had pulled down his head for a demanding kiss.

Her ardor took him by surprise, as it had once before, then her tongue was between his teeth. It was stunning to realize that she could give him so much more passion than she already had. Rolfe was so overwhelmed by her lusty kiss that it was all he could do to return her embrace and simultaneously stay on his feet.

Annelise was heady tonic indeed.

When she ripped open his shirt and ran her hands hungrily over his skin, he thought the fire she had launched through his veins would be the end of him.

Annelise granted him no reprieve, though, for her agile fingers dove into his chausses to investigate their contents. Rolfe was certain he would explode beneath her gentle touch. He gasped her name as she caressed him, then met the gleam in her eyes.

"Temptress," he growled.

Annelise laughed. "I give you no more than you have given me."

It was all the reminder Rolfe needed. He grasped his wife around the waist and lifted her to her toes. "We shall see," he whispered in mock threat. Annelise gasped and grasped his shoulders as his fingers began their own dance of temptation between her thighs.

Rolfe watched with delight as Annelise arched her back in pleasure, and he wondered what had possessed him to sacrifice the sight of her in lovemaking. Her skin pinkened with a rosy flush as she approached her crest, her nipples tightened, her lips parted as she moaned.

Rolfe could not resist her allure. He kissed her greedily, loving how she returned his homage in kind. He swallowed her moans, savored her trembling, was enticed by the way she twined her legs about him.

It was magical how her own arousal fanned the flames of his own.

Then Annelise tore her lips from his. Her fingers gripped

his shoulders tightly and her blazing golden eyes locked upon his own.

"I want you within me," she said huskily.

Rolfe could not shed his chausses quickly enough.

He lifted his wife, her buttocks filling his hands. She wrapped her legs around his waist and Rolfe was surrounded by her sweetness. Her scent tantalized him, her arms and legs embraced him, her breasts were crushed against his chest, her warmth drew him deeper within her.

Rolfe moved slowly at first, but Annelise soon began to echo his rhythm. Her slick curves slid against his own flesh in an intoxicating manner.

He could think of nothing but his desire, his Annelise, and his pulse throbbed to a crescendo. Rolfe struggled to stretch out the moment, to make it endure until she had had her pleasure, but when she cried out, he could wait no longer.

He roared with the force of the explosion within him. He saw colors, he strained for the heavens even as he felt Annelise do the same. He gave her his all, his heart warming with the awareness that she matched him in every way.

In the wake of everything, there was nothing. Rolfe was barely aware of himself falling to his knees in the shallow pool. He gathered Annelise protectively to his chest and they sank together into the gently lapping water.

His next awareness was of little butterflies nibbling on his ear.

He opened one eye to find Annelise's lips responsible for the attack. She grinned unrepentantly, then stretched in a most intriguing fashion, apparently quite satisfied now that he was awake. The moonlight painted her curves with silver, making her look ethereal.

But Rolfe had no doubt that the lady was real. Annelise splashed her toes in the water in a very earthy manner and tapped her fingertips lightly on Rolfe's chest.

"Is your name Ethelbert?" she asked pertly.

The question recalled Rolfe to his senses as nothing else could have done. He scurried to put some distance between them, even as he tried to gather up his sodden chausses.

"Annelise! You cannot guess my name!"

She slanted a glance up to him. "Then you should simply tell me what it is."

Rolfe had never waged such a battle between what his desire demanded of him and the path he knew he must take. And worse, there was no way to explain the truth to Annelise. "You know that I cannot," he satisfied himself with saying.

Annelise's full lips thinned and Rolfe saw that she would not abandon the matter without a fight. "No, I know that you *will* not."

Rolfe's temper flared and he got to his feet angrily. "I cannot! You do not know what is at stake."

Annelise pushed herself up in turn and braced her hands on her hips as she regarded him. "And I am unlikely to know, if you refuse to tell me anything at all."

Rolfe shoved one hand through his hair. There was no convincing the woman. He turned to walk away, his boots sloshing in the pool, as he tried to decide how to proceed. "I refuse to have this argument once more."

"Oh! You *refuse*, do you? Well, I refuse to live in ignorance any longer! What have you to say about that?"

Rolfe glanced back at his wife. "I say you will have to become accustomed to it."

"No!" Annelise retorted. She darted after him and shook a finger beneath his nose. "No, you will have to make a change. As long as you tell me nothing, our days will continue one after the other without cease, and your curse will persist."

"I told you about the curse." Rolfe knew his tone was defensive, but he could not have made it otherwise.

"Yes, but I suspect that you confided only half the tale," Annelise snapped.

Rolfe's gaze flew to hers in panic, for he had been unaware that he had been so transparent. Annelise nodded
sagely.

"Yes, I saw the truth in your eyes, husband of mine.
There is more to this tale than you would have me believe,
and I demand to know the truth. Our lives are tied together,
no matter how much you would prefer that they were not."

"I do not prefer that!"

Annelise's eyes brightened in challenge. "And how
would I know that? I made this match of my own will,
although, granted, it was with limited options. But despite
that, I at least am willing to make the marriage work. You,
sir, show no such inclination."

"Annelise! You are unfair!" Rolfe flung out one hand
in the direction of the tower. "Just last evening I confided
in you. Do you imagine that that was easy?"

"Do you imagine that it was easy for me to tell you my
tale?"

Rolfe swallowed, unable to argue with that. He frowned
down at his wet boots, then met Annelise's eyes. "I cannot
tell you my name," he said tightly.

Annelise inhaled sharply. She folded her arms across her
chest, her gaze unwavering from his own. "I must have
my freedom," she said, and he feared suddenly that she
meant to leave him.

Rolfe's mouth was so dry that he had trouble forming
the words. "You mean to seek an annulment?"

Annelise frowned as though she did not understand him,
then she shook her head firmly. Fear flashed in her eyes
and her lips parted as she stared at him. Rolfe watched her
swallow and marveled that her voice, when she spoke, was
thin. "Is that what you desire?"

"No, Annelise." The response came quickly to Rolfe's
tongue, but he had neither the time nor the inclination to
question it. "Never that."

She smiled then, her change of expression warming

Rolfe like the sun coming out from behind the clouds. A cord tightened between them, though it was clear neither was ready to acknowledge its existence, much less discuss it.

"Neither do I," Annelise confided simply, taking a step closer to him. She laid one hand lightly on his arm, and Rolfe was certain he would drown in the warm pools of her eyes. "But I must be able to come and go."

"You mean to leave?"

"Yes, but just for some time during the day." She cast a glance over her shoulder to the palace, and her brows tightened slightly. "It makes me mad to be trapped within these walls, as fair as this place may be." She looked back at Rolfe and smiled with such charm that he knew he would be hard-pressed to deny her. "I wish only to go outside the walls, to know that I can leave."

"But you mean to return?"

Annelise glanced up at him quizzically. "Do you not trust me, husband?"

*Trust*. There was that word again. Rolfe's gut clenched and he looked to the gates in indecision.

The gates, like all the palace, heeded his dictate alone. And if they opened for Annelise—which he knew they did not—it must be by his command.

Only now did Rolfe realize that it was his own fear that kept Annelise imprisoned. Fear. He was afraid that Annelise would flee, when it was clear the lifting of the curse had to do with her. There was nowhere else Rolfe might have found the elusive love necessary.

He was *afraid*. Now there was a word he liked not, especially when applied to himself. Rolfe had never acknowledged a fear of anything in his life.

He was not going to begin now.

He looked down, saw the appeal in his wife's eyes and realized that this imprisonment would eventually steal the fire from them. He understood that he must grant her freedom or lose all that he admired within her.

In truth, the realization showed him that he had no choice.

Rolfe bent and brushed his lips across Annelise's, savoring her slight shiver of desire. "I would not have you abandon me, my lady," he murmured. "Our fates are tied most firmly together."

"Yes," was all she had time to whisper before he kissed her fully. Annelise melted against him in a most reassuring manner.

When Rolfe lifted his head, she was slightly breathless. "May I, then?" she asked with such childish delight that his heart was warmed.

"Yes, but return within the walls by nightfall," he said, and tapped her nose for emphasis. "The woods are not safe for a woman alone in the evening, as you should know by now."

Annelise grinned and cuddled against his chest. Rolfe caught the glimmer of mischief in her eyes before her lashes hid her intent. "But I had thought to meet you at the tower tomorrow eve," she murmured seductively. "You had said that you did not wish to return here."

Rolfe's body responded with a vengeance to the idea of such a tryst. And Annelise was evidently so pleased with her plan that it would be churlish to refuse. "If you bring food and a blanket, then we can make a night there," he agreed, loving the way she laughed.

"Oh, you will have more of a feast than you bargain for, husband of mine," she teased before she kissed him once more.

It was only the next morning, as he left the palace, that Rolfe realized now granting Annelise her freedom amounted to much the same as trusting in her.

He trusted her to not abandon him.

He inhaled sharply with the awareness of what he had done. Fool again! He had left himself open to betrayal! What was it about Annelise that so addled his wits?

Would she betray him? Would the jinni's curse come true? Would this be the deed that brought a killer to his side? Rolfe had to talk to Annelise again! He had to find the truth of her intent!

He spun on his heel, but the gates slammed resolutely before his face. Too late! He hammered on the gates with his fists, but they did not heed him.

Suddenly he understood why. The eastern sky turned a rosy hue and the sun tumbled forth from its slumber.

"No!" Rolfe bellowed, knowing all the while that it was futile. "Not on this day! Not yet!"

But the sun continued relentlessly to dawn, as he had feared it would, consigning him to his daily fate once again, despite his protests.


The morn dawned sunny and bright, although Annelise could scarcely have expected differently. She fairly danced out of the palace, dressing as she went. Her feet flew across the gardens wet with dew, until she stood breathless before the great, heavy gates.

Would they open?

Annelise took a deep breath, straightened and stared at the portals that had foiled her every effort to depart. "Open," she commanded simply.

To her amazement, the gates did precisely that.

They swung open in the silent majesty that she recalled only too well, gradually revealing a wedge of snow-clad forest to her view. The sunlight made crystals in the snow sparkle like jewels, and a bird called to its mate as it swooped low through the barren branches of the trees.

Annelise was delighted. She clasped her hands together and smiled.

"Close."

The gates obeyed her once again, and she could not resist doing a little jig of victory on the verdant grass of the palace garden. She cavorted back to the gates and flung her arms wide once more.

"I command you to open!"

It worked again. This was perfect! Annelise continued her merry dance through the broad archway of the gates, hesitating only when she made to step over the line that the closed gates marked.

A wintry wind stole around her bare ankles, reminding her only too well that the weather outside varied markedly from inside. What if the gates closed and locked her out?

Annelise scampered back inside and raced back to the palace with a rare disregard for her impulsiveness. She donned all her traveling garments—even the wool stockings, which clung to her skin in the heat of the palace—and draped her fur-lined cloak over her arm. Heart in mouth, she returned to the gates, which still stood patiently ajar.

Her heart began to pound as she stepped through the portal. Annelise realized as she walked how tall the gates were, how broad the entryway, how high and unassailable the palace walls.

She felt very small and questioned again whether these massive gates would continue to obey her. She eyed the clear line where the snow of the outside world began and the green grass of the courtyard ended.

But she would discover nothing by simply standing here. Annelise took a deep breath and stepped into the snow. It crunched as her foot sank into its whiteness.

And the gates slammed immediately behind her.

Annelise stumbled forward a few steps from the force of their closing, then spun to face the broad expanse of smoothly fitted wood. A panic far greater than she had anticipated flooded through her. She was trapped outside again!

"Open!" she cried, hearing the desperation in her own voice.

The gates opened with nary a moment's hesitation.

Annelise plunged back through the portal, clasping her hands together in relief as the gates closed behind her with a thud. She inhaled deeply of the fresh garden scent within the walls, then smiled.

Her husband's will had worked its way once more. She could come and go as she wished. Annelise danced triumphantly in the warm sunlight.

He cared about her; she simply knew it. He had trusted her enough to grant her something she desired.

It seemed the least she could do to show her gratitude would be to take Mephistopheles for a decent ride.

The winter air was bracingly cold, the wind welcomingly crisp in Annelise's face as she rode. The sky arched overhead in flawless blue; the snow sparkled and glinted as Mephistopheles thundered through the forest.

The cold air was invigorating, and Annelise savored the change from the garden's springtime. She imagined that the great horse enjoyed the stretch as well, for he ran with an abandon rare for a one so large.

They rode until the sun was high above the trees, then just before it reached zenith, Annelise turned Mephistopheles back toward the palace. She remembered all too well the elusive tendency of this woods' pathways.

Annelise kept the sun on her left, as it had been on her right before, and was reassured that the fresh imprint of the destrier's hooves were still readily visible. The sun was heating her shoulders through her cloak and her cheeks felt rosy when the palace's smooth walls appeared, shrouded by the forest ahead.

She had found her way home again! A surge of satisfaction rolled through Annelise and she urged Mephistopheles onward.

Then she heard the clink of horses' trappings.

Mephistopheles flicked his ears, and it seemed to Annelise that his pace slowed slightly at the unexpected sound. She peered through the dark silhouettes of the trees, wondering whether her ears had deceived her.

But no. Among the trunks she caught glimpses of color as someone or something moved back and forth before the palace gates.

Someone waited there. Perhaps admission had been requested, but there had been no response. Perhaps a lone traveler sought shelter for the night.

Annelise pulled the destrier to a halt while she watched carefully. She saw green, and flashes of silver caught the sunlight. She guessed there were no fewer than four steeds, although it was difficult to see them clearly through the forest.

A man called out and a pair responded, their voices making Annelise feel curiously vulnerable.

Voices, not a single voice. Her heart skipped a beat with the realization that there was more than a solitary traveler waiting outside the palace gates. Annelise peered through the trees once more and confirmed that at least one man had dismounted.

Clearly, they had no intention of leaving soon. Fat flakes of snow began to tumble from the sky as she hesitated.

Perhaps they had business with her husband. She might learn something more of him.

That thought sent Annelise's heels digging into her steed's side. She had a responsibility as lady of the palace, after all. Her spouse would find neither her manners nor her boldness lacking.

And surely no harm could come to her within the walls of a palace so bent to her husband's wishes. He had shown her nothing but goodwill. That conviction alone was enough to lift her chin as Annelise drew near.

The men turned, but their helmets concealed their faces

from her view. She rode through the last of the trees proudly, noting the green and silver colors of their leader.

There was something familiar about his garb, about that deep green, about the silver diamond emblazoned in the midst of his shield. Annelise struggled to recall, but the details of life before her arrival here eluded her like quicksilver.

Then he doffed his helmet and her heart sank to her toes. "Lady Annelise de Sayerne!" Enguerrand de Roussineau murmured in soft delight. "Well met indeed, my lady!"

Annelise swallowed her shock and inclined her head politely. "Good day, Enguerrand. What brings you to this part of the world?"

Enguerrand dismounted smoothly and strolled through the falling snow. His two accompanying knights watched avidly, their trio of squires peering out from behind the party's mounts.

Dark clouds were gathering overhead, and the sun disappeared momentarily from view. Annelise shivered as the wind's chill crept through her cloak.

Enguerrand lifted a gloved hand to stroke Mephistopheles' neck, admiration gleaming in his eyes. The destrier snorted and sidestepped with uncharacteristic nervousness.

Enguerrand arched a brow as he met Annelise's gaze. "A surprisingly skittish creature for his size."

Annelise smiled as sweetly as she was able. Oh, she disliked this man! It was more than his evident self-interest, for her distrust of him was deep and instinctive. "He is rather particular," she confined herself to responding.

Enguerrand's smile thinned slightly. "Yet a markedly fine beast for a lady." His gaze flicked to hers. "Especially one destined for a convent. Do the nuns ride such valuable destriers these days? Or have you found an accommodating patron?"

The insinuation was most inappropriate.

"You, sir, have a foul mind!" Annelise snapped. She

jerked Mephistopheles' reins, and the steed stepped smartly away from Enguerrand. "Surely you have some business being abroad this time of year? I have already asked what brings you this way, yet you have given no response."

Enguerrand bowed low. "And it was most churlish of me not to answer, fair Annelise." He straightened, although this time he did not touch the black destrier.

He folded his hands behind his back and regarded her steadily. "It seems that Bertrand, and hence Tulley, were concerned about your arrival at the convent. No word returned, you see, and there were *doubts,* shall we say, as to your safety."

"I am perfectly safe, as you can see."

"Sweet Annelise, you should have wed me when you had the chance." Enguerrand leaned forward intently, his gloved hand closing securely on Mephistopheles' reins. His voice dropped and his eyes gleamed. "Where is your brother, Yves, Annelise?"

"I do not know." It was not reassuring to realize that this man knew she was alone here.

Enguerrand arched a brow. "Just as you evidently know nothing of the convent." He shook his head, his gaze dancing over Mephistopheles and the palace gates before them. Too late, Annelise realized that her destination was only too clear. "What cozy nest have you found for yourself, Annelise?"

Her mouth went dry. "Make your accusation clearly."

"I make no accusation." Enguerrand's eyes grew cold. "I have only questions. Why are you not garbed as a nun? Yours is lavish attire for a bride of Christ."

"I am no bride of Christ!"

"I thought you chose the convent over me?"

"I changed my mind!"

"And chose to warm some man's bed rather than take your vows?"

"I took vows of another kind," Annelise snapped. "I chose my husband over both convent and you!"

"Husband?" Enguerrand's features contorted with rage before he managed to hide his response. He was so surprised that Annelise was able to snatch the reins from his grip.

She charged toward the palace gates with Mephistopheles, then turned the horse adroitly. The party of men watched her in astonishment. Enguerrand's gloved hand clenched in a fist as he glared at her.

Annelise wondered whether it had been wise to blurt out the truth. What trouble had her impulsive tongue made worse? Annelise did not believe for a moment that Enguerrand had come out of concern for her safety.

Then Enguerrand's dark eyes narrowed, and Annelise knew with dreadful certainty that Quinn had not yet returned to Sayerne.

And Enguerrand sought the prize he had desired all along. Selfish cur! He cared nothing for her, and Annelise knew instinctively that once Sayerne was under his hand—if indeed that possibility ever came to fruition—he would have no use for the woman who had brought him the prize.

And should Quinn return home, even more woe would have fallen upon the sorry bride Annelise might have been. As Enguerrand's wife, she might have shared her mother's fate. Gratitude flowed through her that she had not been fool enough to accept his offer.

"You are wed in truth?" Enguerrand demanded hoarsely.

"Yes."

Enguerrand's face contorted. "No, it cannot be so. You have evaded the convent, but not wed. You could not have wed another."

"I have."

Enguerrand folded his arms across his chest and smiled as he watched Annelise. "No. I will need more than your bold assertion to convince me, Annelise. Already have you denied me once.''

Annelise held his gaze as she tugged her glove from her left hand. The cabochon garnet winked merrily in a flash of sunlight as she held it up to view. One of Enguerrand's knights coughed under his breath, evidently impressed with the token.

"This is my husband's ring, granted to me at my nuptials." Annelise asserted coldly. "And this is our home."

Enguerrand's gaze roved over the high walls. "You lie," he said quietly. "If this place is your home, why then are the gates barred against you?"

Annelise took a deep breath, hoping against hope that the gates would not choose to be fickle at this precise moment. She glanced over her shoulder and whispered her command.

"Open."

Enguerrand's eyes widened in shock as the broad gates swung back without apparent assistance. Annelise savored the moment and rode through the portal at her leisure.

"You were wrong, Enguerrand," she called over her shoulder. "This *is* my home."

Annelise had not expected Enguerrand to recover so quickly. He dove suddenly for the gates and slipped through them before they closed behind her.

"You!" Annelise was shocked when he popped up suddenly before her. Mephistopheles snorted in disdain.

The knight, though, smiled with suave charm. "Annelise, I must ask you to forgive my rudeness."

"Enguerrand! How dare you simply force your way within these walls? I have not invited you into my home!"

"Fair Annelise!" Enguerrand clutched his heart as though wounded and gestured to the darkening sky. "I never would have imagined you to be so callous as to abandon my party to a wintry night."

She had no ready argument for that. The knight must

have seen her hesitation, for he pressed on, every word dissolving a bit more of her determination.

"Surely you and your husband could endure the burden of granting our small party your hospitality this night? It is too late to return to Beauvoir before the twilight, and it is said there are hungry wolves abroad this year, since the winter came so early."

Annelise fidgeted in her saddle, unwilling to grant Enguerrand sanctuary, for she knew his motives to be less than pure, yet unable to deny his party shelter from the elements this night. She had a responsibility to uphold her spouse's reputation, which would surely suffer if she turned this party away so late in the evening.

As much as she might dislike the man, she could not be so uncharitable as to consign him to a frozen demise.

She cleared her throat. "I apologize for my rudeness, Enguerrand. You must understand that your appearance surprised me."

"But of course, my lady." As he bowed low, Annelise glimpsed his eye roving in assessment of what he could spy from here. "There is no need for apologies between friends such as you and I."

Friends. The very idea made her shudder. Annelise could not bear the thought of having a troublemaker like Enguerrand within these walls any longer than absolutely necessary, but there was little choice. Surely first thing on the morrow, he could return to Beauvoir.

Annelise would be sure the suggestion was raised at dinner.

She inclined her head. "I thank you for your understanding. My home is yours."

Enguerrand beckoned to his party with a flick of his wrist, sending both knights and squires scrambling to gather their belongings. He appeared to notice the springtime garden before the palace for the first time, sniffed the air, then cast a questioning look in Annelise's direction.

When he spoke, his tone was sharp. "No doubt Yves and the others remain in these comfortable surroundings rather than return to chilly Beauvoir?"

"No," Annelise admitted, hating that her cheeks were burning with the embarrassment of the wealth around her. No doubt Enguerrand would discern her expression as guilt of some unnamed crime. "Our party was scattered by a pack of hunting wolves. My husband saved my life."

"How touching." Enguerrand's lips twisted. "And Yves was killed?"

"I told you that I do not know his fate."

Enguerrand's expression turned considering, then he glanced out over the lush gardens with a thoughtful frown.

"And we shall meet your inimitable spouse this evening at the board, I suppose?" he asked with feigned casualness.

Annelise stiffened slightly and hoped he had missed the telltale reaction. "Unfortunately, my husband enjoys the hunt this week. He will not return this evening."

"In such weather?" Enguerrand's doubt was more than clear.

Annelise looked away to hide her lie. "He enjoys the winter air."

"Ah, how unfortunate that we shall miss him."

But Annelise did not miss the speculative gleam that lit Enguerrand's dark eyes before he turned away to his steed. Dread boiled within her as she led the way to the stables, and Annelise wondered what manner of difficulties she had created by allowing Enguerrand admittance.

It was unsettling to have him within these walls, and Annelise knew she would not sleep this night.

An instant later, she realized that she could not keep her tryst with her spouse. She could not risk leaving Enguerrand alone in the palace, nor could she afford to lead him to her spouse, for she did not know the new arrival's intent.

It was disappointing, but her husband would see the reason for her actions when she explained. Annelise was certain of it.

Rolfe was at the tower before the sun even touched the western horizon. Clouds scuttled across the sky and a few snowflakes meandered out of the sky. He bit back his disappointment when he discovered that Annelise was not there.

Of course she had not arrived. He scolded himself silently as he paced. She knew that he did not change shape until dark, and he had forbidden her to watch his change.

But still Rolfe paced, impatient for night to fall. The kernel of dread that had lodged within him this morn outside the palace gates had haunted him all the day.

What if Annelise left him?

What if she betrayed him?

What would he do without her?

The sun took its leisurely time descending into darkness, and Rolfe was certain that the elements taunted him on purpose. Night's inky darkness slowly spread its cloak over the land, rising from the east to chase the last shimmering colors from the western sky. The stars glinted in the cloak's fathomless lining, and a thin crescent of silver moon rode high in the sky.

Rolfe paced as he watched the western sky, relief flooding through him when the last vestige of the sun's light was gone and he became himself again. He leapt to his feet and charged up the tower's stairs. Hauling his shirt over his head as he crossed the room, he peered anxiously toward the palace.

There was not a sound.

But she would come. Rolfe had to believe that his trust was not misplaced. He marked off the width of the tower room restlessly, haunted all the while by recollections of loving Annelise beside the small fire here.

When next he glanced out the window, the sky had dark-

ened to deepest indigo from horizon to horizon and was
filled with myriad stars.

Nothing moved in the forest below.

She had to come! She had given him her pledge. When
else had Annelise broken her word to him?

Rolfe groaned, only too readily recalling her trick with
the candle on the night he had fallen asleep. Had she not
pledged never to look upon him?

She must come on this night. Surely she must know of
what import this was to him?

But Rolfe had not confided that in her. Guilt suffused
him as he strained his eyes against the shadows below.
Annelise had consistently demanded explanations, and
Rolfe had just as consistently denied them to her. If she did
not come this night, he could not lay all the blame at her
door.

Still nothing moved in the forest. Rolfe shifted his weight
impatiently from foot to foot.

Why would she not come? He knew the gates had
obeyed his dictate, although he should have expected nothing else. He had not been able to resist the impulse to
covertly watch Annelise this morn. The radiant smile that
resulted from her newfound mastery over the gates had encouraged Rolfe that his move had been a good one.

At the time, her obvious joy had been enough to dispel
all of Rolfe's doubts. Now, in darkness and solitude, he
was no longer certain.

What could keep her from his side, other than a lack of
regard for him? Perhaps she felt she had no need of him
any longer. Perhaps she did not burn with the same desire
for his company that he felt for hers.

Perhaps she shared more with the grasping Rosalinde
than he would have liked to believe.

Every passing moment fed Rolfe's doubts.

He had followed Annelise and Mephistopheles at a distance this day, marveling all the while at this new protective

instinct dawning within him. When Annelise drew near the castle again and Mephistopheles' steps continued unerringly in the right direction, Rolfe had known he should fully indulge his fledgling trust. He had turned away then, but now he wondered if impulse had led him astray.

What if Annelise had not returned to the palace? What if she had abandoned him? Surely there could be no other reason for her failure to appear?

Rolfe stared into the blackness as the snow began to fall, and his hands clenched on the base of the window. He had pledged to wait for her here, to seek her out at the palace would imply that he thought little of her word.

No. He had chosen to trust the lady and trust her he would. No doubt she had fallen asleep or some such and would come along shortly.

Rolfe hunkered down against the cold stone wall and scowled at the doorway, wishing he could summon greater conviction in his conclusion.

# Chapter Ten

Annelise grimaced at her reflection in the polished brass mirror. She looked every bit as strained by Enguerrand's visit as she felt.

Five days and nights.

Closing her eyes, she leaned her forehead against the cool brass surface and tried to forget the troubles awaiting her outside the haven of her room.

What curse had brought a blizzard to their gates on the morn after Enguerrand's arrival? And what manner of unholy storm could rage so long? Each day, Annelise had peeked through the gates hopefully, only to find a dizzying whirlwind of snow and ice.

None could ride out in such conditions, but Annelise was nearly ready to cast Enguerrand to the elements, regardless of the consequences. The man would drive her mad with his insinuations.

She was tired of inventing answers to perfectly reasonable questions. She had explained the lack of an ostler with a vague wave, saying that the man must be slumbering. She excused the lack of squires with the suggestion that they would be along momentarily. Enguerrand's knights had been clearly skeptical as they set their own squires to the task of unsaddling and brushing down their steeds.

It was most inhospitable, but Annelise could do nothing about it. To her immense relief, meals had been laid regularly for the entire party, although she could not guess how this had been managed. Usually what she desired was supplied, and she could only conclude that her urge to feed the lot was strong enough to have it done.

But even the first night, Enguerrand had not been so quickly satisfied by the sight of a hearty meal. His questions had been piercing, his curiosity relentless and his suspicion open. Annelise had even resorted to her husband's ridiculous fable of fine servants who worked efficiently, yet out of view.

And she was well aware of the avarice in Enguerrand's dark eyes as he openly assessed the treasures of this place. It was enough to keep the most forthright soul from sleeping.

Over these past days, Enguerrand had pressed Annelise mercilessly for details she did not know. What was the name of this holding? When had it been built? From whence had her husband's family earned its wealth? How many brethren had he? Why had none heard of their existence in this forest?

Indeed, Annelise's head spun from the web of lies she had wrought. She had fought to create evasive answers that told her curious guest nothing, knowing full well that the others attended her every word even as they ate.

And now she could not keep track of what she had said and what she had not.

For Annelise was not accomplished in the art of deception. Her head throbbed with the effort. Under other circumstances, she might have simply blurted out the truth and let consequences fall as they may, but she felt obliged to protect her spouse.

It was illogical, but she sensed that Enguerrand posed a threat to her husband that she could not readily name. And she had no intention of being less than true to the man who had shown her nothing but kindness.

On this night, she had been forced to flee Enguerrand's concerted assault and seek momentary refuge in her room. But she knew she could not evade him all evening.

And she did not trust him enough to leave him alone. Annelise opened her eyes and looked toward the doorway, reluctantly acknowledging the rumble of the men's voices in the hall.

She replaced the mirror on a small inlaid chest and braced herself for another assault from Enguerrand before striding from the room.

But Annelise had never expected Enguerrand to find the book. She nearly gasped aloud when he saluted her with the old tome, a glint of malice bright in his eye.

"And what is this, fair Annelise? A collection of secret potions? We have decided that your hospitality here reeks of involvement in the dark arts, for nothing else can explain all we see around us."

"I do not know what you mean," Annelise responded as smoothly as she could. She kept her eyes on the table as she slid into her place and resumed her meal.

Enguerrand leaned closer. "It is clear that something most unnatural is at work within these walls," he hissed.

"Do not be ridiculous," Annelise scoffed.

"Ridiculous? Explain to me if you will, fair Annelise, why the clime within these walls varies so much from outside?"

She swallowed her bite of bread with difficulty, then took a long draught of wine, hoping the delay would give her time to conjure a response.

"It is a trick of the wind," she said finally, feeling the explanation to be hopelessly inadequate. She smiled at the surrounding knights, hoping to cajole them with her explanation. "We all know that there are places in the mountains where warm winds are trapped and the weather markedly different from the surrounding area.''

Enguerrand shook his head with impatience. ''You speak of isolated valleys, not simply the space within a wall arbitrarily constructed.''

Annelise forced a laugh. ''Who are we to say what is arbitrary and what is by design? Perhaps the builder of the palace simply took advantage of a natural effect.'' The knights murmured to each other, one shrugged, and they returned to their meal, much to her relief.

Enguerrand, though, pursed his lips and shook his head slowly, his gaze unwavering. ''It is not so and you know it as well as I.'' He leaned forward and she caught her breath. ''Why will you not admit as much? Who do you seek to protect?''

''No one! Do not be ridiculous!''

''There is no one else here and only the rumor of your spouse. Is he truly at hunt, Annelise? Or does he hide from his guests?''

Annelise did not trust the gleam in Enguerrand's dark eyes.

''What does he want to keep us from knowing?'' he whispered, before tapping the book firmly. ''Is this his collection of black spells?''

''The wine is clearly going to your head,'' Annelise snapped, and one of the knights chuckled.

Enguerrand put up his hands in mock surrender. ''Annelise! I think only of your safety and happiness! Surely you can understand that this situation is most unusual and that my concern is only for you.'' He leaned closer, his eyes wide with mock innocence. ''If you had fallen into the hands of some sorcerer, who better than I to rescue you?''

Annelise barely kept herself from shuddering visibly at the thought. It was time to put this nonsense to rest. She held Enguerrand's gaze and her voice was firm. ''You have nothing to worry about upon that score. My husband is no sorcerer. The man is at hunt.''

With that, she bit into a delightful piece of cheese, although it might as well have been wrought of dust for all she tasted.

Enguerrand's fingertips slid over the book. ''Then this is not a book of spells?''

Annelise laughed aloud. ''Spells? What manner of nonsense fills your head, Enguerrand? It is nothing but a book of tales gathered from other lands to entertain children.''

The others in Enguerrand's party relaxed visibly at both Annelise's bold tone and her explanation. She reached for the volume, but Enguerrand flipped it open.

''Why then is it written in coded script?''

The weight of the knights' and squires' gazes fell heavily upon Annelise. She saw immediately that the book had reverted to its original form. Annelise hesitated to touch the page and make it change, for that would only serve to fuel Enguerrand's suspicions that there was magic afoot.

Instead, she closed the book and claimed it before Enguerrand could protest.

''It is not coded!'' she scoffed. ''This is written in the language of the Moors. Did I not mention that my husband reads in many languages?''

Enguerrand's eyes narrowed. ''Then how do you know what lies within these pages?''

Annelise shrugged as easily as she could and slid the book onto her lap. ''My husband has entertained me with these tales on many occasions. I suppose you have only my word as to its contents.''

With that, she held Enguerrand's gaze steadily, hoping that she guessed aright his unwillingness to challenge her.

''Unless you do not trust me, Enguerrand?'' she asked pointedly. Her gaze met that of each of the others in turn. ''Although why a man would propose to a woman he found untrustworthy, I cannot guess.''

The pair of knights nudged each other, the gesture breaking the tension in the room. To Annelise's relief, Enguerrand cleared his throat and looked away for a moment before glancing over the company. His voice dropped and his manner became disconcertingly confidential.

"You may think my suspicions unreasonable, Annelise, but there have been strange tales afoot of late. Those may well be fanciful stories for children, but these tales are reputed to be true."

"Indeed?" This crisis apparently past, Annelise nibbled on a delectable piece of venison and dared to relax slightly.

"Tell us a tale, Enguerrand!" One of the knights lifted his goblet and took a long draught. "The night is a good one for a rousing piece of fancy."

The other knight settled back with a full goblet of wine, clearly more than ready for entertainment. The pair had shed their mail on that first night, the weather and the wine combining with the evident security of the high walls to make them relax as fully as men of war were capable.

Night had fully descended in the springlike garden and there was a pleasant hum of insects carrying through the arched and open windows. Had it not been for the company, Annelise might have thought the setting idyllic.

Enguerrand took a swig of wine and frowned as he gazed into the courtyard. "I am reminded of one tale in particular, told by a bard visiting Tulley's court. It is a tale of a vengeful jinni. This minstrel insisted he had been told the tale by the jinni herself when he had the misfortune to cross paths with her."

A jinni? Only too recently had Annelise heard a tale of those mischief makers. Surely Enguerrand could not know...

She set the piece of meat aside, unable to summon further interest in eating.

"A jinni?" A squire wrinkled his nose in confusion. "And what might that be?"

"A jinni is an evil creature, a spirit from the East, invisible for the most part but able to wreak havoc upon the lives of men when she chooses," Enguerrand said with surprising enjoyment. Annelise watched him through her lashes. "This one was said to have been of particularly foul temper, although whether that was the cause or the result of her imprisonment, the bard did not know."

The squire's eyes gleamed with anticipation as he settled in to listen. Annelise's mouth was painfully dry and she shared little of the boy's enthusiasm, although she strove to hide that fact.

"You see—" Enguerrand leaned back against the wall, his bright gaze lighting on Annelise "—it was said that she was imprisoned in a bottle before 'once upon a time' and cursed with the demand that she give her finest palace to whoever opened the bottle and granted her release. The jinni was evidently a selfish sort and schemed all the years she was locked away as to how she would take vengeance.

"The bard insisted that a knight returning from the Crusade had somehow acquired this bottle, perhaps in innocence, and opened it near Tulley's estates. The jinni had been compelled to grant him her palace, but then she took her revenge."

Enguerrand sipped at his wine, clearly enjoying how the men leaned forward in anticipation of his words.

Annelise felt slightly ill.

"What did she do?" asked the squire.

Enguerrand's eyes gleamed with malice. "She cursed the knight and made him a wolf. Imagine, to be condemned to take the form of a wolf when a wondrous palace had been granted to you as a gift! The bard insisted that the jinni had forbidden the knight from entering the palace, yet condemned him to prowl around it for the remainder of his days."

His gaze drifted out the window to linger on the enchanted splendor of the spring garden. All eyes followed his, then Enguerrand cleared his throat. "How fortunate we are to wait out the blizzard under such fine circumstances," he murmured pointedly.

To Annelise, at least, his implication was startlingly clear.

"But why would she do such a thing?" demanded the wide-eyed squire.

"It was meant to be a reminder of what he had been," Enguerrand supplied. "And a curse most vindictive, for he was doomed not to forget his lost state."

"God's blood!" breathed the squire. "That is foul indeed!"

The knight beside him smiled and ruffled the lad's hair. "You cannot believe all you hear when tales are told, boy. Undoubtedly, this bard had need of a warm meal in his belly and concocted the tale on the spot to tempt the lord's hospitality."

The boy looked crestfallen, but Enguerrand held up a finger. "No! Not this time, for he gave us the name of this unfortunate, and there were those in the hall who knew of him. They confirmed that he had departed for the Crusade, and as far as all knew, he had not fallen there."

Annelise was dying to ask the man's name, just as she knew she could not risk it. Enguerrand took a leisurely sip of wine, and she had the sense that she played the mouse to his hunting cat.

"Well? What was his name?" the squire demanded.

Enguerrand toyed with his chalice for a moment, his gaze locked on Annelise. "It was said to be Rolfe," he said with relish.

Annelise knew that nothing showed in her expression, although secretly she wondered.

One of the knights snorted. "A common-enough name in these parts. How could any know for certain that the Rolfe of their acquaintance was this same one? Did the bard not supply the name of the knight's estate?"

"No," Enguerrand admitted.

The knight rolled his eyes, muttering "bards" under his breath, and reached for another joint of meat.

"But this Rolfe was said to ride a great black destrier," Enguerrand added. "Indeed, Annelise, your spouse's steed in the stables reminded me of the tale. Why ever would that beast remain here while your husband hunted?"

"He took another," Annelise prevaricated hastily.

Enguerrand raised a brow. "Indeed, I saw evidence of no beast other than the palfrey and destrier there."

She laughed lightly and waved a hand. "His favored steed is scarcely here long enough to leave a mark."

The other knights looked less than convinced by Annelise's explanations, and she swallowed nervously.

Enguerrand gestured toward the courtyard without looking away from her. "I must admit that this place, with its Eastern air and enchanted clime, also made me think immediately that we had stumbled upon the very place of which the bard sang."

The knights, to Annelise's dismay, shifted in their seats and glanced uneasily about themselves, unwillingly swayed by Enguerrand's words.

The candles flickered and the wail of the winter wind could be faintly discerned. Enchantment was thick in the air, and it would be too easy—especially under the influence of the wine—for even the most levelheaded individual to give consideration to Enguerrand's conclusion.

That man leaned forward. "And what, fair Annelise, is the name of your husband?"

The entire party caught their breath and waited.

Annelise shoved to her feet in her best display of indignation. "This is how you reward my trust and my husband's hospitality?" she demanded, forcing her voice to rise shrilly. "How dare you enter our home and make such allegations? How dare you sit at this board and eat and drink for the better part of a week, then insult the lord of this holding with your petty rumors and insinuations?''

Annelise propped her hands on her hips and let her lip curl. ''A man changed to a wolf. What foolery! You should be ashamed of yourself, Enguerrand de Roussineau, for planting such nonsense in the minds of these boys granted to your care and training! You have a responsibility to both them and their parents, and if no one else will remind you of it, then I certainly will.''

The knights looked embarrassed that they had been so gullible, and Enguerrand apparently discerned the shift in his support within the group. ''I would apologize, fair Annelise, for I had no desire to upset you—''

''On the contrary, sir! Your intention has been none other since you arrived! I will not tolerate your disrespect in my home any longer! If this is how hospitality is to be rewarded, then I rescind my offer to grant you shelter!''

Enguerrand paled. ''Annelise! You cannot do this!''

''I can and I will. It is not long to the dawn now.'' Annelise pointed imperiously toward the stables. ''Saddle your horses and collect your belongings. I care not whether the snow has stopped, for if you put your mind to the matter, you can be within the walls of Beauvoir before midday.''

''But you cannot cast us into the forest!'' one squire protested. Annelise granted him a sharp glance, but he continued nonetheless. ''There are hungry wolves out there.''

''And if your lord is to be believed, they are no more than men transformed by a jinni's spell,'' Annelise snapped. ''Enguerrand can surely *reason* with them if you are attacked.''

''And what of the blizzard?''

''It will have done its worst by now.'' Annelise swept away from the table with her chin held high.

The two knights regarded her carefully, a measure of approval in the eyes of both. Enguerrand had clearly overstepped the bounds of acceptable behavior in an uninvited guest. Their manner bolstered Annelise's conviction in her decision.

"But, Annelise!" Enguerrand protested once more. "We cannot travel through the forest during the night!"

She spun to face him, crossing her arms angrily across her chest. "And where did you plan to stay when you left Beauvoir? You knew nothing of this place, yet arrived here just before twilight and on the brink of a storm. Where did you plan to sleep that night?"

Enguerrand's lips tightened, for he clearly had no answer, but Annelise was not finished with him.

"Unless," she asked sarcastically, "you had intended to bed with the nuns at the convent?"

Enguerrand flushed scarlet and indignation made his mouth gape open like that of a freshly hooked fish. The knights muttered under their breath to each other and the squires fidgeted.

Annelise stalked away. "I shall meet you at the gates immediately," she commanded over her shoulder. A scurry of movement followed her words, and she smiled to herself once she knew that Enguerrand could not see her expression.

It would be good riddance to see the last of him. The man's presence had done nothing but reassure Annelise that she had made the right choice, for her spouse's thoughtfulness was a far cry from this knight's self-interest.

Not to mention that five nights of being alone was more than enough for Annelise. She longed to feel her husband's warmth around her once more, although first she had need of some decent sleep.

Today she would sleep, then tonight, her husband would savor the fullness of her enthusiasm for him. Annelise's heart skipped a beat in anticipation.

Enguerrand could not saddle his steed quickly enough for her taste.

\* \* \*

Enough was enough.

Rolfe's patience with Annelise was exhausted. He had to know whether she was within the palace walls or whether she had fled, and he had to know immediately. He knew he could not bear another day—or night—of uncertainty.

Surely he had shown inhuman patience in waiting five nights for her to come to his side.

And all this because he had been unwilling to risk losing the sparkle in her eye. He watched the falling snow slow to a flurry and wondered.

Rolfe feared he had been a fool.

Again.

Rosalinde should have taught him all he needed to know about trust. Rolfe forced himself to recall the pretty smiles she had cast in his direction, all the wiles she had used to beckon him closer. He had been smitten by her beauty when first he saw her, and her coy encouragement had served only to fuel the flames of his desire.

Rolfe's ears burned with the recollection of how adroitly Rosalinde had toyed with his affections, how he followed her into the garden of her father's home for a promised tryst, how one chaste kiss had granted him the boldness to propose marriage to the gracious goddess he so worshipped.

Rosalinde had coldly inquired after his wealth. Rolfe had been naive enough to think that unimportant on the field of love.

Now he cringed with the memory of Rosalinde's lip curling in response to his confession that he was a younger and unlanded son. Her beautiful features had been transformed into a malicious mask before his very eyes; her laughter had been harsh as she mocked his intent to seek a small holding from his brother.

Rosalinde had informed Rolfe that he was not worthy of cleaning her shoes, much less wedding her.

While he struggled with this revelation, she had called

in mock anguish for assistance from an attacker. Her eyes had gleamed when her father's guards appeared. Rolfe had stood back, astounded at the change in her, as Rosalinde pointed him out as a lecher who had attacked her in her sire's own home.

The guards had chased him from the property with dogs, like some common thief, and Rolfe had pledged never to play the besotted fool again. He swore that Annelise would not compel him to dance to that tune, regardless of the strength of her charms.

For deep in his heart, he knew that Annelise had captured his heart more thoroughly than Rosalinde could ever have done. His gut wrenched as he wondered what he would do if Annelise betrayed him. Rosalinde's deception had burned, but the thought of life without Annelise's smile was infinitely worse.

Annelise was different from Rosalinde, despite Rolfe's earlier suspicions. Her beauty was more than skin-deep and her concern extended beyond simple material luxuries. Rolfe suspected she had spoken the truth when she confessed to wanting no marriage without love.

He was beginning to wonder whether it was only his inability to trust her that was keeping them from having that love match. What if he confessed everything to her? What if they worked together to remove the curse laid upon him? Annelise was quick of intellect, Rolfe had already seen, and her assistance would be an aid, indeed.

But what if Annelise turned away, just as Rosalinde had done, when she learned Rolfe's true worth? The palace was an illusion, he knew well enough. Even if the curse *could* be removed, Rolfe would still be a younger son, dependent upon Adalbert for some crumbs from Viandin's table.

Rolfe drummed his fingers impatiently on the window-sill. He could not bear the thought of seeing Annelise's sweet features twisted into a mask of disgust.

Had she ever shown disgust for him, though? Even the

threat of some horrible disfigurement had not swayed her from trying time and again to get a glimpse of him. He smiled despite himself.

Rolfe recalled the delight on Annelise's face when she rode out of the gates on Mephistopheles, the purposeful gleam in her eyes when she had turned back to the palace. His trust had pleased her, he knew. And she had fully intended to return to him, Rolfe was convinced.

There had been an unholy blizzard these past days and nights. Surely he should grant his lady the benefit of the doubt. Surely he should not be so prepared to accuse her of the sins of another.

As Rolfe stood at the tower window, sorely missing his wife, and the snow faltered to a stop, he considered for the first time that some ill might have befallen her.

Why had he not thought of that sooner? Rolfe was out the tower in a flash, striding through the snow with purpose despite the late hour.

What else could have kept her from his side? Every step increased Rolfe's conviction that it was circumstance, not design, that kept Annelise away. He cursed himself a hundred times that he had been unable to see past his own fear of betrayal. His heart began to pound as the palace's smooth walls came into sight.

But the sound of men's voices made him hesitate at the periphery of the forest.

"Farewell, my sweet Annelise!" cried a man garbed in silver and green.

*Whose* sweet Annelise? Rolfe frowned at the knight who led a small party out of the opening palace gates. Annelise hung back in the courtyard, huddled in her cloak, her features hidden within the shadows of her hood.

Rolfe's frown deepened to a scowl as the knight danced back to her, dropped to one knee and planted far too thorough a kiss on her hand. Annelise, Rolfe noticed, did not pull her hand away. He straightened indignantly and glared at the oblivious couple.

Any fool could see what had kept Annelise occupied these past days—and nights!

Rolfe chafed with the knowledge that his fair wife had played him for a fool twice over. Not only had she convinced Rolfe to let her come and go freely, but he had given her the benefit of the doubt when she had not kept their tryst.

How black was the heart of a woman who could stare innocently into a man's eyes and pledge to meet when she had no intention of ever doing so? Rolfe's hands clenched by his sides, but he could not turn away from the unfolding scene.

He had trusted Annelise. And she, in return, had made him a cuckold. Rosalinde had been typical, after all! Rolfe should have heeded both warnings he had been given!

His traitorous wife stood silently watching her lover stride back to his mount. The knight swung jauntily into his saddle—and well he should, after five nights in Annelise's passionate company!—waved and gave the beast his spurs.

Annelise gave no sign of disappointment, indeed of any emotion, as her lover rode away. Rolfe savored that fact with satisfaction. It was small consolation that she cared just as little for the departing knight as she did for her spouse.

She shivered, and Rolfe wondered suddenly if she wore anything beneath the fur-lined cloak wrapped so securely about her form. It was too easy to imagine her tumbling from bed to wish her lover farewell, her soft bare skin brushing against the fur lining of the cloak, her auburn hair hanging like unbound silk beneath the hood.

How long had her lover lurked in the forest outside the palace? How long had she schemed to have him join her within the palace's sheltered warmth?

Fury flared through Rolfe as the gates closed smoothly. He stormed out of the forest, glad that he had plenty of time left before dawn to get to the bottom of his wife's deception. He had been seven kinds of a fool to be lulled into trusting her.

And now Annelise would pay the price of her deceit.

Annelise crawled back into bed with relief.

Enguerrand was gone. And she could finally sleep in peace. She was exhausted beyond compare after these nights of keeping watch on her guests and could think of nothing but catching up on her lost rest.

But it was worth it all. Enguerrand, whatever his malicious intent, knew nothing of her spouse. Annelise dared to relax for the first time in days.

Tonight, she told herself as her eyes drifted closed, she would tell all to her husband. He would understand, she knew, for she had had little choice in the matter and he was a compassionate man.

Something tingled within Annelise in anticipation of how they would compensate for the week of loving they had lost.

"What manner of fool do you think I am?"

Annelise frowned, her world hazy as she drifted to sleep. If she had not known better, she might have thought her husband bellowed from the doorway. But he had pledged not to return here. Clearly, she but dreamed of him.

She smiled and snuggled beneath the linens, only to have them abruptly torn away. Annelise blinked in surprise as the cool air of the room settled over her skin. She stared down at herself in astonishment and found the bed linens completely gone.

"Do you think I have no eyes in my head, woman?"

Annelise rolled over cautiously, her eyes widening at the sight of her furious spouse. He jabbed a finger toward her and his eyes snapped angrily.

"Do not imagine that you will get around me, Anne-lise," he growled. "You may look as fetching as you choose, and keep those beauteous eyes wide with feigned innocence, but I know the deception you have practiced these past days!"

Annelise blinked carefully, but her husband remained before her—infuriated as she had never seen him before. It was clear he had lost his wits, for she had no idea what he was talking about.

She patted the bed and smiled. "Come to bed, husband of mine. I am tired beyond all, but would welcome your warmth for what remains of this night."

"Ha!" He cast the linens on the floor and trod upon them with a vengeance before glaring at her. "Do not imagine that I will console you after your lover has left you exhausted! Do not imagine that I will be grateful for his leavings!"

Annelise propped herself up on her elbows to regard him. "You have gone mad."

"Mad?" He paced the length of the room and back, flinging his hands out angrily. "Yes, I must be mad to have put my trust in a woman who brings me nothing but grief!" Annelise's heart skipped a beat, but he ranted on, ignoring her. "I was better left a brute beast in the forest with no chance of reprieve, for at least then I did not know how deeply deceit could burn. Even Rosalinde could not hold a candle to your duplicity!"

Annelise cleared her throat. "What deceit, precisely, do you mean?"

Her husband glared at her. "You should know well enough about that," he snapped. "Not that you care anything for what you have wrought."

It was clear he blamed her for some imagined crime. Annelise swung her legs out of the bed, eyeing him cautiously all the while. She stepped closer to her spouse, not liking in the least the hostile glance he fired in her direction.

Annelise laid one hand on his arm, but he shook off her touch as though it burned.

The gesture annoyed her as nothing else could.

Enough was enough. She had done nothing to deserve such treatment. Annelise folded her arms across her chest and returned his baleful stare.

"What is amiss?" she demanded.

He shoved his fingers through his dark mass of hair. "Do not imagine that you will make me explain to you what you already know, Annelise. Especially while you stand before me, dripping with your lover's seed."

Annelise gasped. "What?"

He propped his hands on his hips. "Do not play games with me. I know what I saw, and what I saw can mean only one thing."

Annelise heard the chill in her own voice. "What did you see?"

Her spouse's eyes flashed. "I saw your lover parting from your side just moments past!"

"Lover?"

"Do not imagine that I do not have eyes in my head," he declared with uncharacteristic savagery. "He could have been no one else."

Annelise suddenly made the connection. "Surely you cannot mean Enguerrand?" She stifled a giggle of surprise by clapping her hand over her mouth. "You think *Enguerrand* is my lover?"

Her husband was markedly less than amused. The corners of his lips turned down and his eyes were as cold as steel. "I am glad to see you find the matter amusing," he snapped, then turned to leave.

"No!" Annelise darted after him. "No, it is the idea alone of Enguerrand..." Her face worked as she sought a word to describe her repugnancy at the idea of coupling with that knight. Her spouse watched her impassively. "I mean, *Enguerrand*." Annelise winced. "Do you think I am blind?"

"I might ask you the same, *madame*," he said coldly. "There could be no other reason why you stayed away from the tower these past nights, and that knight's departure from these gates early this morn is proof enough that you were…occupied."

The way he uttered that last word dismissed every vestige of Annelise's amusement. Her spouse looked at her with such disdain that Annelise's blood simmered. How dare he assume she was guilty of such a ridiculous crime?

"At least have the grace to tell me the truth!" he snapped.

"You addlepated fool!" Annelise slapped him so hard that her palm stung.

The coldness in his eyes did not thaw. "Do not lie to me, Annelise," he growled.

"Lie to you?" Annelise sputtered at the unfairness of his accusation. "I have *never* lied to you. I have never taken a lover. I have never been untrue to you in any way."

Doubt wavered in his eyes. "Then who was that knight?" he demanded.

"I would gladly have explained, had you but given me the chance!"

Her husband's forbidding expression was less than encouraging. Annelise decided that she would rather he raged angrily than stand so still and cold. "I grant you the opportunity now to do so."

"And I refuse to dance to your dictate any longer!" Annelise tossed her hair. "You have lied to *me* for too long for me to stand aside and let matters be!"

Her husband's eyes flashed like lightning. "I have *never* lied to you!" he roared.

"No? Then you have kept the truth from me, which amounts to much the same."

His eyes narrowed and his voice dropped dangerously. "What are you talking about?"

"I am talking about your name." Annelise scooped up her chemise and hauled it over her shoulders before turning on him once more. "What manner of man would expect a woman to wed him without knowing his name?"

"A man who has much to lose."

"So you say. I have no more proof that this potential loss exists than you have of my faithlessness."

He eyed Annelise warily as though he was not quite certain what to think. Then he shook his head. "You befuddle me again with your charms," he muttered. "I am a man who cannot afford to risk all in this."

"You are a man who refuses to trust the one he should trust above all others," Annelise corrected.

"Unfair!" her spouse declared. He stalked across the room to wag a strong finger beneath her nose. She lifted her chin proudly, her gaze unwavering. "I trusted *you* enough to let you come and go from this palace, just as you asked, yet you rewarded me with deception!"

"I never deceived you. In truth, I have not slept these past five nights—"

He flung his hands skyward and stomped away. "Spare me the sordid tale of your faithlessness."

"You!" Annelise ran after him and clutched at his sleeve. He flicked a glance back at her as though he wished to be convinced, and Annelise was encouraged. She must make the truth clear to him.

Because she loved him.

The truth stole her breath away momentarily, and Annelise stared into his distinctive eyes as she struggled with the fact of it.

She loved her husband.

There was so much at stake here. If he walked away, convinced of her deception, Annelise knew that she would likely never see him again, marital vows or no.

His gaze chilled when she did not speak, giving her the courage to plunge on despite her fears. "I have not slept because I did not trust Enguerrand alone in your palace!" she told him with all the earnestness she could muster. "Every hour of the day and night I have been vigilant to ensure that he brought you no harm! Where is the faithlessness in that?"

Her spouse regarded her skeptically, though new uncertainty dawned in his eyes.

"You are the faithless one!" she accused, ashamed to find her vision blurred with tears. "You come here and accuse me of foul deeds without even asking for an explanation. What have I ever done to earn your distrust?"

His lips twisted. "Lit a candle to surprise me?"

Annelise hugged herself and granted him a cold glance. "Besides that. I apologized for that deed already and you are beyond churlish to cast it at me once more."

Her husband shuffled his feet, though he did not openly agree with her. He cleared his throat and frowned down at Annelise, but when he spoke, his tone was more gentle. "Then grant me an explanation."

"You do not deserve it!"

"Annelise..."

"No! You make cruel accusations and do not apologize! You tell me nothing—why should I tell you anything?"

"That is unfair."

"It is not! How many times have I asked you to tell me your name?" Annelise lifted her chin, but her spouse averted his gaze guiltily. "What have you to lose by telling me that? What nonsense it is to be wed to a man without knowing his name! This is a simple enough thing to ask, but you have no time to grant me an answer."

"It is not so simple as that."

"It is as simple as you make it. You talk about trusting me, but clearly you never have and never will." Annelise heard the bitterness in her own voice, but could not quell it. It was beyond cruel to realize she nursed tender feelings for a man who had not even the lowest regard for her. ''Surely it is not too much for a woman to know the name of her own spouse.''

His gaze locked with hers for a long moment, and Annelise saw that all the fight had ebbed from him. He shook his head abruptly and looked away. ''I cannot tell you that.''

''No, you *will not* tell me.''

He shrugged, apparently unwilling to rise to her challenge. ''Then I will not tell you. Either way, that secret remains with me.''

''As shall the full tale of our guest, then,'' Annelise retorted.

Her husband's head snapped up and he stared at her for a long moment. Then he scooped up the bed linens and tossed them toward her. He turned to leave, but Annelise could not bear to let them part company on such a sour note.

''Unless,'' she called as he reached the doorway, and his footsteps faltered to a halt. He did not turn, but he did not leave. Annelise took a deep breath.

''Unless your name is Rolfe.''

Her husband swiveled, and there was no doubting the truth when his gaze burned into hers.

# Chapter Eleven

"How could you know such a thing?"

Annelise saw the fear flash through his eyes. Her husband crossed the room with long strides and grasped Annelise's upper arms to give her a shake. "Who told you?" he demanded.

Annelise stared up at him, shocked both that she had guessed the truth and that he was so frightened in response.

"Who was that man? What did he tell you? What did you tell him?"

"I—I knew him before."

Rolfe's lips tightened savagely. "Yes, I would have guessed as much. What did you say his name was? Enguerrand? Where is his home? And what has he to gain from all of this? Did you summon him here? How do you plan to betray me?"

"Rolfe! Cease your accusations!" Annelise reached up and captured his face in her hands. To her astonishment, the gesture made him fall silent, although he watched her with haunted eyes.

"Rolfe," she repeated again, and smiled slightly. "I like your name well," she whispered.

He took a deep, shuddering breath, and all the resistance drained from him. He closed his eyes, and Annelise marveled that the touch of her hands could have such an effect on this determined knight.

"Annelise." His voice was low. "I beg of you, do not toy with me. Tell me your intent. I must know the worst that confronts me."

Annelise shook her head, uncertain how she would ease his concerns. How could she quickly tell him all she had just realized?

"My intent is to be your wife," she said firmly.

Rolfe's eyes flew open and he stared down at her, his shock clear. "You what?"

Annelise put a finger over his lips. His astonishment left her feeling more sure of herself and of him than she had thus far. Surely this could all be resolved? Surely love would not lead her astray?

Rolfe had only to learn the truth and all would be well. She took a deep breath, knowing that she would have to be the first to make a confession.

"The knight in silver and green was Enguerrand de Roussineau. He offered for my hand some time ago, but I did not trust him. Bertrand de Beauvoir bade me choose between Enguerrand and some knight of whom I knew nothing, but I chose instead to return to a convent."

"You loathed the convent," Rolfe whispered.

Annelise smiled. "Yes. My brother knew that as well, and I thought—mistakenly—that he would understand the fullness of my objection to Enguerrand and the other when I insisted on the convent instead." She looked down as she felt a flush stain her cheeks. "I thought he would relent in his insistence that I be immediately wed."

Rolfe chuckled unwillingly, and she dared to glance up, only to be snared by the familiar twinkle in his eye. "But he did not play your game?"

Annelise pursed her lips disapprovingly. "It was no game. I always pledged that I would wed for love alone."

"Because a man who loved his wife could not treat a woman as your mother was treated," Rolfe guessed.

Annelise gasped aloud that he should have divined her thinking so accurately. "Yes."

He ran a fingertip down her cheek. "And your brother did not care for your concerns?"

Annelise frowned in thought, as much to concentrate on the conversation while Rolfe trailed that warm finger across her lips as anything else. "He insisted that I wed before Quinn arrived home at Sayerne. It is rumored that my elder brother is beyond cruel, and Yves thought only of discharging his responsibility to me."

Now Rolfe frowned. "Quinn de Sayerne? He is not a man to dread, Annelise—" he said firmly, but she touched her fingertip to his lips in turn.

"I do not care for that now. Yves insisted on my wedding someone and I refused."

"Why not return to Sayerne?"

"I will never return there!"

Rolfe looked down at her with amusement in his eyes. "Then what else would you have done, rather than wed or join a convent?"

"I would have gone with Yves!"

"And how old is this brother Yves?"

"Fifteen summers."

"And not even knighted, I would wager." Rolfe shook his head. "Annelise, how could you imagine that you had a place with him? The boy does not even know what fate lies before him. He could hardly have cared for you responsibly."

"You take his side!" Annelise accused in dismay.

"Yes, because it was the only sensible path. Seeing you wed before he left only made good sense."

"How can you agree with Yves?"

"I cannot see that he truly had much choice," Rolfe argued gently. "A guardian without a blood tie would not necessarily see to your best interests and he was wise to see the truth.''

"What would you have done in his place?" Annelise could not help but ask.

Rolfe smiled down into her eyes. "I would have tried to hold fast against your unruly desire and hoped to accomplish much the same thing." His thumbs caressed her shoulders in a most disconcerting way. "I would like to think I might have succeeded as admirably in his place."

And what did Rolfe think of the results? Annelise stared into his eyes, wishing she were bold enough to ask. Certainly she was well pleased, but she could not read her husband's thoughts.

His grip tightened on her shoulders. "You have yet to tell me how you arrived here."

Annelise licked her lips and continued with her tale. "The wolves attacked our party on the way to the convent, and that was how I ended up at the palace gates."

"So, you denied Enguerrand?"

"Then and now," Annelise said firmly. "He insisted that he came here only to seek me out and ensure my safety, but he lied." She pursed her lips in thought. "I suspect that Quinn has not yet arrived back at Sayerne."

"And what matter is that?"

Annelise met his steady gaze. "Enguerrand's estate is sadly failing. I believe his interest is more in Sayerne than in me, for if Quinn does not return home, then I may be heiress."

"Ah." Rolfe tapped his toe for a moment. "And you did not couple with him?"

"Rolfe!" Annelise swatted his shoulder. His continued doubt stung, almost certainly because she was still coming to terms with her recently realized feelings. "Did I not just tell you as much? For a man who professes a desire to trust in me, you have a marked skepticism in my word!"

Rolfe laughed and made to gather her close. "Ah, Annelise. There is a fire within you that warms my heart."

Her heart skipped a beat, but she was not about to be swayed so easily by his sweet words. "Ha!" She struggled free of his embrace and backed across the room. "Ha! You say as much now, when all your questions are answered. Your fleeting trust does not run deep enough for my taste, sir!"

He eyed her warily. "What do you mean?"

"I mean that my questions always go unanswered, while yours earn my response! I mean that I know little more about you now than on the day we first met, although you are privy to much of my life. I have bared my thoughts to you, explained myself, told you of my circumstance, yet I had to guess your name."

His eyes narrowed slightly. "And how did you guess my name?"

"There it is again!" Annelise pointed an accusing finger in his direction. "There is the doubt in your eyes once more! How can you expect me to continue like this? I demand to know the truth! All of it! Immediately!"

Rolfe leaned back against the wall. "I cannot tell you that."

Annelise blinked back tears of frustration. "We have danced around this maypole before, Rolfe. You know the truth is that you *will* not tell me. And you will not tell me because you do not trust me."

Hurt made Annelise bold, especially when Rolfe's expression did not soften. She donned her old traveling kirtle hastily and laced the sides with shaking fingers. "Well, I am no longer prepared to live with your suspicion."

"Meaning?" he prompted coolly.

"Meaning that I will have the entire tale of this curse and how to mitigate it or I shall walk out that gate this very morning." Annelise shoved her feet into her shoes and swept her worn cloak about herself in a regal gesture. She looked up in time to see fear flicker through her husband's eyes.

"You would leave me?"

"You grant me no choice." She was dismayed to hear her voice trembling. "We cannot make a marriage if you refuse to trust me."

Rolfe gestured helplessly. "You do not understand—"

"No, *you* do not understand!" Annelise crossed the room in three paces, grasped the front of his shirt and gave him a shake. "I cannot understand your circumstance simply because you will not tell it to me! I have struggled to guess, I have fought to discern the truth, but the fact of the matter is that you must make at least this gesture. I cannot make this match work alone, especially if you cannot even find it within yourself to give me the benefit of the doubt."

"Annelise!" The strain was evident in his voice, and she looked up to find his eyes haunted. His hands fell on her shoulders and stroked her skin. "Annelise. I cannot risk it," he confessed. "There is too much at stake."

She tightened her lips and shook her head hastily. He might as well have cast her out. It was more than clear that Rolfe held her in little regard. She supposed she would find the convent on her own.

"Then I must leave," she said flatly and turned to go.

Silence dogged her footsteps. She paused on the threshold and glanced back, surprised to find Rolfe looking as despondent as she felt.

She owed him the truth, at least.

"I love you," she admitted softly, closing her eyes to his response before she walked away.

Rolfe blinked.

Annelise loved him.

He frowned at the floor as his heart took an unruly skip. She *loved* him. Three simple words and he felt all warm inside.

Annelise. Only now did Rolfe realize that if any other person had betrayed him as he had believed Annelise had this night, he would have simply turned away. But he had had to come to Annelise.

And he had come in what he now recognized as a jealous rage.

In point of fact, he had been quite unreasonable. In Annelise's place, Rolfe knew he would not have been quite so patient. He had no doubt that her tale was true, for he had seen in the clear amber shimmer of her eyes that she hid nothing from him.

Rolfe's trust had been well placed.

And he, like a selfish cur, had made hurtful accusations where none were due.

Annelise deserved an apology.

No, she deserved an explanation. Rolfe knew as soon as the thought came to him that it was the truth. He had put his trust in her and to his surprise, that had led to no dire consequences. Even though Annelise had guessed his name, fulfilling Rolfe's deepest fear, she had not betrayed him as the curse foretold. His faith in her had left him unscathed.

Save that Annelise had walked away with Rolfe's heart.

She loved him. Rolfe's heart thudded in his chest at the thought. Annelise loved him. And he, who had never before raged in jealousy, who never lost his temper, realized that he loved Annelise.

Suddenly Rolfe realized that he could no longer hear her footsteps on the flagstones. He raced out into the corridor, his breath catching when there was no sign of her.

She was not in the garden, though the sky was lightening with dreaded speed in the east.

"Annelise!" Rolfe bellowed. "Annelise! I will tell you all, if you but grant me another chance!"

There was no response. Rolfe raced to the stables, and Mephistopheles glanced up with a condemning stare.

Rolfe shook his finger at his destrier. "I will find her," he pledged, though the horse looked unconvinced. "I will find her and bring her back."

Mephistopheles snorted his disdain, but Rolfe was gone. He raced toward the palace gates, fearing that he followed Annelise too late. The shadows were thinning as the gates opened silently for him, and the faint howl of a wolf carried to his ears.

No! Annelise could not have gone out alone into the night forest! Rolfe felt the wind rustle behind him and knew his tail had burst forth already, but still he raced on.

He saw Annelise's silhouetted figure as she trudged through the snow ahead, her head bent against the wind.

"Annelise!" he cried. She turned and astonishment crossed her features. Rolfe thought she might have smiled, but the sun chose that moment to peek over the horizon.

He could not have taken refuge anywhere before his transformation began to manifest itself. Rolfe looked away so he would not have to witness the horror in Annelise's eyes as he changed form before her.

Dread shadowed his heart, and in that moment, Rolfe feared the sight of what he was would abolish Annelise's love and send her fleeing from his side.

Annelise caught her breath as Rolfe's shape began to alter. As horrible as it was to watch his nose darken and his ears sprout, it was equally fascinating to witness the change.

She stood and stared in amazement. The rising sun painted the snow with rosy gold as an azure blue slowly spread across the sky. The stars winked out, and the wind nudged the barren trees as it, too, seemed to awaken.

Then the wolf looked up from the garments cast about him in the snow and fixed her with one blue eye and one silver-gray.

Annelise swallowed her fear with difficulty. She had

been so close to a wolf only when her horse had been killed. But this was her spouse. This was Rolfe, the man who treated her with kindness, who granted her shelter, who made her flesh sing with desire, who spoke to her with an understanding she had never known.

This was the man whose ring she gladly wore. Annelise took a step closer. The wolf did not move.

"I wish you could tell me why you gave chase," she said as conversationally as she could manage. The wolf that was Rolfe returned her glance expressionlessly. Annelise took another step. "I would like to think that you intended to confide in me after all."

Rolfe wagged his tail. He barked like a happy pup, and Annelise was encouraged. "Were you going to?"

Rolfe barked with enthusiasm, then ran in a tight circle around her. Annelise spun in her efforts to watch him, laughing aloud when she became so dizzy that she collapsed in the snow.

Immediately a dark nose appeared in her peripheral vision. Annelise gazed into those unusual eyes. "It is you in truth," she marveled.

The wolf bent slowly, his gaze fixed upon Annelise as though he meant to reassure her, and licked the back of her hand.

Another wolf howled in the distance and Rolfe's head snapped up. Annelise gasped aloud when she saw the yellow gleam of a pair of eyes in the fading shadows. Rolfe stared into the forest and his lip lifted in a menacing snarl.

The soft pad of footsteps told her that the second wolf had abandoned her to seek other prey.

Rolfe nudged her elbow with his nose, impatiently urging Annelise to her feet. She glowed with the memory of his assertion that she would always be safe in his presence, and wondered how she could have ever doubted his feelings.

She should trust in results, not fleeting words, as he had

told her on the first evening of her arrival. And his deeds showed that he held her in esteem.

With the exception of his refusal to tell her his tale, but that looked to be an issue that would soon be addressed. Annelise could not have been more delighted.

Rolfe trotted to the gate, then back to her, his determined manner telling Annelise precisely what he intended.

She stood her ground stubbornly. "I am not going back in there without you."

Rolfe growled with what might have been frustration and increased his pacing between Annelise and the gate.

"No," she insisted. "I will not go in there. As long as you remain out here, then so will I."

Rolfe snarled pointedly in the direction that the other wolf had disappeared, then growled at Annelise. She leaned over and tapped him smartly on the snout. "You do not frighten me, husband of mine. I have no intention of letting you out of my sight until you have told me this entire tale."

Rolfe dove behind Annelise and pushed her in the direction of the gate with his head. She shook her head at his determination, pivoting to face him.

"If I go in, we both go in."

Rolfe backed up, shaking his head from side to side as he did so. He settled on his haunches and dropped his nose to rest on his paws.

Annelise braced her hands on her hips. "I will not go in without you," she said firmly. "There is absolutely no reason why we cannot wait in the garden until sunset and then you can confide in me. I see no point in remaining out here in the cold."

Rolfe did not move.

Annelise rolled her eyes. She stomped across the snow and grasped Rolfe by the scruff of fur on the back of his neck. Then she began to drag him back toward the gate. "Of all the stubborn nonsense you might come up with, this takes it all."

He snarled and twisted, but Annelise had too good a grip on his fur for him to wriggle free. "Why on earth would you insist on waiting out here with all this snow and cold? *Open!* As if there are not enough obstacles before the two of us without freezing to death in the process...."

Rolfe yelped as the gates swung open, and his struggles became much more concerted.

"What is the matter with you?" Annelise demanded, but then she noticed a black cloud wafting around her ankles. A heavy, unfamiliar, yet exotic scent teased her nostrils, and she knew there had been no such scent when she left the palace moments before.

She looked up, straight into the malevolent gaze of a woman who was there and yet not there.

Annelise was so astonished that she loosened her grip on Rolfe, who stepped out in front of her, teeth bared as he snarled.

The insubstantial woman laughed at his show of bravado, exhibiting a terrifying array of brass teeth in the process. She slowly grew taller as Annelise watched, until she towered over the walls of the palace like a storm cloud.

"And who," she asked Annelise deliberately, "might you be, demanding entry to my palace?"

Those few words told Annelise much more than she wanted to know. Her heart went cold with the certainty that she could accurately guess exactly who—or perhaps more precisely *what*—stood before her.

"I am Annelise de Sayerne, wife of Rolfe. We are coming into the palace." The jinni glared and the fur on the back of Rolfe's neck bristled. Annelise swallowed as she defiantly held the jinni's gaze. "If you will excuse us?"

"Excuse you? *Excuse you?*" The jinni reared back and bellowed, a foul cloud of darkness filling the air around her. "I most certainly will not excuse you!"

Her face was before Annelise's with an abruptness that

stole Annelise's breath away. "You, mortal, are not going to enter my palace, and that is final."

Annelise cleared her throat. "I believe that you have given this palace to my husband," she said carefully.

The jinni's eyes flashed like lightning. "Do not remind me!" She swirled, and the wind swept around them, pelting Annelise and Rolfe with cold chunks of snow.

Annelise was forced to shout, though she was uncertain the jinni would even hear her. "I do not mean to be rude, but he and I would like to return inside. As I see it, *madame,* if the palace is Rolfe's, there is no reason why we should not enter its gates."

The squall halted abruptly. Annelise glanced up as the jinni smiled at her with an amusement that made her blood run cold. "No reason?" she inquired.

Annelise straightened warily. "None at all."

The jinni's smile broadened as she swept her arm out in a parody of a welcoming gesture. "Then, by all means, do come in."

Annelise took a cautious step forward. Rolfe growled and glanced back and forth as he walked beside her. The jinni watched hungrily, but Annelise could not discern her trick.

Until they reached the gate itself. Annelise stepped easily over the threshold, but Rolfe yelped in sudden pain.

Annelise spun just as he darted forward again. He yowled as his head butted into an invisible wall.

His eyes flashed when he saw Annelise inside, and he dove for the gate again, only to fall back dazed once more. Annelise leapt toward him and confronted that same invisible wall. She could not reach him! She could not penetrate its sheer strength, either, though she beat upon it in desperation.

She was trapped inside, while Rolfe was locked out.

Rolfe was not ready to surrender, by any means. He leapt at the unseen barrier with renewed force, but fell back in evident pain. His legs were shaky as he regained his feet, though he lunged forward once again.

"Stop it!" Annelise cried. But it seemed he could not hear her, for she saw him eyeing the wall once more. He snarled and charged again.

"Stop it!" she shouted, and spun to confront the smiling jinni. "Stop it now!"

She examined her nails insouciantly. "His pain troubles you," she commented easily.

"Of course his pain troubles me! I love him! Stop this immediately!"

"Stop?" The jinni arched a dark brow, then shook her head. "I have no intention of stopping." She leaned closer, and the cruel gleam in her eyes did little to reassure Annelise.

"You see, love was not part of my plans for Rolfe." Her lip curled. "A mortal man spurned me, and I vowed a mortal man would pay. Rolfe is doomed to render the debt of humans to me, and he will do so by living out his life in misery."

"And what does that gain you?" Annelise demanded impatiently.

"Satisfaction," the jinni hissed.

"If you gave him the palace, then why can he not enter it?"

"Because he is a wolf," the jinni snapped. "I might have had to give him the palace, but I did not mean to let him enjoy it! That was a mean spell I wove, condemning him to live out his life as a wolf, pacing around this place!" She laughed aloud.

So how had Rolfe managed to change to a man by night? Annelise wondered. It was easy enough to see that this was not the time to ask such a question. She had no doubt that this jinni would take more vengeance on Rolfe if she learned that somehow he had thwarted her.

Now the jinni's gaze slipped assessingly over Annelise.

"It is evident you care for Rolfe, for whatever foolish mortal reason, and just as evident that I intend for him to have no consolation in his misery. My condition that the first person to enter the palace must wed him was designed, after all, to torment him even further with the reminder of what he had lost." She examined her glittering nails, then the cloud reared up once again. "Clearly, you will have to spend the remainder of your days locked within these walls."

That is not fair!"

"Fair?" The jinni chuckled softly to herself. "What an enchanting mortal concept." Then she glared at Annelise with sudden vigor. *"Fair has nothing to do with the workings of this world!"* she bellowed. "And it is about time you learned as much!"

She flung out her arms. As Annelise ducked, the wooden gates slammed shut, then suddenly the garden was silent.

Annelise raised her head to find herself alone.

She straightened and ran her hands over the wooden portal. "Open," she commanded firmly.

The doors shuddered as though they fought between two conflicting minds. Annelise thought for a moment that they might swing inward; indeed they fairly bowed with the force bent upon them.

Then abruptly, they stilled, leaving her barricaded inside.

And Rolfe, no doubt, alone outside.

Annelise spent the next few days aimlessly wandering the halls of the palace. She already knew that she could not go over the walls, and the jinni had ensured that she could not go through the gate.

A lifetime here, despite her fine surroundings, was more than Annelise was certain she could endure.

And she was worried about Rolfe. Was he changing to a man by night and forced to live out in the cold? Or was he condemned to remain a wolf all the time?

Annelise did not know which would be worse.

Mostly, she chafed at the fact that she was doing nothing. There had to be something to do. There had to be a solution or a way to trick the jinni. Every puzzle had a key, that much she knew.

But Annelise did not even know where to begin.

She stumbled over that mysterious book time and again, but this was a time for action, not leisure reading.

Even though there was precious little action to take. Annelise racked her brains and took to lingering in the stables. Mephistopheles usually kept an eye upon her, his tail swishing at the flies.

Annelise imagined that he liked her being here, too. Certainly, both he and the palfrey enjoyed being brushed. Despite the palace's comforts, Annelise found herself here most often and imagined it was because in all of the palace only in the stables could she find another living being.

The smell of the hay in the sun and the rustle of the horses in their stalls reminded her of days at Sayerne, when she had spent time in those stables. The ostler's wife had given her sweets to chew, and the ostler, between tasks, had recounted fanciful tales. It had been an escape for Annelise, and the source of most of the happy moments she had had upon returning to her father's home.

She tried not to remember the ostler's gray puppies, for they made her think of a certain wolf.

One sunny afternoon, she wandered into the stables and tripped over the book again. "Get out from under my feet!" she declared with no small measure of frustration. "I have no time to read now!"

Annelise hooked her toe under the book and hefted it across the stable floor. It landed in a stack of hay, its gilt catching the sun and taunting her to come closer.

Annelise eyed the book and wondered anew how it had come to be here. She was certain she had left it in the foyer.

It was almost as though the volume was following her. At the thought, the hair prickled on the back of her neck, and Annelise knew she had been in her own company for too long.

When she heard a throat being cleared, Annelise jumped in shock. She spun around, to find a short, plump woman beside Mephistopheles' stall.

"Greetings!" The woman gave Annelise a cheerful wave, then stepped forward to scratch the destrier's ears.

Her kirtle and cloak were commonplace enough, but she wore the most peculiar fur hat Annelise had ever seen, and Annelise could not have easily guessed her age.

Mephistopheles seemed markedly untroubled by her presence. He leaned his head against the stall so she could scratch his other ear. The woman smiled and complied.

"Who are you?" Annelise asked.

"I might ask the same of you." She laughed and strolled around the stall. Annelise noticed a faint rosy cloud hovering around her and took a cautious step backward.

"Are you that jinni again?" she asked warily. "Or another one altogether?"

"Dear me, I seem to be hearing that a lot lately." The woman grimaced. "Do not tell me that you met *her* first, as well? Not much of an ambassador for our kind, is she?"

Her expression of distaste made Annelise suspect that she and this stranger shared the same opinion about the malicious jinni, but for once Annelise was determined to be careful. Impulse had steered her false often enough that she should know to bide her time.

"Her?" she asked carefully.

"Yes, *her*. The troublemaker herself." The woman sighed. "But there was a time when I had wondrous dreams for her and what she might become." She shook her head, as though dismissing a sentiment that had no place in this conversation and smiled brightly at Annelise. She waved a

hand at their surroundings. "Surely you know by now that
this is her palace?"

"You mean the jinni that cursed Rolfe?"

"Oh!" The woman's expression was one of delight.
"You know Rolfe? He is, of course, mortal, and western
as well, which gives a man a measure of intolerance, if I
might say so. But all the same he has a certain charm. Do
you agree?"

"Yes." Annelise thawed slightly. "He is my husband."

"Truly?" At Annelise's nod, the jinni began to speak
eagerly. "Oh, that is fine luck indeed. I had never imagined
he would make such progress in such short order. He originally looked quite grim at the prospect of marriage."

Annelise noticed only one word in the jinni's commen-
tary. "What manner of *progress* do you mean?"

"Progress against the curse, of course, my child!" The
jinni shook her head, setting into motion the curious little
red balls along the perimeter of her hat. "You must know
about the curse—after all, you *wed* the man. Did he not tell
you?"

"Perhaps not all of the tale," Annelise acknowledged
carefully. If she were prudent, this talkative jinni might tell
her more about how to abolish the curse.

"Well, he was cursed to be a wolf, but I—in a markedly
fine spell created entirely on impulse, one that amazes me
to this day with its adept little rhyme—mitigated the curse
so that he was only burdened to be a wolf by day. And
look at you—you are a fine enough looking woman to not
hurt the eyes! What fortune that man has!"

"He has many blessings to count, indeed," Annelise
commented dryly.

The jinni drew herself up taller as her expression turned
skeptical. "Oh, you two do have something in common, do
you not? When dealing with our kind, a sharp tongue is
markedly less than an asset, though I am surprised to have

to remind you of that. The pair of you would not be in the fix you are had Rolfe been a little less quick to express his skepticism.''

"Yes, he told me as much.''

The jinni looked impressed. "He did? Well, that is progress indeed. Better late than never, I would suppose the motto here to be. You know, he was decidedly less than impressed that I had not been able to remove the curse entirely, as I recall, although—'' she laughed lightly "—how anyone could expect *that* I truly do not know. I thought I did rather well, under duress. It was no pleasure to be cloistered with *her* all these centuries.''

"I can imagine it would not be,'' Annelise said with heartfelt sympathy. Just a small taste of the other jinni had been sufficient for her.

The jinni met Annelise's gaze and smiled pertly. "That is a marked improvement in your tone,'' she said warmly.

Annelise knew an opportunity when she saw it. The jinni was well disposed to both her and Rolfe; Annelise should make the most of a moment that might be a fleeting one.

She smiled, summoning every vestige of charm she possessed. "Might it be possible for you to intervene now to aid Rolfe?'' When the jinni's gaze hardened, Annelise hastened on. "Not that I would show any lack of appreciation for your efforts thus far, but the other jinni has returned and made our situation rather worse.''

"I can imagine she might.'' The jinni shook her head. "No, I cannot risk incurring more of her wrath. I think I have done quite enough.''

Enough? Annelise's irritation flared, though she fought valiantly against it. The burden of being cautious when she was itching to demand the truth was a challenge indeed.

"What exactly must be done to end this curse?'' Annelise asked as calmly as she could.

The jinni shrugged. "Rolfe's salvation must be earned.''

"But how?" How Annelise would love to tell these meddling two what she thought of what they had wrought! "I have tried everything imaginable and now matters are only worse."

The jinni considered Annelise for a long moment. "You love him, do you not?"

"Of course, I love him! He is my husband."

"Then *you* may be his salvation."

There was an empty promise! How could such nonsense possibly be true? Annelise's strained control snapped at that one measured comment.

"I should think not! Each time I think of a solution, some jinni changes the rules of play." She flung her hands skyward in frustration. "I cannot talk to Rolfe, I cannot touch him, I cannot see him—not even as I could before! I have no idea what I might do to aid him, much less how his freedom might be *earned!*"

There was silence in the stable for a long moment. Mephistopheles swished his tail and a few flies strayed, buzzing, into the sunlight.

"Perhaps you are already doing it," the jinni said finally. Annelise glanced up in surprise, and the jinni smiled. "I cannot believe that you wed a man who was half wolf," she mused in a dizzying change of subject. "It cannot be as though you were lacking in offers."

That hit a little too close to home for Annelise's taste. Her situation and this conversation were not improving her temper any favors. "Circumstances were unusual," she retorted. "As they still are."

"Ah." The jinni strolled closer, her feigned casual air not fooling Annelise for a moment. "Having regrets, are we?"

"No. I simply wish Rolfe could have been honest with me at some point."

"Perhaps he was afraid of losing you."

"Losing me?" Annelise snorted her disagreement with that idea. "I was trapped within this palace from the start, just as I am right now!"

"Losing your support, then," the jinni corrected gently. "Her spell was a wicked one, you know."

"No, I do not know," Annelise retorted, her patience with this spell nonsense well and truly expired. "I know nothing about it, and no one will tell me anything!"

"*Her* curse said that anyone he trusted would betray him."

Annelise's anger ebbed out of her with a single breath as she stared in the jinni's fathomless brown eyes. "That is dreadful," she whispered.

The jinni nodded ruefully. "And far from all of it, though I had best leave the telling of the remainder to Rolfe. It is easy to imagine how concerned he might be." She flicked a glance Annelise's way. "I suppose you are thinking that things have not been easy for the pair of you?"

Annelise grimaced. "I would guess our obstacles to be rather worse than those in most marriages."

"As perhaps may be your reward," the jinni said quietly. Annelise glanced up to find the woman smiling gently at her. "Can you say in honesty that you have ever met a man like him?"

"No," Annelise confessed.

"I see the rest in your eyes, child. Do not be dismayed by the task set before you." The jinni touched Annelise's hand, and the brush of her fingertips sent renewed hope surging through her. "We must all fight for what we believe to be of import."

"But the other jinni has come back! And she has locked Rolfe out and me inside!"

The jinni brushed her fingertips over Annelise's brow, and Annelise felt a sense of calm replace her frustration.

"It is easy to see that Rolfe is blessed with a wife of rare courage and wit," the jinni murmured soothingly. "You have the will within you and the means around you to solve all of this. Every puzzle, after all, has a key."

"Surely you can aid us?"

The jinni shook her head. "I have done all that I can."

Tears rose in Annelise's eyes and she turned away. Despite the jinni's confidence in her, she could not begin to imagine how to save Rolfe.

"You will need this," the jinni said quietly.

Annelise blinked at the black bottle cradled in the woman's hands. There was something fascinating and simultaneously repulsive about the dark lights that seemed to move over its surface.

"Do not look overmuch upon it," the jinni counseled. "This is the only thing I can grant you that you might need."

"But she—"

"Leila." The jinni's voice was firm, and her gentle gaze grew suddenly fierce as she pressed the bottle and its stopper into Annelise's hands. "Her name is Leila." The jinni looked suddenly a great deal older than she had at first.

"You knew her before being confined with her?" Annelise guessed.

"Only too well." The jinni shook her head and turned away, her gaze brightening when it landed on the discarded book. "So that is what happened to it! I should have known that *she* would have claimed it for her own."

"But why is the book worthy of note? Surely it is only a volume of children's tales?"

The jinni looked back to her, and Annelise thought she saw the shimmer of tears in her eyes. "I suppose we are all destined to become mere entertainment for children," she said.

Her sadness at the thought was clear, but before Annelise could say anything, the jinni walked right through the stable wall and disappeared.

For each room the stone carver... carry off below. Annelise couldn't prevail. The maid walked right through the white wall and disappeared.

# Chapter Twelve

Mephistopheles snorted oats all over the stable floor, seeming to take great delight in his feat. Annelise stared wide-eyed at the wall for a long moment, then looked down at the bottle and the book.

The jinni had said that the solution was in her own hands. Annelise had only to figure it out. The jinni had called the evil jinni Leila, and Annelise vaguely recalled the mention of a Leila on the page of the book she had scanned.

She scooped up the tome, opened it, touched the page and watched with wonder as the foreign words melted into familiar script. She sank down into the hay and began to read a tale for children, well prepared to find a glimmer of truth within it.

There was, there was not, in the oldness of time, twin daughters born to a jinni and his wife. Herein lies the tale of Leila and Kira, twins born to Azima and Azzam. They were matched in looks but not in manner.

This was in the days when man and jinni walked the earth together—one wrought of potter's clay, the other of smokeless fire—in echo of the master's creation. Equal but different, they shared trials and successes, in those times before the jinns were dispatched to the world beyond the world of men. Good and evil stalked the ranks of both man and jinni in those times, as always it did, and as this tale soon will show.

For Leila, being a child of the night, grew to womanhood with an intuitive understanding of the dark arts, while Kira, a child of the day through to her core, was filled with guileless innocence.

Though both children were fair in their way, the sight of Kira made anyone she met feel as though they looked into the warm beauty of the sun itself. People and jinns both smiled when she passed them, even when she was an infant, and Leila's dark heart grew to nurture a dreadful jealousy of her sister.

Leila hid her feelings from all, and the sisters grew, becoming more themselves with each passing day. Kira was good and kind, thinking of others before herself, willing to give the last of what she had to another in need. It was said that diamonds and pearls fell from her mouth when she spoke, and all she gave came back to her tenfold.

Now Leila, though gifted, did not have such abundant charms. As she grew older, her jealousy deepened into a dark and hateful thing. She turned to sorcerers' arts to compete with her sister, but though she could oft mimic her sister's gifts, that wrought of shadows did not stand the test of time. The flowers she created quickly withered and died, while Kira's blossomed with rare vigor and thrived even in adverse conditions.

It was said that Kira had a rare gift, and the parents showered affection on their golden child. All this served only to feed Leila's hatred, though none might have guessed unless they looked into her eyes. Accidents began to befall Kira, and as their severity increased, those outside the family wondered about Leila. Kira smiled away any questions though, and would hear nothing said against her twin.

In time the sisters were of a marriageable age, and a young mortal came calling. He was handsome beyond all, gifted, yet moderate of speech, which pleased the father of the two sisters. The young man fell in love with Kira as suddenly as Leila fell in love with him. His mortality was not an issue, for the nuptial kiss of a jinni welcomes a mortal partner into the ranks of the immortal jinns.

One might easily imagine the jealousy that erupted in Leila once Kira made her affections for the young suitor clear. Leila delved deep into her store of forbidden secrets, and the love of Kira and her suitor were sorely tested in Leila's attempts to drive them apart.

But despite the odds against them, despite the pitfalls laid across their path, the couple's love was of such magnitude that they overcame every challenge. Leila lied and cursed, her attacks on Kira becoming more overt, though that golden child stepped through the worst of calamity unscathed. Each failure made Leila yet more bitter, and she dove deeper into the shadows of arcane sorcery, but to no avail.

Meanwhile, the wedding was planned and no expense was spared. Gifts came from far and wide for the happy couple, and the twin's father, Azzam, built a palace for the newlyweds. It was graced with the gifts and the love of all in the community, and those nearby claimed Kira's smile brought the sun into the central courtyard on the most cloudy day.

Leila, not to be outdone, built a palace so fine that it tugged at the heartstrings of all who came near. Men were drawn to the palace's beauty, like sailors to sirens calling from rocky shores, but Kira's beloved was immune. He remained in his new home, preparing for his nuptials and doting upon his intended.

Leila was infuriated that the object of her love had

spurned her lavish palace. She threatened to cast spells on those who attended the wedding, or those who sent gifts. She struck a man dumb in the marketplace after he commented on her sister's beauty and that man never spoke again. Similarly, those who gazed admiringly upon Kira from afar found themselves blinded shortly thereafter.

Enough was more than enough, the mother declared. Azima knew more than most of the extent of her daughter's stubborn nature. From the beginning, Leila had been a child bent upon her own satisfaction, regardless of the cost to others. Fearing that her spawn might not be amenable to change however artfully the idea was presented, Azima planned for the worst.

A jinni goldsmith fashioned a bottle at Azima's demand. He dictated that any jinni released from the bottle would be obliged to grant a gift to whoever gave that freedom. To the surprise of all, the resulting decanter was blacker than black, yet impossible to break.

Azima took the vessel home, her heart heavy with what she might have to do. She planned to visit Leila in her palace, but Leila would not receive her mother's messengers. Invitations were ignored and even Azima herself was not greeted at her daughter's home.

Azima feared Leila was up to something, but what she could not guess. Fearing disaster, she instructed Azzam on the role he must play, should anything go amiss on the day of Kira's nuptials. As soon as Leila dove into the bottle, he must put the cork in as firmly as he could. Azima reminded Azzam of their responsibility as parents, and made it most clear that all their love would never be enough to control one like Leila should she choose to ignore their appeal for reason. Azima made her spouse swear an ancient oath of uncommon strength to ensure that he would keep his word.

Then she kissed him with great affection, and he wondered at the cause. Perhaps even then she had a feeling of what might transpire.

On the morning of the wedding, Azima was well prepared, though she hoped Leila would stay away and all her plans would be for nothing. Azima hovered near Kira, afraid her other daughter would try one last trick to have her sole desire. When Kira stepped into the carriage summoned to convey her to the nuptials, Azima had an odd feeling. She darted into the carriage just before it pulled away, even though Kira had asked to ride alone.

Azima found Leila holding a wicked dagger to her sister's throat. It seemed she had decided to substitute herself for the bride. Azima talked as quickly as she could, using all the charm she could muster to distract her daughter from her foul deed. Leila was not swayed, and Kira's eyes were wide with fear.

Knowing she had no other choice remaining, Azima casually made her offer.

She remarked that she had a decanter at home into which no jinni could fit. Leila declared that she could do anything she set her mind to, scoffing at her mother's inadequate powers. Azima challenged her to prove it, offering to let whichever daughter could slide into the bottle marry Kira's suitor.

Leila accepted the offer without hesitation. The carriage turned around at Azima's dictate. When the women arrived, Azzam fetched the bottle at his wife's bidding and set it in the courtyard. The stopper he kept hidden.

Now Kira knew the point of the trick, and though she made a good show of it, did not really try to enter the bottle, so was unsuccessful. Leila, gloating, pushed her aside and made a great production of sliding effortlessly into the bottle.

But Azzam pulled the cork from his pocket a moment too soon, and Leila guessed his intent. She tried to squirm out of the bottle, but her mother pushed her the rest of the way in. Leila was overpowered, but, in the last moment, her fingers locked around Azima's ankle. To the horror of all, Azima tripped on her flowing robes and was hauled into the decanter along with her evil daughter.

Azzam fumbled, then recalled his oath and jammed the cork into the bottle with shaking hands. The wedding proceeded as arranged, for all knew Azima would have desired as much, but the day was less than euphoric for all.

Time passed, yet none could figure out a way to let one jinni free while the other remained trapped inside. Heartsick, Azzam hid the bottle away, unable to look upon it without guessing what Azima suffered within its confines. It was not overlong before he died, as a jinni seldom does, his heart broken by the role he had been compelled to play in all of this.

Though Kira looked for the bottle, wanting to ensure that Leila was guarded responsibly, it was never found. Over time, the world grew less tolerant of jinns and their kin, forcing those wrought of smoke to hide from mortals. The possessions of the wondrous house were scattered, the house occupied by mortals. The story of Leila and Azima passed into legend thereabouts and no one ever saw the dark decanter again.

It was thus, it was not thus, in the oldness of time.

Three days later, Annelise had a plan.

Reading the story of Leila and Kira had left her with an overwhelming sense of Leila's obsession with the man who had ultimately become Kira's spouse.

Annelise intended to use that jealousy against the evil jinni. But she required Leila's presence to even begin. Since the only other thing of import to Leila was clearly this palace, Annelise set to work destroying it, simply to gain Leila's attention.

The obsidian bottle rested in the middle of the foyer, waiting.

First Annelise threw a delicate, inlaid table into the shimmering blue pool with all her might. It shattered in a most satisfactory fashion, but she had already darted back into the palace.

A stool flew through a blown-glass window; a heavy chest snapped the carved marble neck of a fountain. Annelise cast rugs and pillows in every direction, sending brass clattering to the tiled floor and trinkets smashing against the wall. She screamed and howled as she did so, breaking everything she could lay her hands on and making as much noise as possible in the process.

It was not long before she had company.

"What is the meaning of this travesty?" shrieked the jinni Annelise now knew to be Leila.

She had come!

"What has happened to my beloved palace?" the jinni demanded.

As planned, Annelise turned to the furious jinni and fell sobbing to her knees. "Thank the heavens you are here!" she cried. "They were destroying your beautiful palace and there was nothing I could do about it!"

"They?" sniffed Leila.

"Yes, there were two of them and they were larger than life. They moved so quickly I could barely keep my eyes upon them, and they were fighting, making such a dreadful noise…"

"Who were they? I shall see them cursed for all eternity!"

"I do not think they were mortal," Annelise admitted carefully. She kept a wary glance on her opponent as she struggled to appear distraught.

''How would you know?''

''They appeared as suddenly as you do and their size changed as they argued.''

''Well, what were their names?''

''I do not know, but the woman...'' Annelise sighed as though recalling a scene of wonder. ''The woman was so beautiful that I felt as though I had stepped into the sunlight when she first smiled at me.'' She flicked a glance at the jinni. ''And you will probably not believe me, but I could have sworn that diamonds and pearls fell from her lips when she spoke.''

Leila hissed angrily. ''Was she here alone?''

''No, no, she came after *he* did.''

Annelise could almost feel the jinni's piercing gaze upon her and did not dare look up lest she be caught in her lie.

''He?''

''Yes, he came first, and oh, he was so handsome that I nearly lost my heart on sight. He wandered through the palace, not touching anything, only calling a woman's name.''

''Who? Who? *Who* did he call?'' The jinni leaned over Annelise, her face contorted with her demand.

Annelise shrugged. ''Some woman named Leila.''

''He came,'' the jinni whispered to herself. She drifted away for a moment, a delighted smile upon her lips. ''He came for me.''

Annelise almost smiled herself at the apparent success of her ruse, but the matter was hardly resolved as yet. ''Then *she* came,'' she added pointedly.

The jinni jumped, then spun to lean anxiously over Annelise. ''Yes. Yes, tell me all! I have to know exactly what happened!''

''She smiled at me first, but then she saw him. He ran.''

''He did?''

''He did. As though he had demons at his heels! She chased him, grabbed him by the hair, begged him not to leave her. She cried and sobbed, but he struggled to get away from her, screaming all the while that he loved Leila alone.''

"Aha!" The jinni's voice was triumphant. "Aha! I knew it well all these years!'' She flung out her hands and stretched high in the sky. "He loves *me!*" She shouted, so loudly that Annelise thought her eardrums would break.

Abruptly, there was silence. Annelise found the jinni huddled in front of her, looking her straight in the eye, her dark gaze bright. "Where did they go, mortal?" she whispered.

Annelise was deliberately coy. She took a step backward and folded her hands behind her back. "It seems to me that this matter is of import to you," she mused as she wandered away.

Leila darted quickly in front of Annelise, and her eyes snapped. "Do not imagine that I will grant you any favors for telling me this, little mortal," she snarled. "Confide in me or I shall make your miserable life much, much worse.''

Annelise did not have to pretend to tremble in trepidation. She pointed one shaking finger to the bottle, as though the information were being dragged from her unwillingly. "She hauled him in there when she heard you coming.''

Leila dove onto the bottle victoriously. She grasped it in both hands and shook it. Nothing came out. She peered into its depths, called into it, but there was no response.

She turned on Annelise with suspicion. "Where is the stopper?''

Annelise contrived to look as innocent as she could. "Why would such a pretty vase have a stopper?''

Leila smiled with cruel satisfaction. The dark cloud swirled about her, narrowed into a plume that swallowed up the jinni, then dove in its entirety into the bottle.

Annelise snatched the stopper out of her stocking and jammed it into the neck of the bottle. The decanter shook back and forth, and Annelise inadvertently dropped it. Her eyes widened with horror as it rolled about, the anger of its occupant more than clear.

Annelise hoped desperately that the stopper would hold. Her imagination busily conjured fears of what Leila might do to her if she escaped, and Annelise wondered if what she had done was truly wise.

Then the bottle abruptly grew still.

Annelise waited, but it did not move again. She released a breath she had not known she was holding. Leila was contained in her prison once more.

When Annelise moved to retrieve the dark bottle, her shoe crunched in the snow. She looked around in alarm, to find that the palace was gone so completely it might never have been there. Nothing but snow and trees surrounded her on all sides.

Annelise's old cloak was cast on the snow just a few feet away, its location roughly corresponding to the site of the room she and Rolfe had shared, where she had left the garment. The fancy raiment Rolfe had given her had vanished into thin air, from whence it evidently had come.

Beyond her cloak, Mephistopheles and the palfrey glanced about with apparent astonishment, their trappings and Rolfe's armor scattered about them.

The spell was broken! Rolfe was saved!

Annelise had earned his freedom, just as Azima had said she could! Annelise had found the key and solved the riddle!

She cavorted through the snow as playfully as a child. Delight with her accomplishment made her whistle as she packed Rolfe's belongings into his saddlebags and saddled the two steeds. Wherever Rolfe was, he would return here soon, looking for her, and they would begin their life together.

Annelise grinned at Mephistopheles as she dropped his saddle on his back, but the steed's gaze flicked over her shoulder. His ears twitched, and Annelise knew that her spouse was returned.

"Rolfe!" She spun with a bright smile of greeting on her lips.

A lone wolf stood at the perimeter of the forest, his gaze fixed eerily upon her. Annelise's heart sank to her toes.

"No," she whispered unevenly. "No, it cannot be thus."

But the wolf began to walk toward her, and Annelise's heart filled with dreadful certainty.

Rolfe could not be trapped forever in wolf form! There must be another explanation. It must be another wolf. She fought to find a reason why this wolf picked his way toward her, knowing it was futile all the while. The wolf was so dejected in his carriage that Annelise knew it could be none other.

She had failed.

She had failed Rolfe and consigned him to a prison of enchantment for the remainder of her days. It was unfair!

"Rolfe!" Annelise had meant to call out his name, but instead the greeting fell from her lips in a tormented whisper.

The wolf's footsteps slowed as he drew near, and he paused a dozen paces away. Annelise stepped closer, a part of her still insisting that it could not be so.

The wolf had one blue eye and one silver-gray.

She choked back a sob. How could she live out her life, knowing that she had condemned Rolfe to such an existence?

How could she have so betrayed his trust? She had assumed that trapping Leila would make her spells void, but Annelise had clearly been wrong.

The wolf that was her spouse pushed his dark muzzle under her hand. Annelise looked into his eyes, saw the pain there, and wondered how she could bear to see her beloved in such agony for the remainder of his days.

He sat down before her, understanding gleaming in his

eyes, understanding that made her ache with responsibility. It was so much worse to think that he knew the fate ahead of him. She held him close, savoring his warmth, and wished she was not so cursed with impulsiveness.

She should have waited until the night, when Rolfe was a man, before she trapped the jinni. The logic of it all came to her far too late to make amends.

"Somehow," Annelise whispered unsteadily, "we shall find a way." She took a deep, shuddering breath and clutched Rolfe's furry face in her hands. She looked deeply into his eyes.

"We will find another jinni," she told him bravely. "We will convince another to aid us, or seek out a magician in the hills. It is said there is an old witch near Tulley, and she might be able to cast a spell...."

Annelise's voice faded as her resolve crumbled. She was fooling herself and Rolfe. There was no respite from what she had wrought. The jinns were gone, and only the result of their labors remained. No one, jinni or mortal, could change that fact.

Annelise buried her face in her hands and wept.

Rolfe licked her cheek.

It tickled and she pushed him away, but he persisted. He wriggled his nose against her neck and tickled her again while tears ran down her cheeks.

"Rolfe! This is most serious!"

Rolfe licked her ear in response and that tickled even more. Annelise pushed him away, but he pursued her, his tail wagging, his tongue mischievous. She smiled just a little, despite herself.

"Stop it!" she cried, but to no avail. There was snow sneaking into her old kirtle and creeping into her shoes.

"You make a joke of something beyond serious!" She formed a snowball and cast it at Rolfe in frustration. He leapt and caught it in his mouth, cavorting in the snow and bringing it back to her as playfully as a pup.

He tossed the snowball into her lap and wagged his tail anew. Annelise suddenly realized he was trying to encourage her, and she reached out to scratch his ears. "Do you think that we might find a way together?" she asked wonderingly.

He wagged his tail and barked. Then he ran in a circle around Annelise, and she spun to watch him again and again. Mephistopheles eyed the pair of them skeptically, while the palfrey looked decidedly nervous. When Annelise fell dizzyingly in a heap, Rolfe licked her face with abandon and she laughed aloud.

"If you believe, then so shall I," she whispered when he stopped to look down at her. The wolf that was Rolfe appeared to grin.

Then a hunter's horn sounded in the woods.

The sound brought their heads up with a snap. The horn blew again, the sound bouncing through the forest with increasing vigor. Annelise heard the hunting party crash through the undergrowth. Men shouted to each other, and gradually she discerned a cry that made her blood run cold.

"Wolf!"

Rolfe must have heard the call at the same moment as she, for he dug his nose into Annelise's knee. He shoved her toward Mephistopheles, his agitation making it clear he intended for her to mount.

"But what of you? If they hunt wolves, then you are prey!"

Rolfe did not respond but pushed at Annelise until she was mounted. Then he snarled at the horse's heels, and Mephistopheles danced away from him. Rolfe kept up his attack, urging both horses onward until they galloped away from the hunting party.

At least they would flee together, Annelise thought with relief. The two horses crashed through the woods, while Rolfe snarled behind them, compelling the intimidated beasts to greater speed.

Annelise clutched the reins, glad she had already packed their belongings. The sounds of the hunting party grew louder behind them, and her heart leapt to her throat.

Would they be able to escape in time?

Annelise spied a path ahead. Should she follow it to the left or the right? She glanced back to ask Rolfe, only to find that he was gone.

Mephistopheles snorted indignantly when Annelise reined him in sharply. She turned and peered into the shadows of the trees. Was that flicker to her left the silhouette of a quickly moving wolf? What about the one far to her right?

The hunting party's dogs began to bellow as they found a scent.

Annelise's heart skipped a beat. Where was Rolfe?

She could not leave him to be hunted!

Annelise dug her heels into the destrier's side and tried to retrace their route. The snow was glazed with a crusty surface that left no mark. She could not tell where Rolfe had broken off and could not pick out the point where she had last seen him.

So intent was she on seeking her spouse that she did not see the hunter burst from the woods ahead of her until she was directly before him.

"Well, good afternoon, Annelise," Enguerrand purred.

She caught her breath as she stared at the unexpected arrival. "What are you doing here? I thought your mission done?"

"As did I." Enguerrand gave her a chilling smile. "But it seems the people hereabouts are troubled by wolves this winter. I have organized a hunt to eliminate the beasts from this forest."

His gaze was too knowing as it fixed upon Annelise. "It is said there is a particularly evil one with one eye blue and one silver-gray," he said with relish. Annelise fought to hide her revulsion and was not certain she was successful. Enguerrand's voice dropped confidentially. "You may rest assured that I shall take that one with my own hand."

"You cannot!"

"Why ever not?"

Annelise sputtered as she sought an excuse. "There are no people hereabouts. For whom do you perform this service?"

Enguerrand's eyes gleamed. "For those who are threatened. Surely you, Annelise, know better than most who they are."

"What do you mean?"

Enguerrand only smiled.

Annelise sat up straighter in her saddle. "You have no jurisdiction here! This is not even Tulley's holding! I demand to know what grants you the right to hunt these lands."

"As I might demand to know your right to ask." Enguerrand arched a brow. "Knowing how your spouse enjoys the hunt, I intended to invite him to join our party. Oddly enough, it seems his palace has completely disappeared."

"Perhaps you grew confused as to the direction," Annelise retorted.

Enguerrand's slow smile did not reassure her in the least.

"Perhaps you might show me the way, then." He flicked a glance over his shoulder as the hounds' barking grew markedly more agitated. "*After* the hunt, of course."

"No!"

"Of course, you are welcome to join us in his stead?"

Annelise forced herself to swallow the lump in her throat. "I am afraid I have little taste for the hunt."

Enguerrand smiled maliciously. He urged his horse closer, and Annelise held her ground, though she longed to flee. "Do you think me a fool, Annelise? I saw with my own eyes that enchanted palace and know it was the one in the bard's tale. Your brother Quinn has yet to arrive at

Sayerne, and I have already mentioned to Tulley that he should consider granting the property to you."

"I am wed already!"

"Precisely. But by the end of this day, you may rest assured, sweet Annelise, I will see you widowed." Enguerrand's smile flashed. "That way you can bring me your spouse's wealth, which will go far toward restoring both Sayerne's and Roussineau's charms."

"You cannot do this!"

"But I will." Enguerrand bowed slightly. "Until later then, fair Annelise. I look forward to enjoying your... hospitality."

Any response Annelise might have made was cut short when Enguerrand gave his steed his spurs and disappeared into the woods. The dogs were in a frenzy and not far enough away to be reassuring. Mephistopheles stepped nervously at the sound of their barking.

Too late, Annelise wished she had accepted Enguerrand's offer, just so she might see what was happening.

"I wish there was something I might do!"

"Wish?"

Annelise found the friendly jinni perched on a tree branch to her left. She swung her legs and granted Annelise a friendly smile. "I might be able to help with that," she offered.

"You already said you had done all you could."

"Ah, but that was before you trapped Leila in her bottle again. A very nice piece of work, I must say, and accomplished at not inconsiderable risk to yourself. Such an unselfish deed surely deserves a reward, and I, my dear, am precisely the jinni for the job. You cannot imagine what a relief it is to know that I no longer have to either endure her company or fret about her retaliation."

Annelise remembered only too well all she had read in the curious book. It was gone now, too, she suddenly realized, along with the rest of the palace.

"You could have left Leila free," she commented.

The jinni grimaced. "I suppose, but one has a certain responsibility, you know, and can only ignore that at one's own peril. I was responsible, at least for bringing that one into the world, and I owed a debt to every other being once it was clear how she had turned out. I could not have stepped aside and let the blood of my blood wreak havoc upon the great goodness around us. It would have been wrong."

The jinni gave herself a shake and summoned a perky smile. "But enough of that. What will your wish be, child?"

Annelise blinked. "Are you serious?"

"Well, of course I am! Good deeds must not go unrewarded. Think quickly now, for the dogs have cornered something and I have a rather good idea what—or who—it is."

Impulse brought an answer immediately to Annelise's lips. "I wish for a stag of such beauty, grace and speed that hunter and hound will forget all else to pursue it."

The jinni's gaze was assessing. "I cannot create a life from nothing," she murmured.

Annelise swallowed, knowing full well what she had to say. The life of her beloved was at stake.

"Then make me the stag."

The two women's gazes held for a moment, and Annelise imagined that the jinni hesitated. The dogs barked impatiently.

"Quickly!" Annelise urged, and the jinni stretched her hands to the sky. She wiggled her fingers, crinkled her nose and closed her eyes as Annelise watched impatiently.

Just as she was going to urge haste again, the jinni spoke. "As she wishes, so shall it be. Make this stag of Annelise."

Annelise felt a curious tingling pass over her flesh, and

she slipped from Mephistopheles' saddle. She looked down and saw her flesh darkening to a rich hue of brown.

Hooves grew on Annelise's hands and feet, her arms lengthened and she found herself on all fours as naturally as could be. A great weight was on her brow and she knew she sported an impressive rack of antlers.

"That was quite good, was it not?" the jinni asked in apparent awe of her own abilities. But Annelise had other matters on her mind.

A dog howled as it caught scent of the stag Annelise had become. Annelise's heart leapt and she dashed into the forest, directly toward the hunting party and the dogs. She must save Rolfe!

It was exhilarating to run at such speed. Annelise felt her long legs stretch out, and savored the agility of her new form. She ran with a grace and speed untold, her nose catching the scent of dogs, men and steeds with uncanny accuracy.

They spotted her all at once, it seemed. The dogs turned from whatever they had cornered, their noses high as they strained for her scent.

"God's blood, what a creature!" a man breathed. All turned as one, and Annelise fled with all the speed she could muster. The horses thundered in pursuit, and the dogs' barking made her pulse race.

Annelise had effectively exchanged her life for Rolfe's, and she felt not one regret.

# Chapter Thirteen

The dogs closed around Rolfe, fangs bared. They barked and growled as they backed him into the undergrowth. Rolfe's heart pounded in his ears as he snarled. He lunged at first one dog and then another, keeping them at bay even as he knew his time was limited.

He was vastly outnumbered, and when he heard more dogs behind him, Rolfe knew he could not hold them off for long.

But he must grant Annelise enough time to escape.

Rolfe prayed that even now she was riding away, that Mephistopheles would guess his master's will as that stalwart beast had oft before and would carry Annelise out of danger. Rolfe knew that Annelise would prefer to join the fray and defend him, but even together they would have had no chance.

And Rolfe did not want Annelise left to entertain this enthusiastic hunting party in the wake of their kill.

The dogs edged closer, first one then another nipping at Rolfe. Their circle tightened; their eyes glittered in anticipation of the kill. Hoofbeats echoed as the hunters arrived. Men's voices carried to his ears, then one rose above the others.

"This one is mine!"

The dogs backed reluctantly away, growling all the while. Rolfe looked up into the cold gaze of the same man who had visited Annelise.

Enguerrand de Roussineau's dark eyes gleamed with animosity. In an intuitive flash, Rolfe realized that this man understood fully what he did. He knew what Rolfe was; he knew that he would be killing another man, not a wolf.

And Rolfe knew that Annelise had nothing to do with Enguerrand's understanding. She had not betrayed him.

He should never have doubted her.

Rolfe suddenly could not accept his death so easily. He needed to apologize to Annelise.

Teeth bared, he lunged toward Enguerrand.

The destrier shied away, Enguerrand cried out in fear, but Rolfe had no intention of granting him any quarter. Just before his teeth closed on the man's forearm, Enguerrand jerked away. Rolfe's teeth grazed the steed's neck. When a hunting knife slashed Rolfe's shoulder, he snapped and twisted, and the knife fell to the ground.

The fallen dagger glinted on the snow, and Rolfe wished he had the ability to use it.

But no. He must work with the tools he had been granted. In this form, he had wickedly effective teeth, agility and sharp claws.

Enguerrand unsheathed another blade and gathered up his steed's reins purposefully. No, Rolfe thought grimly. He would not leave this man to claim Annelise as his prize. He would not abandon her to the cruel hand of such a villain.

Rolfe eyed the knight's mail as they circled each other. Enguerrand's hauberk hung to his knees, but it was slit on either side from the hip down. He wore heavy leather boots, but no other protection on his legs than his wool chausses.

And for this hunt, Enguerrand had left behind his helmet.

Fool! His bare neck gleamed with promise for a wolf's sharp teeth.

Rolfe leapt suddenly for Enguerrand, latching into that man's thigh. The horse shied wildly and reared when it felt the weight of the wolf upon it. Enguerrand screamed as he and Rolfe fell from the steed, their limbs entangled. The horse fell awkwardly, then stumbled to its feet.

To Rolfe's surprise, the other knights did not rally around to defend their leader. Rolfe felt the dogs' attention waver, heard something thunder through the brush nearby, but did not turn from his goal.

This man intended to force Annelise to become his wife. Rolfe had no doubt that her life in that role would not be markedly different than her mother's had been. If he accomplished nothing else, he would ensure that this man could not kill the sparkle in Annelise's eyes.

Enguerrand raised the knife. Rolfe bit hard into his palm before the blade could be planted. Rolfe's teeth slid easily through the heavy leather, and he savored the other man's scream of pain. The knife bounced to the forest floor. Rolfe dove for Enguerrand's chest and felt his claws find their way through the links of the knight's mail.

Rolfe bared his teeth and snarled, wishing he could tell this knave exactly what he thought of him. Enguerrand blanched, then Rolfe's sharp teeth were buried in his throat. The villain shuddered within Rolfe's grip, then went still.

The nervous destrier lifted its nose, and Rolfe was suddenly aware of the baying of the dogs on a scent. He struggled to peer through the woods, but one of the knights whistled a summons.

The horse shied and reared, then lost his footing on the icy forest floor. Rolfe darted away just before the destrier's weight crashed to the ground. The horse fell noisily atop its master, its head cracking loudly on a jutting boulder.

Neither moved again.

But what had distracted the dogs? Despite his wound,

Rolfe trotted in pursuit as quickly as he could manage. To his astonishment, the dogs had cornered a stag of such majesty that his breath caught in his throat.

But there was something unnatural about the desire the beast aroused within the breast. The hunters and dogs clustered there had an unusual gleam in their eyes, as though they were bewitched.

Suddenly the stag leapt nimbly over the barking dogs. The animal bolted through the woods, and Rolfe heard a splash as it plunged into some running stream out of sight. Dogs and hunters immediately gave chase, the sounds of pursuit fading quickly into the surrounding forest.

Then speculation fled as Rolfe felt himself changing. He gasped in delight as his own flesh appeared before his eyes, as the fur disappeared, as dark nails rescinded and he stretched to his full height under the midday sun.

The spell was broken! Rolfe knew not how or why, but it was done. He let out a whoop of delight and danced through the forest, uncaring who heard or saw his jubilation.

He could be the husband Annelise desired!

He had only to find her. Rolfe hastened to the tower, hoping against hope that he would find her waiting for him there.

The sight of Mephistopheles and the palfrey standing outside the tower made Rolfe's heart leap with joy. Both horses were saddled and apparently ready for the road. Ah, Annelise was a marvel! Rolfe patted the destrier's rump on the way past and took the stairs three at a time.

But the tower room was empty. Indeed, it did not look as though anyone had been here since his last visit.

Rolfe stared out the windows, certain he would catch a glimpse of Annelise outside. Nothing moved in the surrounding forest. He darted back down the stairs to confront Mephistopheles.

"Well? Where is she? Where did you take her?"

The steed eyed him for a long moment, then snorted and looked away. It was almost as though he were disgusted with his master, though Rolfe could not fathom why.

"Look! I am myself again!" He gestured to the sun overhead. "The curse is broken! Is this not wondrous news?"

Mephistopheles nibbled on a bit of moss clinging to the tower wall, apparently disinterested in anything his master might say.

Rolfe frowned, then shivered. He glanced at the wound on his shoulder and dismissed it as insignificant. It was no more than a graze. Perhaps Annelise would tend it for him. The prospect made him smile, then frown anew.

Where could she have gone?

He opened the destrier's saddlebags, found his garments neatly folded there and proceeded to dress. It was a delight to don familiar garb, to feel the weight of his hauberk over his shoulders and know his lethal blade hung ready at his side.

But where was Annelise?

Rolfe propped his hands upon his hips and stared about himself. He started when he noticed the good jinni sitting on the tower stoop.

She had not been there before, he knew.

"Good day to you, *madame*."

She smiled with apparent pleasure. "Well, if nothing else, you have learned manners from this little adventure."

Rolfe cleared his throat. "Then it is over?"

The jinni nodded with an enthusiasm that made all the balls on her hat jiggle merrily. "That it is indeed. Just as I foretold."

Rolfe bowed deeply. "I must thank you for your intervention in this matter. It is impossible to imagine how bleak it would have been to spend my entire life alone as a wolf."

The jinni eyed him carefully. "I did not do the deed

single-handedly," she said. "Though I appreciate your thanks, it is not I to whom you owe the greatest gratitude."

Something about her tone made Rolfe suddenly dread the truth. "Why exactly did the curse end?" he asked carefully.

The jinni stood up and brushed her kirtle with studied casualness. "It was exactly as I foretold. The curse was ended by the power of love."

"Whose love?"

"Why, Annelise's love for you, of course!" The jinni shook her head. "Did you not see any of what happened this day?"

Rolfe fought to dismiss the lump rising in his throat. He sensed it was not good that Annelise was not here. "Perhaps you could be so kind as to review events for me."

"Yes, you were busy with that troublesome Enguerrand, were you not?" The jinni shrugged and took a light step toward him. She produced a familiar dark bottle, its cork firmly in place, and tossed it between her hands before Rolfe's amazed eyes.

"You see, Annelise managed to trap the evil jinni within the bottle again, which, naturally, is why the palace disappeared."

"But how?"

"It does not matter." The jinni waved her hand dismissively and the bottle danced from her grip. Both knight and jinni gasped, and Rolfe snatched the bottle out of the air just before it hit the ground. He handed it back to the jinni, relieved beyond all that it had not shattered, and she smiled. "Suffice it to say that Annelise used the tools she had at hand to solve that dilemma."

"What will you do with the bottle?"

The jinni eyed the dark decanter and pursed her lips, though Rolfe sensed she had already made up her mind. "I shall appoint myself as its guardian. There truly is no other way to ensure that it remains corked."

Rolfe was less certain of that than she, but kept his doubts to himself. "But why would you want to take such a task upon yourself? I had thought there was no love lost between you and the other one."

The jinni trailed a fingertip down the neck of the bottle, her gaze averted from Rolfe's. She appeared to be lost in recollection, and for an instant, Rolfe thought her much older than he had originally believed. "There was a time when we were close," she said huskily. "I owe her no less."

Then the jinni shot a sharp glance Rolfe's way. "Annelise is a most clever and resourceful woman. I should hope you appreciate that."

"Yes." Rolfe felt a glow of pride.

"Which is why it is all the more tragic what has happened," the jinni continued conversationally, restoring Rolfe's fear to its fullest.

"Tragic? What do you mean? What has happened?"

"I granted her a wish," the jinni confessed. "It was only fitting after what she had done, but truly, I could have guessed what she would have asked me to do." Her gaze was fixed upon Rolfe with a steadiness that told him she had finally arrived at her point.

"What?" His voice had become a croak.

"She chose to become a stag of such beauty that the hunters were distracted from their intent to kill you."

The breath left Rolfe's lungs so suddenly that his knees gave out beneath him. He stared at the snow surrounding him without comprehending what he saw.

It was only too easy to recall the dogs and hunters bent on their pursuit of that stag. And Rolfe remembered his own sense that there was something enchanted about the stag to so capture their interest.

There were no sounds of hunters in the woods now, and Rolfe knew, deep in his heart, that the hunt had been completed.

The stag, which was truly Annelise, had been killed.

The world suddenly seemed to be a very flat and color-less place. Rolfe's recovery from his spell was no longer an event to celebrate, for the one person with whom he might have rejoiced was lost to him forever.

"She traded her life for mine." Even Rolfe's voice was flat.

"Exactly!" the jinni confirmed, with a pert cheer that was decidedly inappropriate. "And that is why you are freed. The power of love, of self-sacrifice, was what ended your curse."

"But Annelise is dead!" Rolfe sputtered angrily. "How can you be so dismissive? She gave her life for mine!"

"Annelise made her choice," the jinni retorted. She spun on her heel and started to walk away. "As we all must make our own."

Rolfe stumbled to his feet. "Is there not something we can do? Can you not make another spell?"

The jinni glanced over her shoulder and her expression was pitying, to Rolfe's mind. "What is done is done," she said quietly. "I would suggest you make your peace with it."

"This is unfair!" Rolfe roared. "It was not Annelise's curse, nor her battle! Why should she be compelled to pay the price?"

The jinni shook her head. "I have told you already that she chose her path. There is nothing else to be done." She sniffed and lifted her chin. "I should think you would be glad to see the last of jinns in your life."

With that, she snapped her fingers and disappeared in a rosy puff of smoke.

She was gone. Annelise was gone. And Rolfe was more alone than he had ever been in his life. A hollow ache took up residence where his heart should have been as he faced the fact that he would never again hear Annelise's laughter.

It was humbling to realize that she had given her all just to see him safe.

Rolfe had never even told her that he loved her. She had passed from this world lacking the one gift he might have given her. Love, Rolfe knew well enough, was the only thing that Annelise had held to be of value, and he had denied her the knowledge of his love.

He was a knave of the lowest order.

Rolfe dropped his head into his hands and, for the first time since he had been knighted, permitted himself to weep for what he had lost.

Long moments later, he thought he imagined the brush of fingertips on his shoulder, the fleeting touch was so light.

"It is not so bad a wound as that," Annelise whispered, and Rolfe could not believe his ears. "See? The blood runs clearly. You have but to discard your tunic and let me cleanse it."

"Annelise!" He rose in wonder and drank in the sight of her. Annelise it was, disheveled and short of breath, but Annelise all the same.

She smiled at him and touched her fingertips to his cheek. "You are not cursed any longer."

"No!" Jubilation flooded Rolfe's heart. With a bellow of relief, he scooped her up and spun her around.

And kissed her with all his love.

Annelise, to Rolfe's delight, kissed him back. Her arms twined around his neck and she pressed herself against him with a sweetness he had feared never to savor again.

"And you," he murmured when he finally lifted his head, "are not dead."

Annelise's bemused smile fled. "You thought me dead?"

"The jinni said you had asked to become that stag." Rolfe's heart gave a thump as he relived his fears. "I saw the hounds give chase! How did you escape them all?"

Annelise's expression turned to one of confusion and she

shrugged her shoulders. "I do not know. I was running as quickly as I could, splashing through the stream. I was certain they would fall upon me at any moment. But they halted all at once and turned aside, even as I felt myself changing back." She looked uncertainly to Rolfe. "What happened?"

He shook himself in turn. "I cannot say for certain. The jinni said that your sacrifice had broken the spell—perhaps the spell broke for both of us in the same moment."

Annelise smiled at him with a warmth that made him glad she had found her way back to his side. "Perhaps the proof of our love for each other was the love she vowed would set you free."

Rolfe cupped Annelise's face in his hands, his fingertips tenderly tracing a scratch on her cheek. He stared down into those amber eyes, so filled with promise and love, and ached at how close he had come to losing her. "But why would you put yourself in such danger? You should never have taken such a risk...."

Annelise reached up to run her hands over his own face. "Why did you try to lead the hunters away from me, then?"

The answer was so obvious that Rolfe was surprised she needed to hear the words. "Because I had to see you safe."

"Yes," Annelise agreed with conviction. "And Enguerrand had come to kill you—what choice did I have but to lead him away from you?"

The shadows in her eyes wrenched Rolfe's heart and he felt her shiver as he gathered her closer. "You have nothing to fear from Enguerrand any longer. He is dead, by my own hand."

"Truly?" Rolfe nodded and Annelise tightened her grip around his neck as she smiled. "Thank you! Oh, I do love you, Rolfe," she said with heartfelt sincerity.

Rolfe's heart skipped a beat as he stared down at Annelise. Never had he imagined he would win the heart of such a woman. Never had he imagined that he, a landless younger son, would have the opportunity to wed....

Rolfe's world shattered around him at that thought. He was a man again. He was still a younger son, still landless, still without the right to wed.

The specter of Rosalinde's disgust reared its head once more, and Rolfe feared to see that same loathing in Annelise's amber eyes.

Annelise smiled with feminine delight. "This is the part where you tell me that you love me, too," she prompted playfully. "What *were* you coming to tell me this morning?"

She had risked all for him, Rolfe knew. The least he could do was risk his pride.

He bent and brushed his lips across hers, loving the way she melted beneath his touch. "Annelise, I love you with all my heart and soul," Rolfe murmured. "Indeed, I cannot imagine how I could have lived my life without you by my side. I was coming this morning to tell you all, just as you suspected."

Annelise smiled sunnily and pressed herself against him. "I quite like this confession," she teased, then traced the line of his jaw. "But why are you so serious?"

"Because I am nothing but a younger son." Rolfe looked into Annelise's understanding eyes. "I have no land or title. I am beholden to my elder brother for all I have." He smiled sadly down at his wife. "In truth, I have little to offer you but myself."

"But that is all I want!" Annelise exclaimed, and Rolfe could barely believe his ears. Then she reached up and took his face in her hands, her golden eyes gleaming with sincerity.

"There could be no other for me but you, Rolfe," she whispered. "I do not care where we live or what we eat or what manner of clothes we wear, as long as we are together." She tapped one finger in the middle of his chest, and Rolfe's heart began to sing. "My home is wherever you are."

Rolfe smiled and ruffled her auburn hair. "It will not be a rich life I offer you, my Annelise, though I do not doubt that Adalbert will be convinced to grant me some small holding to call my own."

"It will be the only life I want," Annelise said fiercely, "for it will be with you."

Rolfe wondered how he could ever have doubted her. He crushed her in his arms and kissed her with abandon. His spirits soared with the faith inspired by Annelise's love, and suddenly the world seemed full of possibilities.

He owed his newfound optimism—and the restoration of his life—to Annelise. And Rolfe vowed silently that he would spend the rest of his days showering her with his gratitude and love.

He could not wait to get to Viandin.

# Chapter Fourteen

Desolate Beauvoir rose from the road ahead, and Annelise confronted her doubts. She imagined that she had transposed roles with Rolfe, for while he pushed excitely onward, she harbored doubts of the future.

She recalled Enguerrand's assertion that Quinn was not yet home and wondered what path Tulley would insist she follow. There was evidently no way to Viandin without passing through Tulley's holding, and Annelise knew they could not transverse its breadth without stopping.

What if Tulley insisted she govern Sayerne? What if he did not believe she and Rolfe were wed in truth? Certainly any who heard the full tale of what had transpired might doubt its validity.

What if Tulley compelled Annelise both to return to despised Sayerne and to take another spouse? Annelise could think of nothing worse that might befall her.

It was too cold to snow by the time their horses climbed the steep road to Beauvoir pass, and the wind was biting. Annelise watched Rolfe covertly as they rode, seeing him fully garbed for the first time and afraid this might be the last time they rode together and at ease.

Her heart swelled with love for the proud lines of his profile, the resoluteness of purpose in his grip on the reins.

She remembered only too well the caress of those hands upon her own flesh, the press of those firm lips against her own.

"Hail, gatekeeper!" Rolfe called boldly as they reached the barred gates. "We seek shelter this night!"

"We have no more shelter for travelers," growled the gatekeeper. "But should you have coin for the toll, you are welcome to pass."

"But this lady is of your overlord's own nobility," Rolfe argued. "Surely a place might be found for her out of the wind?"

A slot in the gate slid open and the gleam of eyes could be discerned in the darkness revealed. "Who is she?" the keeper demanded.

"Annelise de Sayerne."

"And you?"

"Rolfe de Viandin."

Viandin. Annelise frowned to herself, temporarily distracted from her concerns. She was certain she had heard the name of that estate before, but could not recall where or when.

There was a scurry of activity behind the gates and a flurry of whisperings. Footsteps clattered as someone evidently ran across the bailey to the keep itself.

Annelise watched the snow gather on the pine trees around the gates and wished she could make this moment last forever. To her astonishment, she suddenly felt the weight of Rolfe's gloved hand over her own.

He smiled down at her, as though he guessed her trepidation, and his fingers tightened on hers. The gates opened before Annelise could say anything.

"The Lord de Beauvoir grants you welcome, Rolfe de Viandin and Annelise de Sayerne," the keeper declared with ceremonial flair. "And the Lord de Tulley awaits Lady Annelise in the hall."

Tulley was here. It was the worst possibility she could

have imagined. Annelise swallowed carefully, knowing the moment she dreaded was upon her. They rode through the gates and dismounted in the bailey, Rolfe moving to accompany her.

Her heart stopped when a guard raised his hand to halt him. "The lord requested the lady come alone."

Frightened, she exchanged a glance with Rolfe, but he smiled slowly, obviously intending to reassure her. "I shall see to the horses," he murmured, his gaze warm upon Annelise. "Doubtless Mephistopheles will welcome some attention from me."

Annelise could not repress a fleeting smile of her own before the guard led her firmly away. As she crossed the threshold and stepped into the shadows of a corridor, Tulley's aggrieved tones carried to her ears and her heart began to pound.


Rolfe waved off the squires and brushed down his steeds himself. This was a task he had missed, for the rhythmic motion helped him compose his thoughts. He thought of Annelise and their future together and whistled to himself as he worked.

"You seem in fine spirits for a man deemed missing," a familiar voice commented.

It could not be! Rolfe spun around, not believing his ears. His mother, Hildegarde de Viandin, stood at the end of the stall.

Her ebony hair was dressed in glossy coils only faintly tinged with silver; her carriage was still proud. Her sapphire wool kirtle highlighted her coloring and her slender form admirably. She smiled and twirled a piece of mistletoe in her fingers when he said nothing.

"Surely you have a kiss on the cheek to spare for your dame after all these years? It is the season, after all."

"Mother!" Rolfe stepped to her side, noticing that the years had been kind to her, and pecked her on both cheeks.

"What are you doing here? Why are you so far from Vian-din?"

His mother ruffled his hair affectionately, as though he were but a boy and not a man who towered a good foot taller than she. "I never thought to lay eyes upon you again," she whispered unevenly. "When they said a Rolfe de Viandin had come to the gates, I could scarce believe my ears...."

Her voice broke, and Rolfe gathered her into an impulsive hug. "I am here, Mother, and as real as might be."

His mother pulled back slightly and looked questioningly into his eyes. "Never were you so quick with affection before." She shook her head as she gazed upon him, and the confidence with which Rolfe was more familiar seeped back into her gaze. "And here I thought you dead."

"Dead? Why would you fear such a thing?"

His mother grimaced as she spun the mistletoe posey. "You did depart on Crusade," she commented. "And it is not so unheard of for men to not return from such endeav-ors."

Rolfe picked up the brush and turned back to his task. "Mother, you fret too much about such matters," he accused in a teasing tone. "Here I am, hale and hearty, and on my way home, none the worse for wear."

"And on a different steed."

"Sebastien did not take well to the heat."

Hildegarde followed Rolfe into the stall, eyeing Mephistopheles warily. "Could you have found one any larger or blacker? He looks as fearsome as a demon."

"Then you will well appreciate his name," Rolfe jested. He winked at his mother and told her. She frowned in disapproval and rapped him sharply on the shoulder with the posey.

"It is most unfitting to ride a beast cursed with such a name! Ill fortune could only dog your footsteps! Have you no regard for your own luck?"

Rolfe smiled to himself, knowing immediately that his mother and Annelise would see eye-to-eye on more issues than this. "And have you no regard for your health?" he retorted cheerfully. "What madness has you far from home in the dead of winter?"

His mother's face fell, and Rolfe knew suddenly that something was amiss. "What is it? What is wrong?"

"I came to seek you out, but the snow stopped us here. Bertrand, you may know, trained with your sire, and he kindly offered my party accommodation for as long as required."

"But why did you leave Viandin? Surely nothing is amiss there?"

"No." Hildegarde cleared her throat and looked away. She watched the posey as she tapped it against the side of the stall. "Viandin runs as ceaselessly as always it does."

She glanced up at Rolfe, dismay gleaming in her eyes. "I was concerned when you did not return home," she confessed.

Rolfe had no intention of telling his mother precisely what had delayed his return. It would not serve any purpose for her to know by how narrow a margin he had managed to come home at all.

"Mother, there are many yet returning from the East. The journey is long, far longer than one might think." He gave the lady's hands a shake. "You should have awaited me at home. After all, there is no need to hasten."

"But there is. Last fall, Adalbert took the ague."

Rolfe frowned with concern. "He is recovered?"

To his dismay, his mother shook her head. "He is dead, Rolfe."

Adalbert dead. It was impossible to believe. Rolfe swore softly and stepped away. He let himself replay the homecoming he had imagined, the way that Adalbert would stalk out to the bailey, complaining all the while about his lot. They would have shaken hands, as they always did when

Rolfe returned. They would have looked into each other's eyes for a silent moment and seen the admiration each had for the other.

Then Adalbert would have winked. He would have turned away, bellowing for the ostler and the cook, complaining heartily about the trouble caused by those who arrive unexpectedly.

Then he would so plague Rolfe with questions about where he had been and what he had seen that Rolfe would be hard-pressed to eat anything before it was stone cold.

It was unthinkable that Adalbert was not at Viandin, waiting to do precisely that.

Rolfe looked to the ceiling and blinked a suspicious glimmer from his eyes. He cleared his throat and glanced back to his dame. "He did not suffer?"

"It was quick," she admitted. Rolfe's shoulders sagged in relief, but his mother was not finished. She laid a hand upon his arm.

"I am not up to the task of administrating Viandin, Rolfe, though I have endeavored to do my best in your absence." Her voice was low with concern, though Rolfe was confused at her intent. "I hope you will not be disappointed in my efforts when you take the reins of the estate."

Take the reins? Rolfe blinked and stared uncomprehendingly at his mother for a moment. She gave his arm a shake and smiled at him.

"You are heir, Rolfe," she said with sudden force. "Viandin is yours."

All the breath left Rolfe's lungs in a rush. He was no longer a landless younger son, but Lord de Viandin.

He had something to offer his fair bride.

His mother's thoughts had already run off on another tangent, and she frowned as she spoke. "I must apologize, though, for despite my finest efforts I have not been able to procure a bride for you as yet. Even Bertrand tried, without success, to convince a local noblewoman, name of Annelise de Sayerne, to take your hand.''

She patted Rolfe encouragingly on the cheek. ''Perhaps the ladies have need of a taste of your own charm.''

Rolfe's lips twitched at her confession. They had tried to match him with Annelise? He was the other suitor she had deemed unfitting? It was the threat of wedding him that had driven her to the convent...and hence to him? The coincidence could only make him laugh aloud.

His mother frowned at him uncomprehendingly. ''I should hardly think the matter amusing,'' she said stiffly. ''Despite the wound that witch Rosalinde granted you, you are going to have to consider marriage, whether you like it or not. It is part of your responsibility to Viandin to ensure the bloodline continues....'' Her tirade suddenly stopped and she glared at Rolfe. ''Where is your ring? Surely you did not lose the token I granted you?''

''No, Mother,'' Rolfe said with a smile. ''It was used to seal the vows between my wife and I, one Annelise de Sayerne.''

Hildegarde's eyes widened in astonishment, then, as Rolfe watched, an unwilling smile curved her lips.

''Well, does that not take all?'' she murmured. ''I always knew you had the devil's own charm, should you only choose to use it.'' She tweaked his ear playfully, and Rolfe abandoned his brush, beckoning for the ostler to finish the task.

''Come along, Mother. There is someone I would like you to meet.''

''I should think so,'' his mother retorted. ''A wife. And without telling me first.'' Her manner was indignant, but the sparkle of delight in her eyes revealed her true feelings.

Yes, Hildegarde and Annelise would get along just fine. Rolfe's step was buoyant at the promise of the future he and Annelise would share.

* * *

Annelise was shown to a room just off the great hall. She glimpsed the boughs of cedar hung there and realized suddenly that it must be near the Yule. The concerns of the real world seemed distant to her, even as Tulley's bright gaze locked upon her.

"Come in, Annelise," he said tightly.

Annelise swallowed her fear and did precisely that.

"I had understood that you were to join the Sisters of Ste. Radegund a short time ago," the slight overlord said. His gaze flicked over her garments. "Without my permission, I might add. But now you do not appear in nun's garb."

"I did not join the convent, sir." When dealing with the indomitable Tulley, it would only be wise to redouble the polite manner Annelise had learned from the jinni. This man held her future in his hands, and Annelise had no intention of annoying him unnecessarily.

"Why not?" he snapped.

"Our party was beset by hunting wolves, sir, after we had lost our way. The man I travel with granted me refuge."

Tulley arched a brow. "And the others?"

"Scattered, sir. I have seen nothing of them since."

Tulley leaned across the desk. "But why did you abandon Sayerne in the first place? I did not grant you leave to do so."

"I had no intention of waiting for Quinn to return home and take his vengeance upon us!"

Tulley's gaze turned assessing and he settled back in his chair. "You have nothing to fear from your brother, you know."

That was an assertion Annelise was tired of hearing! Her patience snapped, for she alone knew the deeds of which Jerome and his spawn were capable.

"I know no such thing! I have heard nothing of him but tales of his cruelty!"

"From whom did you hear those tales?"

"From my sire!"

"A man we both know to be of somewhat unsavory character."

Annelise looked into Tulley's gaze and saw understanding of what had transpired at Sayerne all those years past. "You knew!" she breathed. "You knew and yet you did nothing!"

"On the contrary, I did all that I could!" Tulley's tone was savage. "Law maintains that a man cannot be accused of a crime without evidence or witness. There was neither. I had no option but to send you away and secure your safety, and that was what I did."

Silence reigned in the little room while Annelise came to terms with this news.

"And now you would compel me to return to that accursed place," she accused.

Tulley looked surprised. "Why would I do that?"

"Because Quinn is not home and I am the only other legitimate child. I am not a fool, sir, so pray do not treat me as one."

Tulley's lips quirked in a smile before he sobered again. "Trust me, Annelise, even if that were the case I have well learned my lesson about leaving a woman—heiress or no— in charge of an estate. No, I would find a man I could trust and grant the estate to him on the condition he wed you."

Tulley stared into space for a moment and frowned, then shook his head. "But my other concerns are not of import here. I have had word that Quinn will shortly return home to claim his legacy." The overlord drummed his fingers on the desk. "Which leaves the issue of what to do with you. Perhaps Quinn had best resolve the matter."

"I will not wait for my brother, regardless of what you deem his character to be!" Annelise retorted.

"Well, you will not wed Enguerrand de Roussineau, regardless of how well worded his entreaties may be!" Tulley pounded his fist on the desk. "If you have your mind set upon that path, then abandon it now! The line of Roussineau is so badly tainted that I can only justify letting its seed die out."

"I never wanted to wed Enguerrand," Annelise informed her overlord. "And he is dead, at any rate."

"Truly?" Tulley's gaze sharpened. "How?"

Too late, Annelise realized her slip. "I heard he was killed accidentally while at hunt in the forests south of Beauvoir."

"Fool!" Tulley snorted. "All know those woods to be unsafe." He frowned thoughtfully. "Perhaps you should return to the convent. Although frankly, I would be more inclined to spend gold for a dowry than a convent donation." His bright gaze flicked to hers. "At least then your allegiance could yield tangible benefits."

At that meager encouragement, Annelise took a deep breath and dared to present her own solution to the dilemma. "Perhaps, sir, my marriage to the man who granted me refuge should be recognized. I am sure that such a dowry would assuage any doubts there."

"Marriage!" Tulley shoved to his feet in indignation. "You were already wed without my permission? Do you not know your place?"

"It seemed only fitting, sir, especially as the knight and I were sequestered alone together."

"Then who performed the nuptial mass?"

"We exchanged a pledge with each other," Annelise said defiantly. "I have heard that such vows hold weight."

"Yes," Tulley admitted with evident reluctance. "Among commoners it is prevalent enough. Who might this knight be? Is the match fitting?"

Annelise feared suddenly that Tulley would not approve of her wedding a younger, landless son.

"Rolfe de Viandin is his name." Annelise held up her hand. "I wear his ring."

"Rolfe de Viandin!" To her astonishment, Tulley threw back his head and laughed. "Annelise! You are the most stubborn woman I have yet encountered! He was the knight you already refused!"

"When?"

"When Bertrand presented his mother's offer for your hand and you chose the convent."

Annelise stiffened. Surely Tulley was mistaken? "Well, how could I guess what manner of man would follow his mother's will so readily?"

"A man who knew nothing of his mother's schemes."

Tulley leaned across the desk, his eyes gleaming with mingled amusement and satisfaction. "To think that news of your arrival had me endeavoring to plan how I might encourage you to make this match. It is a good one, Annelise, and an alliance I deem most fitting to make."

Rolfe had been the other knight offered to her! Annelise choked back a delighted laugh, not certain it was appropriate in her overlord's company. Then Tulley grinned, and Annelise could not help but smile in return.

"Come along, child. Bertrand must have a priest here somewhere, and the hall is even festively garbed. It is a good day for a wedding, and we shall see those vows of yours exchanged again before witnesses. I want none to question the alliance your spouse and I will make."

Annelise fairly danced from the small chamber. How could she have doubted that all would come right in the end? She spied Rolfe across the hall, and her heart leapt with the promise of the days they would share together.

"Rolfe! We can wed!" Annelise ran across the great hall, and he swung her up into his arms with a grin.

"We *are* wed," he corrected, and punctuated his words with a kiss. "And we shall stay that way forevermore."

Indeed, Annelise could not have hoped for greater promise than that.

# *Epilogue*

It was in the spring of 1103 that Annelise's labor contractions began.

To his dismay, Rolfe was shooed from the solar and found himself in the hall with little to do but wait. His wife's screams made him cringe, but he avoided both drink and companionship. Rolfe paced the length of the hall and back, time and again, and thought.

Every moment he had spent with Annelise filtered through his mind as he walked, and he knew that there had not been enough of those moments to satisfy him. She had taught him so much about love, given him a faith in the unseen, shared with him her passion for life and all its joys.

Twilight crept into the hall and lengthened the shadows. A servant silently lit an array of candles, then departed, leaving Rolfe with his thoughts. Annelise's cries reached a new crescendo, and Rolfe halted, his mouth dry, and stared up the stairs.

If he should lose her this night, there was nothing that could fill the gap her departure would leave in his life. His mother's voice, low and reassuring, carried to his ears as Annelise's scream subsided. Rolfe shuddered to think what his wife endured.

And what had he given her in return? His love, his com-

mitment, his protection. The balance seemed rather thin to
Rolfe, especially in light of the sacrifice she made on this
night. A new mother deserved a gift, but Rolfe knew well
enough that Annelise would not care for jewelry or other
finery.

He must grant her a gift from the heart. It must be in-
tangible, to show her that he had learned the value of things
unseen. It must be something she could not hold but that
might make her life more complete.

Rolfe thought suddenly of Sayerne, of a knight he had
known, and wondered. Annelise had never spoken again of
her childhood, and that alone hinted at the depth of her
wound.

Annelise screamed, and Rolfe lunged up the stairs to the
solar. He was not going to wait below while his wife suffered, regardless of the clucking admonitions of women.

This ordeal could not be over soon enough for his taste.

Annelise awoke as the last rays of the sun were slanting
through the solar window. The room was painted in a rosy
gold well suited to her relieved satisfaction.

She had given Rolfe a son.

Blue lights danced in Rolfe's dark curls as he rocked his
son at the foot of the bed. Annelise watched him make
faces at the babe for a few moments before her smile revealed that she had awakened.

Rolfe smiled back at her and she saw the exhaustion in
his eyes. Her heart swelled that he had been with her at the
last and most difficult part of the delivery. His strength had
made the pain easier to bear. They smiled silently at each
other until the babe let forth a healthy yell.

Rolfe flicked a glance at their child. "I think he is hungry."

Annelise opened her arms. "Undoubtedly so. He did not
take much the last time." Rolfe lowered their son into her
embrace, and her flesh tingled everywhere her spouse

touched her. The babe settled in to suckle, and Annelise looked up to find Rolfe's gaze warm upon her.

"Thank you for coming at the last," she whispered. "I cannot tell you how much it helped."

Rolfe sat on the side of the bed and captured her free hand within his own. "I could stay away no longer."

"Despite your mother's demand?"

Rolfe's lips quirked, but his gaze was warm. "It would take more than that to keep me from your side, Annelise."

She ran her fingers over his warm skin, savoring the stillness and the strength of his hand. "You said before that I would be safe while in your presence," she murmured.

"That is a pledge I mean to keep."

The heartfelt declaration brought unexpected tears to Annelise's eyes. Her grip tightened on his hand and he leaned forward, concern in his eyes. "What is it?"

She shook her head and tears coursed over her cheeks. "I am simply so happy," she declared, to Rolfe's evident confusion. "I never imagined that I would have a husband such as you, or a home such as this, or a family." She sniffled and bit her lip in a bid for control. "This is what I have always wanted most of all, and you have granted it to me."

Rolfe moved so that he sat alongside her, and the welcome weight of his arm slipped over Annelise's shoulder. He leaned down to whisper in her ear, his hand still cradling hers. "You had a family before."

Annelise shook her head stubbornly. "No, I had no family. I will not accept that man as a part of my life."

The babe stirred against her breast, then opened his eyes to gaze blearily upward. To Annelise's shock and dismay, his eyes were the same amber hue as her sire's. She gasped, and Rolfe's grip tightened around her.

"What troubles you?"

"The babe, our son—his eyes are the same as my sire's!" Annelise turned an anguished gaze on her spouse.

"What if he has inherited more than the shade of his eyes from Jerome?"

Rolfe's finger flew to Annelise's lips and his touch silenced her. "Annelise," he said in the low tone that always reassured her, "our son has *your* eyes."

Annelise took a shaking breath. "But what of the other? I would hate to know that such evil flowed through his veins because of me."

"But you share nothing of your sire's character."

"But what of my brother Quinn? He was said to be worse than my sire. Perhaps it is a curse upon the men alone!"

"Annelise." Rolfe gave her a little shake. "What of your brother Yves? You see? There are men in your family who do not share your sire's curse."

Annelise shook her head again. "Yves was only a half brother. It could well be that his dame's goodness overwhelmed my sire's evil. My mother, it is more than clear, was dominated by Jerome in every way." She straightened and looked Rolfe squarely in the eye. "No, you, our son and your dame are my sole family. That is more good fortune than most have to call their own."

A considering glint lit Rolfe's eye, but then he looked away, and Annelise wondered whether she had imagined it.

"What shall we name the new arrival?" Rolfe tickled the babe's chin and the child squirmed. He belched with a volume that surprised them both into laughter, and Annelise forgot the conversation of families.

Had she known that Rolfe picked up a quill and parchment after she had fallen asleep, much less that a messenger left Viandin in the middle of the night, she would not have been so inclined to forget.

A fortnight later, Rolfe sauntered into the solar. Annelise knew immediately that he was up to something, but anticipated only that he had found his son a new toy.

Or thought of a name. Between the two of them, they could not find a name they both liked. Family names were few, especially as Rolfe was not interested in using those from his side and Annelise had no family she cared to claim.

"What mischief have you been making?" she asked with a smile.

Rolfe grinned. "Me?"

"Yes, you. You have the devil's own glint in your eye."

Rolfe folded his hands behind his back and strolled to the window with feigned casualness. "A messenger delivered something for you today."

"For me?"

"Yes. It was a twisted little root that I have asked the gardener to plant in the herb garden you favor."

"What kind of root?"

Rolfe swiveled to look at her, his eyes gleaming. "One from the East. I sent word to a merchant in Lyons when we first arrived back at Viandin, and he finally had success in locating it."

Annelise clasped her hands in delight, intuitively guessing what he had obtained. "Those flowers," she breathed.

Rolfe smiled at being found out. "Yes. Roses. Now you shall have one of your own."

"But not an enchanted one," Annelise scolded in a teasing tone. "So you had best not even think of cutting all the blooms to cast across the bed!"

Rolfe laughed and Annelise launched herself into his arms.

"Thank you," she whispered. "But you had no need to fetch me a gift for bearing you a son. He is my son as well, and his very presence gives me joy."

"No, that was not my intent," Rolfe maintained, much to Annelise's surprise. "This is a nuptial gift that took much longer to acquire than ever I expected."

"And a welcome one all the same," Annelise purred as

she lifted her lips for his kiss. As always, Rolfe's embrace stirred her blood and made her toes curl within her shoes.

"No," Rolfe whispered into her hair. "Your gift for bringing our son into the world awaits in the garden as well, but is not the rose."

Annelise looked out the window in surprise.

A knight strolled among the greenery below. His cloak flicked in the wind, but it was difficult to see him clearly because of the healthy growth in the garden and the sunlight glinting off his mail. His auburn hair, so like her own in shade, gleamed brightly, its hue making Annelise nervous.

A knight. Come to see her. He was too tall and broad of shoulder to be Yves, and his hair was not of Yves' sunny yellow. Indeed, he moved like a man older than Yves.

The cloak fluttered and Annelise went cold when she realized it was the robust wine color of Sayerne's standard.

An older knight from Sayerne could be only one man.

Annelise spun to face her husband, not surprised to find his gaze fixed upon her. "You did not!"

Rolfe contrived to look innocent. "Did not what?"

"Invite my brother Quinn to visit!" Annelise felt hot with disappointment and trepidation. What would she do? What would she say? "What did you tell him? What does he want?"

Still worse, what would Quinn do and say? Would he bellow at her? Would he pick up where their sire had laid off?

Would he silence her so that she could not tell anyone else the crime she had witnessed? It was too easy to imagine that a son and heir would not want that tale to come to light.

"Annelise," Rolfe said sternly. "Quinn and his wife are our guests."

"Guests?"

"Yes. I sent for them."

"How could you? You know how I feel about both him and my sire!"

Rolfe crossed the room and gripped her shoulders. She refused to look at him.

"Annelise, I know how you feel, just as I know your feelings are unjustified. It is time you learned the truth."

His voice echoed with the force of his conviction, and Annelise could not help but glance into his eyes. What she saw there made her doubt her certainty for the first time. "What do you mean?"

"You are wrong about Quinn."

Annelise shook off his grip and stalked across the room. "How could you know such a thing? There were tales aplenty of his cruelty. My own sire thought Quinn beyond evil, which is saying something indeed."

"Your father used rumor to his own end."

Annelise glanced up, having no problem imagining her father doing precisely that. In fact, Tulley had made much the same charge.

Could she have been wrong?

Rolfe smiled reassuringly and crossed the room to stand before her once more, his gaze unwavering. "I knew Quinn de Sayerne in the East—not well, but well enough to know that your opinion of him was undeserved."

"You summoned him without telling me!"

Rolfe shook his head. "Would you have approved?"

Annelise was forced to concede that point. "But how could you know I was wrong about him? What proof have you of his character? You already admit that you do not know him well!"

Rolfe's thumbs traced soothing patterns on Annelise's shoulders. "Some correspondence with Tulley confirmed what I had suspected since you confessed your tale—that Quinn and your sire fell out over the abuse of your mother."

Annelise's gaze leapt to meet her husband's. Could this be true? Clearly Rolfe believed it to be.

"Quinn apparently sought to defend her, until Jerome tried to cast Quinn out. Tulley intervened and urged the boy to leave for his own protection, never imagining that your mother would bear seed again."

A lump rose in Annelise's throat. "But how could Quinn abandon her there? He had to know that my father would raise his hand against her again, and without a defender, she could only be more hurt."

"Perhaps you should ask him that yourself."

Annelise's mouth worked for a moment and she clenched her hands as she thought. "I cannot do this," she said finally.

Rolfe pulled her into his embrace, and Annelise did not resist. She closed her eyes and leaned against his chest as his fingers slid into her hair.

"Where is my fearless bride now?" Rolfe teased softly.

Annelise shook her head. "I am afraid," she admitted in a small voice. "What if you are wrong?" She took a deep breath. "What if he has charmed you? What if he wishes only to silence the truth about my sire's crime once and for all?"

Annelise pulled away from Rolfe's warmth and looked up into his eyes. "I was the only witness, and you are the only one in whom I have confided the tale."

Rolfe cupped her face in his hands. "There is nothing to fear, Annelise. You wanted proof that our son is not doomed to repeat your father's crimes. That proof awaits you in the garden."

"But what if—"

Rolfe tipped up her chin so that his gaze bored into hers. "Do not imagine that I would let anything befall you now, wife of mine," he said fiercely.

Despite herself, Annelise smiled at the reminder of his pledge to protect her. She straightened and looked toward the window.

Rolfe was right. It was time she confronted her fears and laid the past to rest.

She took her husband's hand in hers and smiled up at him. "Will you come with me?"

Rolfe grinned. "Do not imagine that I would be anywhere else."

The knight in the garden spun around at the crunch of Annelise's footsteps on the gravel. His gaze locked with hers, and she found herself staring into eyes that were familiar, yet not. His amber eyes were so like her babe's, so like her sire's, yet filled with a compassion alien to Jerome de Sayerne.

That compassion emboldened Annelise to move farther into the garden. Rolfe waited behind as she approached her brother one step at a time. Annelise had never met a man who could keep his true feelings from reflecting in his eyes, and Quinn's were so warm that she felt her doubts melting away.

Quinn smiled a slow and encouraging smile. "Blood of my blood," he whispered, as though he could not believe she was real. He dropped to one knee before her and took her hand in his.

With that gentle touch, Annelise knew her fears had been unfounded. Quinn intended her no harm.

This man, she could already see, was the complete opposite of Jerome. Quinn was so still, so thoughtful, so resolute. There was not a line of cruelty in his face, not a glimmer of harshness in his demeanor. That Rolfe thought highly of him could only mean that Quinn shared her husband's high moral code.

It was a marvel to her to look upon Quinn's features, to see the echo of both sire and dame, as well as a faint reminder of her own babe's face.

Family. Blood of her blood, as Quinn had said. She and he shared a legacy—one that had had its pain, to be sure, but the bond between them was not one easily dismissed.

"Annelise de Sayerne, I am most pleased to finally make

your acquaintance,'' Quinn said, and brushed a kiss most appropriately across her knuckles.

"As am I to meet you, Quinn de Sayerne.''

Quinn smiled up at her, his wondering gaze dancing over her features. "You look so much like her,'' he marveled.

Annelise's heart skipped a beat. "Who?'' she asked, knowing all the while who he must mean.

"Our dame, of course.'' Quinn shook his head as he studied her. "But there is a strength about you that she never had. I can see it in your eyes, feel it in your grip.''

Quinn's fingers tightened slightly on Annelise's hand and he flicked her a telling glance before he rose. "I am sorry that you were forced to learn that strength so early and while so alone.''

"Why did you leave her?'' The question that haunted Annelise fell gracelessly from her lips. "How could you have abandoned her? You had to know that he would strike her again.''

Pain filled those amber eyes, and Quinn looked away in an obvious effort to compose himself. His voice, when he spoke, was strained.

"She would not come.'' He cleared his throat and looked back to Annelise with a new intensity burning in his eyes. "She refused to leave him. We argued long over the matter, but she insisted that I was but a child and could not understand. I believe now that she feared none other would have her, that Jerome alone would see her kept and fed.''

"She was wrong! You should have forced her to leave!''

Quinn's expression turned sad. "She refused, Annelise. And Jerome swore before Tulley that the beatings would stop. Tulley insisted that I leave immediately.'' He shook his head. "There was nothing I could do but hope for the best.''

Annelise clutched at his hand, seeing how he blamed himself and how the responsibility was not his to bear. Her vision blurred with unexpected tears. "You could not have known.''

Quinn frowned. "I could have known, if Tulley had sent word. For whatever reason, he told me nothing of what happened at Sayerne, though he kept a close eye on my whereabouts." His gaze bored into Annelise's own. "Perhaps he feared that if I had known the truth, I would have challenged my sire more seriously."

"And what would have been the harm in that?"

Quinn shrugged. "I was too young to rule Sayerne effectively, especially after our father's lax administration. Even now, if I did not have Melissande at my side, the task would be insurmountable."

Annelise must have looked puzzled, for Quinn smiled slightly. "My wife, Melissande d'Annossy. Tulley did us the great favor of insisting we wed. She awaits in the hall, at Rolfe's bidding. I think you might find you have much in common with her."

Annelise recognized the name of Sayerne's highborn and reputedly beautiful neighbor. But because of Annelise's long years in the convent, the two women had never met.

"What would I have in common with your wife?" Annelise demanded with a smile.

"Your doubt of my character," Quinn retorted with a smile of his own. "It took me many months to convince her that I was as different from our sire as could be."

He turned then and strode to Rolfe, shaking his hand with hearty vigor. "I thank you, Rolfe. Who would have thought that a tankard of ale lifted in a tavern so far afield would have brought me a sister so fine?"

Rolfe's gaze was warm upon Annelise. "Yes, fine she undoubtedly is." He extended a hand to Annelise and she danced to his side, her heart swelling with joy.

She had a brother again, she marveled—a family both past and present. This was more, so much more, than she had ever dreamed she might call her own. And she had Rolfe to thank for it all.

"I have thought of a name for our son," she whispered as they turned back toward the hall.

Quinn continued to stroll through the gardens, and Annelise had no doubt he only pretended to be oblivious to the fact that he now walked alone.

"Yes," Rolfe murmured, unsuccessfully trying to hide a smile. "I imagine it is one I long thought appropriate."

"Do not tell me that you intended to name our son Quinn?"

Rolfe only winked in response, and Annelise could not help but laugh aloud. "But you said nothing to me!"

"A wise man knows when an idea must be his wife's own," he teased and gave her fingers a squeeze.

Annelise grinned at the truth in that, then sighed with satisfaction. "Oh, Rolfe, you have made me happier this day than I ever imagined I might be. Thank you."

Rolfe cupped Annelise's face tenderly with his hand, and she forgot her newfound brother. She stared into Rolfe's eyes, one blue and one silver-gray, both gleaming with heartfelt sincerity.

"Surely I owe no less to the woman who so completely enchanted me with her love," he murmured. Then he smiled with that slow sensuality that warmed her right to her toes.

"This is one spell from which you will never wriggle free," Annelise threatened playfully.

Rolfe laughed as his arms tightened around her. "I will not even try," he vowed, before his lips closed possessively over hers.

\* \* \* \* \*

## *Author's Note*

The wild roses that are native to Europe are flat with five petals, much like wild roses elsewhere in the world, and bloom in shades of white and pink. In fact, Rolfe is a bit before his time in bringing roses back from the East—it was Thibaud IV who brought the red Apothecary Rose, or Rose de Provins, to France on his return from the Seventh Crusade in 1250.

These roses were cultivated extensively near Thibaud's château in Provins, outside Paris, and were renowned for their strong fragrance and rich color. Although not as rounded as the cabbage roses bred in the nineteenth century, Provins roses are sufficiently different from the native wild rose in hue, scent and shape that Annelise—not a gardener, by any means!—would not have realized they were the same flowers.

A medicinal preserve was also made from Provins roses, leading to their name Apothecary Rose. In the late thirteenth century the red rose was associated with the Virgin Mary and the purity of her love. As her cult grew in popularity throughout the Middle Ages, so did that of the Provins rose. Eventually, the troubadours linked the blossom to more secular love, and the red rose evolved into a symbol of romance still recognized today.

# And the Winner Is...
## You!

...when you pick up these great titles
from our new promotion at your
favorite retail outlet this June!

### Diana Palmer
*The Case of the Mesmerizing Boss*

### Betty Neels
*The Convenient Wife*

### Annette Broadrick
*Irresistible*

### Emma Darcy
*A Wedding to Remember*

### Rachel Lee
*Lost Warriors*

### Marie Ferrarella
*Father Goose*

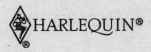

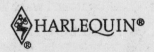

*You are cordially invited to a*

# HOMETOWN REUNION

*September 1996—August 1997*

Bad boys, cowboys, babies. Feuding families,
arson, mistaken identity, a mom on the run...
Where can you find romance and adventure?
Tyler, Wisconsin, that's where!

So join us in this not-so-sleepy little town and
experience the love, the laughter and the
tears of those who call it home.

## WELCOME TO A
# HOMETOWN REUNION

Tyler's vet, Roger Phelps, has had a crush on
Gracie Lawson for fourteen years. Now she's
back in town and he still wants her madly. But
Gracie couldn't possibly carry on romantically with
the boy who used to pack her groceries. Even if
the man he turned out to be is gorgeous, gentle,
funny and passionate.... What would people say?
Don't miss *Puppy Love* by Ginger Chambers,
tenth in a series you won't want to end....

June 1997
at your favorite retail outlet.

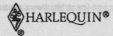

HARLEQUIN®

HTR10

*It's hot...and it's out of control!*

**BLAZE**

Beginning this spring, Temptation turns up the
*heat*. Look for these bold, provocative,
*ultra*sexy books!

**#629 OUTRAGEOUS**
by Lori Foster (April 1997)

**#639 RESTLESS NIGHTS**
by Tiffany White (June 1997)

**#649 NIGHT RHYTHMS**
by Elda Minger (Sept. 1997)

**BLAZE: Red-hot reads—only from**

HARLEQUIN® *Temptation*

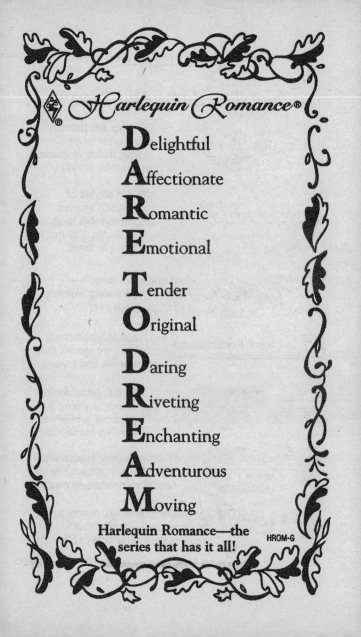

**_Harlequin Romance®_**

# **D**elightful
# **A**ffectionate
# **R**omantic
# **E**motional

# **T**ender
# **O**riginal

# **D**aring
# **R**iveting
# **E**nchanting
# **A**dventurous
# **M**oving

**Harlequin Romance—the
series that has it all!**

HROM-G

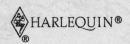

# *Not The Same Old Story!*

 Exciting, emotionally
intense romance
stories that take readers
around the world.

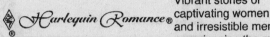 Vibrant stories of
captivating women
and irresistible men
experiencing the magic
of falling in love!

 Bold and adventurous—
Temptation is strong women,
bad boys, great sex!

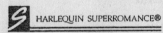 Provocative, passionate,
contemporary stories that
celebrate life and love.

 Romantic adventure
where anything is
possible and where
dreams come true.

HARLEQUIN®
INTRIGUE® Heart-stopping, suspenseful
adventures that combine the
best of romance and mystery.

 Entertaining and fun, humorous
and romantic—stories that
capture the lighter side of love.

Look us up on-line at: http://www.romance.net          HGENERIC